C000128038

YORKIE BOYS

DAVID CLOUGH

Michael Terence
Publishing

First published in paperback by
Michael Terence Publishing in 2019
http://mtp.agency

ISBN 9781913289294

David Clough has asserted his right to be identified as the
author of this work in accordance with the
Copyright, Designs and Patents Act 1988

Copyright © 2019 David Clough

All rights reserved. No part of this publication may be reproduced,
stored in a retrieval system, or transmitted, in any form or by any
means, electronic, mechanical, photocopying, recording or otherwise,
without the prior permission of the publishers

Cover image
David Clough

Cover design
Copyright © 2019 Michael Terence Publishing

To my family…

POSTED

1957 was a great year for me, although it didn't start too well.

Dad came home from work to our house in Knaresborough and announced, "I've been posted!"

My little brother Richard and I had no idea what this meant, but we soon found out as our mum and dad had a row about it. Being 'posted' meant that we would have to leave Knaresborough, where we were born and had always lived, and instead we would move away to Ravenscroft, because the Army were sending my dad to work at somewhere called Catterick Camp. Catterick Camp sounded exciting.

Our mum did not seem quite so enthralled at the prospect. We were living happily in Knaresborough, where my dad's family had lived for generations. We had a nice new semi, which my mum and dad had saved for years to buy.

"Our dream house!" wailed my mother. And now we were going to have to sell it and move north to Ravenscroft, somewhere we had never been before.

1

***

And so it came about that our furniture went off one day in a big Pickford's lorry, while my mum and dad, my little brother Richard, aged four and me, aged seven, set off by train.

At Ravenscroft railway station, my mum took one look at the great grey castle, the lowering clouds and the steeply-wooded hillsides and exclaimed, "What a Godforsaken hole!"

My dad grinned. "It's not as bad as it looks."

Ma then began the row which was to simmer for the next few years, boiling over occasionally into ferocious battles, until she could persuade my dad to get himself posted to somewhere more civilised.

Richard and I took one look at the woods, the fields, the castle and the river and immediately loved it.

Ravenscroft, where we had come to live, was going to be one adventure after another, but little did we realise as we stood there in the rain outside the station, just what lay in store for us all.

RAVENSCROFT

Ravenscroft is perched high on steeply-wooded hillsides, clinging precariously to the banks of the River Swale, the fastest-flowing river in England. It is dominated by a huge Norman castle, with a great square Keep glowering over the town, which has grown up round a cobbled marketplace outside the castle walls. In the middle of the marketplace is a church. There is an ancient cross. Red buses with United on the side line up on the cobbles to take people up to the little towns and villages of Swaledale: Reeth, Marske, Muker, Leyburn – or down to Darlington, the nearest big town, which is many miles away on the River Tees.

Ravenscroft clings to the side of the valley. Every street is a steep cobbled hill. The river curls round the town, from the bridge by the railway station, to the high bridge on the back road to Catterick Camp. There is a spectacular waterfall, and a walk alongside the river, beneath the towering castle walls.

Ravenscroft has only a few thousand inhabitants, is fifty miles from the nearest city and in 1957 was at the absolute dead end of a railway branch line.

3

Ravenscroft is also very high up, although you have no idea of just how high it really is until you make your tired way to the top of Swinegate or Hubberholme hill and look out across the valley of the Swale. There are huge views in every direction, across to the Vale of York, up to the windswept moors above Catterick and far north way up to Teesdale. Everywhere you look you sense the presence of the castle, which looms over the town and has done for a thousand years. And on the skyline above the town is the Green Howards barracks, squatting like a mediaeval fortress over the town. The streets around the barracks have ancient names like Threapland, Watlass and Gunnerton. Living in Ravenscroft feels like being on the end of the civilised world, with the wilds beyond.

To my mother, who had spent years living in the sophistication of London, it was like being exiled to the bleakness of Dartmoor.

OUR HOUSE

Our house, on Chestnut Grove, had only just been built. All around it was the debris of a building site. The road was not made up, there were no pavements. It was the last house at the top of a very steep hill, and beyond it there was nothing but open moors.

My mother, who had entrusted the buying of the house solely to my father, and had not seen even a picture of the house before her arrival, took one look at a half-built house and a massive building site and burst into tears.

My dad said plaintively, "Well, I like it."

This had the immediate effect of transforming mum's tears into threats of violence and abandonment.

We left them to it. To us it was paradise.

***

There was only one other family with kids living in Chestnut Grove. These were a boy, a year or two younger than me and big gangling girl of about ten. These were the

Greensits, Norma and Kenneth, who we met later that first day.

SCHOOL

I had been looking forward to school, but school in Ravenscroft came as a bit a surprise. It was tough, really tough.

My first school was on Durham Street, near the library, right in the middle of Ravenscroft. It was held in an ancient stone building, behind some tall iron railings. These were to keep the kids in, we discovered, not to keep predators out. Ma delivered us both there on that first day. The playground was already covered with kids, kids playing football, kids chasing each other, girls throwing balls against the wall, girls in little groups huddled talking and girls with skipping ropes.

"Go on in," said Ma, and shoved us both inside.

We edged nervously into the playground. No-one took any notice. I turned round to look for Ma but she'd gone, probably anxious to get out of the way in case there were tears or tantrums from our Eck, who had already decided he didn't like school.

The first person to take notice of us was a boy with a torn cardigan and a snotty nose. He came up to me, stood very close, looked me up and down, and without speaking thumped me hard in the chest. Winded, but angry, I swung back at him and hit him in the mouth, which bled satisfyingly red.

"Serves you right," said our Eck, taking a boxer's stance in case of another attack on us both. This was good sense as the boy with the torn cardigan, snotty nose and bleeding mouth rapidly gathered a group of friends.

"Who's this new kid?"

"Let's fill him in!"

"Smack him!"

"Gob him!"

"Give him some fist!"

They were a welcoming lot, the Ravenscroft kids.

Luckily for us the school bell rang. Fights stopped, footballs were gathered up and the kids formed into a line. A grey-haired woman with a mountainous chest and a large bell in her hand stood by the entrance tunnel and bellowed, "Quiet!" There was instant silence. There was no messing with this woman. School was about to start.

***

We had both been sent initially to this little school on Durham Street. It had just two rooms, one for big kids and one for little kids. It always seemed spectacularly full of kids, especially as there was only one tiny playground. Break times, when the boys were playing football or fighting and the girls playing with tennis balls against the wall or skipping or playing hopscotch, were dangerously overcrowded.

I don't remember any of the teachers because I was only there for a few weeks, but I do remember one frosty day in autumn. Frosts came early in Ravenscroft.

All the boys had made a tremendous slide on the ice in the playground. It was polished and polished until it was really slippery and fast.

We were all having a great time trying to go as fast as we possibly could, running to get onto the slide and then standing sideways with our arms outstretched, zipping along until the slide ended at the stone doorway to the school. Eventually I managed to go so fast that I slid at great speed straight into this stone doorway, hitting it headfirst and knocking myself out.

For some reason, shortly after that, I was moved away from this little school and up to the proper Junior school. I don't know whether they thought I was excessively stupid, or a risk to others, but I was sent away without ceremony, and had to leave my brother Eck behind.

***

The Junior School was at the bottom of Widdybank Wynd, a very steep and twisty little lane leading from Kirkgate down to the river. This was more like it! I loved it from the start.

I have very vivid memories of the school, presided over by Mr Morley. There was a large school hall, where we had Assembly sitting on benches. At lunchtimes we were served school dinners there. The floor was polished wood and classrooms lined one side of the hall, although at first my own classroom was a temporary hut outside in the playground. The school was a lovely old building and always smelled of polish.

On the wall of the hall was a great big chart. Every lunch time I had to sit in the same seat and look at this chart, which depicted in glorious colour and excessive details, a whole lot of creatures I rapidly grew to dislike.

The chart was called *The Early World* and showed what the creatures which inhabited our world in the Paleozoic Age looked like. One in particular resembled a giant woodlouse, and was called a Trilobite. I have always been interested in most living things, but the creatures of the Paleozoic Age I could cheerfully have done without. Their wiggly antennae and multiplicity of legs put me off school dinners for life. I was delighted to learn at the bottom of the poster that Trilobites had died out entirely in the Devonian era.

Teachers at the Junior school were first of all Mrs Brooks, who taught us to write properly, using ink pens which we had to dip into an inkwell. I enjoyed her lessons and dreamed one day of achieving power – power being one of her two chosen acolytes, whose job it was to collect all the inkwells from the children's desks every Friday afternoon. These would be loaded onto a special tray, which was then taken off somewhere for the wells to be re-filled. What a responsibility!

Miss Somerville was young and glamorous. She drove a two-tone sports car called an Austin Metropolitan. She was the height of sophistication in Ravenscroft and everyone was in love with her – girls, boys and, I suspect, most of the staff. Mr Morley was the Headmaster and was very strict but fair. After a while he started giving me a lift to and from school because his son Peter was in my class. They lived on Elmwood Avenue, next to our road. He drove a fawn-coloured Ford Anglia. I can remember sitting in the back as the little car strained to get up Widdybank Wynd (which was an extremely steep hill.) I used to guess when he would need to change gear, by listening closely to the engine revs.

Mr Morley was very strict, and never, to my knowledge, spoke to me. His wife, however, made real ginger beer from weirdly-shaped alien roots. This was simply the most delicious drink I have ever tasted. She used to give Peter and myself a glass each when we got to his house, so it was worth the slightly frightening lift home to sample this nectar of the Gods.

Ravenscroft Junior School had no sports field of its own, so for our games lessons we all marched off down to the river and along a winding lane through the woods towards Masham Abbey. There in the middle of the wood was a clearing, where we played games. I don't think it was much of a field as we didn't get to play football, but I do remember the whole class of us happily swinging off down this track into the woods. It was an anarchic kind of games lesson, as kids used to disappear and go off climbing trees, while the more romantic boys tried to kiss the girls they liked best, without getting caught by the teachers.

One day the following summer we all went paddling in the river! I don't know what the health and safety people would say nowadays, but I do know that back in the 50s we all loved our games afternoons.

In the playground I soon made friends with other boys and, like them, was either fighting, playing marbles, or fighting about playing marbles. The girls kept to themselves, their games involving playing with tennis balls by throwing them against the walls and juggling them at speed.

It constantly amazed me how the girls could do this with such skill and yet no boys could. I tried it once and fell over, to much laughter. Girls also skipped in gangs, one girl at each end of the rope, with one girl after another stepping into the middle of the skipping rope. They had their own songs and rituals and boys were never allowed to join in.

Fights among the boys flared in seconds, lasted minutes and were usually over and forgotten by the end of break. No-one was ever seriously hurt, it was just the young males sorting out their pecking order, not real violence or bullying.

Kids usually kept to their own year group and to the area of the playground belonging to that group, so that conflict was avoided. The biggest kids played football down at the far end of the playground, while we younger boys congregated around the iron drain covers, to play our games of marbles. The marbles were known as Liggies and the contests were fierce.

There was only one thing I really disliked about school (apart from the Trilobites) and that was Cheese and Bacon Flan. This was a yellowish pie that was served up to us by the dinner ladies once a fortnight. I absolutely loathed the taste of it. The smell of it would start to permeate the building during the morning and I would dread the coming of lunchtime. When the plate was put in front of me I would gag and start to choke at the merest taste of it. Of course this was long before food intolerances were known about, so the only intolerance I got to know about was when one of the teachers clipped me round the ear and told me to eat up. Then I would rush to the toilets and be sick.

***

At the back of the school, in a forbidden place where no-one was allowed, was the Head's secret garden. This was hidden away up some steep steps and was a wonderful, magical place. Rows of bushes grew luxuriantly up the steep hillside. Flowers grew in a colourful abundance none of us had ever seen before. (Our own garden was still mainly builder's rubble, with the odd patch of spinach or mint where my dad had cleared enough rubble to find soil.)

In the Head's secret garden there were bushes heavy with every sort of fruit, and best of all, there was an ornamental pond, which even had fish in it.

Once a week, we were taken up there for a lesson called Nature Study, where we were shown the insects scooting around on the surface of the pond. These were called Water Boatmen, clever little bugs that didn't actually get their feet wet, but which could move with great speed and alacrity over the surface of the pond.

Those were the best lessons I ever had.

OUR TERRITORY

O ur new house on Chestnut Grove was up at the top of Hubberholme Hill. It was an unprepossessing house, a pebbledash and stone semi, part of a new development. The house had only just been built and was the last one on an un-made-up road. For some reason, the builders had stopped working on Chestnut Grove and we were left alone. After our house the fields began and there was nothing but open country until the Goathland estate at Hubberholme, where the noble Marquess of Goathland lived in his mansion. We were very much on the edge of civilisation.

At the bottom end of Chestnut Grove, the road joined Elmwood Avenue. As kids we soon played happily with the other kids of Chestnut Grove and of Elmwood Avenue. The two streets led down a sharp turn and steep hill to the main Hubberholme Road, which formed one boundary to our territory. The Ghyll was the other. This was a steep-sided grassy valley behind Elmwood Avenue and it cut us off from the Army estate perched on the hillside on the other side of the Ghyll.

We were isolated, with the main road on one side, and The Ghyll cutting us off from the rest of Ravenscroft on the other. This was therefore our territory – the top of Hubberholme Hill. Our territory ended at the junction of Elmwood Avenue and the main road, for once you passed that point, you were at the mercy of the gangs from the big estates – the Army kids and the Lord Lovat's kids.

The Army kids lived on the new estate surrounding the Green Howards barracks, on the far side of the Ghyll. They were both numerous and warlike and it was always a risky venture to enter the Ghyll, in case we were spotted by any of them. However, as long as we kept out of the Ghyll, they were relatively harmless, simply because there was no reason for us to go anywhere near them. There was no road linking the two estates.

The Lord Lovat's kids were a different matter. They were a fearsome tribe of snot-caked loonies, filthy-faced and foul of tongue, easily identifiable by their shaven heads (from nits, not fashion.) We inevitably had regular contact with them, because they lived on our route to and from Ravenscroft town centre.

They inhabited a grey and grim estate of unpainted pebble-dashed terraces, just across the main road from the end of Elmwood Avenue. They lay between us and town, and therefore between us and our school. Luckily for us, the Lord Lovat's tribe were restrained by a very high stone wall, which kept them from attacking passers-by and well out of sight of normal human beings.

Occasionally as we were passing they would venture forth without warning, swarming up and over the wall, armed with sticks and stones. The cry would go up, "Lord

Lovat's!" and we would all run like hell for the safety of Chestnut Grove. Lord Lovat's were usually reluctant to follow, not liking the feel of tarmac under their feet, and we would be free to recover our wits and reflect on a narrow escape.

***

The battleground for all the kids of Hubberholme Hill was The Tip. This was an area of wasteland adjoining the Ghyll, the end of Elmwood Avenue, and Hubberholme Road itself. It was accessible by all three gangs: Lord Lovat's could climb up their wall to reach it; the Green Howards kids could march down The Ghyll to reach it, and we lived in the Grove just next to it.

The Tip was unwanted land. As a result, the builders had tipped rubble and all sorts of assorted rubbish onto it. This was to provide the ammunition for our battles.

We were outnumbered by both the other tribes, but we who lived in the Grove had one great asset – we lived at the top of the hill. No matter what our enemies attempted, they always had to fight uphill, while we held the heights and the commanding position. Thanks to O'Briens the builders, we had piles of rocks and debris as weapons, and this we happily rained down upon our enemies.

Many happy days were spent that summer hurling rocks at kids from Lord Lovat's and the Green Howards.

OUR MA

A word of two about our parents. Firstly, Ma. Our Ma was Irish. We always called her Ma, although her real names were Lucinda and Elizabeth. She was born in 1921 in Clones, County Monaghan, in Ireland. Anyone who knows anything about Irish history can tell you that 1921 was about the worst possible time to be born in Ireland, especially in Clones, County Monaghan, because that was the year that Ireland was split in two – 26 counties breaking away from the British Empire to form the so-called Irish Free State, and 6 counties staying loyal to the Crown, in a province that was then named Northern Ireland.

Why was Clones such a bad place to be born? Because the disputed border between the two hostile countries ran not just near Clones, but through Clones, round Clones, and indeed up and down the lanes and streets of Clones. So on one side of the road there was a new country, led by armed Catholic Irish republicans, violently hostile to the British Crown and to the Irish Protestants who supported it, and on the other side of the road there were Loyalist Protestants, passionately loyal to the Crown and both fearful of, and hostile to, the Catholics across the road.

17

To make matters even worse, County Monaghan was historically a county of Ulster- most of which was now in Northern Loyalist Ireland, but was excluded from the new entity for political reasons, thus making sure that the Protestants of County Monaghan, who had been left behind to fend for themselves in the new Free State, would be a threatened minority.

Ma's family were Protestants and lived on the road leading out of Clones to the border, which was a hundred yards past the family's house. Throughout his lifetime Grandad slept with a loaded Webley .45 revolver under his pillow and a loaded rifle stacked against the bedroom wall. He had had many friends murdered by the IRA and wasn't going to take any chances if he could help it.

I have seen both weapons many times. When Grandad died our Uncle Jack threw them into the lough at the back of the house.

Ma was the oldest child. She had a younger brother, John Joseph, known as Jackie, and a little sister, Margaret, known as Peggy. I don't know why they were all known by names different from those they were christened with, perhaps because they were Irish. Ma was known as Linda.

Her father, our Grandad, known to everyone as Johnny, had a bicycle business in Clones, just off Fermanagh Street, the main street. It was a prosperous concern because in those days no-one had a car, but everyone needed a bike. Johnny was a well-known local character, holding court to a lively crowd at his shop. Ma told us that they were the first family in the town to have a car, long before the war.

Her mother Louie was a Chapman. Her family had never recovered from the loss of their son Samuel

Hamilton Chapman, who was killed seconds after leaving his trench on 1st July 1916 at the Battle of the Somme, aged twenty. He was in D company, of the 9th Battalion of the Royal Irish Fusiliers, and attacked the Germans at the River Ancre. The entire battalion was wiped out in minutes.

This massacre had had a huge effect back in Ireland, not just on the Chapman family, but on all the Protestant families of Armagh, Monaghan and Cavan. As many of the dead were the sons of farmers, it meant that in many cases there was no-one left to take over the farm, and they were subsequently sold off and bought up by Catholics. This loss of territory added to the Protestant fears of being driven out of their homes, as they felt threatened and intimidated. Indeed, there was a sense of doom hanging over the whole Chapman family. A beautiful but frail sister died at 22. Louie herself died at 42.

Ma was very intelligent and quick-witted. She attended Clones High school and wanted to better herself. Realising there was little opportunity for her in Clones (other than being married off to a wealthy farmer, which was the last thing she wanted) she left home at 17 and went to Belfast, where she studied at a secretarial college and learned shorthand and typing. A year later, she headed for London, and with her usual immaculate sense of unfortunate timing, arrived there just in time for World War II.

OUR DAD

Dad was Yorkshire. He was completely different in every way from our Ma. He couldn't have been more different if he'd tried. If computer dating was possible back when they met in 1947, they would have been the last pair in the country to be matched together.

Ma was Irish. Dad was Yorkshire.

One was hot-tempered, volatile and quick to take offence; the other was calm, phlegmatic and solid a rock. Yet they married! I couldn't believe it and I often thought that they couldn't understand it either.

My brother and I often wondered what on earth brought them together, as they were so different in interests and outlook. In moments of extreme trial, at the sharp end of my mum's tongue, my dad would often be heard to wonder what caused their union to come about as well! Then she'd calm down, they'd make friends and we knew why. It was because they loved each other, that was why.

Ma was temperamental, full of ideas, prone to disaster, passionate, restless and ambitious.

Dad was quiet, often silent, calm in himself and easy-going.

Dad was Yorkshire to the soul.

"He hasn't got one!" – Ma.

He was calm, methodical and reliable.

"If he was any slower, he'd be dead!" – Ma.

He was universally popular and respected.

"Ach, what do they know? They don't know him like I do!" – Ma.

OUR KID

D ad called him Icky. I called him Eck. Only Ma called him by his proper name, which was Richard. When he was born Grandma had taken one look at him and pronounced to his stunned family, "You'll have trouble with that one!"

This prophecy was taken very seriously as Grandma, in addition to possessing a wonderful singing voice, was regarded as having the gift of second sight. Although this prophecy was often re-told whenever our Eck did something naughty, I doubted if there was any truth to it myself.

"How come if Grandma was able to see into the future, she didn't know that she would die soon after?" I asked Dad. She had died at an early age as a result of medical negligence. Dad couldn't answer that one.

Our Eck was very stockily-built, with a square head which proved resistant to rocks, blows, beatings and even the arrow with which Kevin Batty shot him later that summer. He was very solid, with short, powerful legs. I was tall and skinny. My dad was average in everything, or as Ma would say, "He excels in nothing!" He was five feet ten and weighed eleven stone. Ma was tall and graceful, and looked like Deanna Durbin the film star. Neither of them looked remotely like our Eck.

"Are you sure he's mine?" Dad would sometimes ask.

We all wondered why Eck was so different from the rest of us, and we didn't find the answer for a long time, until one day Ma wanted to go out shopping. Eck didn't. It wasn't anything special she wanted to do. He just didn't want to do it. And when Eck didn't want to do something, he wouldn't do it.

Ma shouted at him, screamed at him, tugged at him, pulled at him. She sat him down and smacked his legs.

"You're coming!" she shouted.

"No I'm not!"

"Yes you are!"

"No I'm not!"

"Now get you coat on and come with me!"

"No! I won't!"

She gave up in despair.

***

When Dad came home Ma told him about Eck's obstinacy. "He takes after your father!" she sobbed. Dad's father had never spoken to her since their wedding. "That's it!" she suddenly shouted. "He's a throwback to your horrible father!"

We all stopped what we were doing and looked at Eck. He sat there, a truculent expression on his face.

"My God!" said Dad. "You're right."

This was the answer we'd all been seeking as to our Eck's character. He was Grandad. The only surprise was that no-one had spotted the resemblance before.

Our Eck, short, pugnacious and obstinate, was just like his Grandad, at one time the terror of his own home town, a rampaging bull of a man.

The discovery cast gloom over the household for days.

THE GREENSITS

The Greensits lived lower down Chestnut Grove. Greensits had a car, the only one in our street.

Norma Greensit was about two years older than me. Norma was a strange gawky creature, fond of galloping around the fields which surrounded our houses, while shouting, "Neigh!" She was about a foot taller than me, and though skinny and unattractive, was both violent and intimidating. She seemed to consist entirely of knobbly bones. She thumped everyone with her hard bony fists and, perhaps not surprisingly, had no girl friends to play with. Consequently we saw a lot more of her than we would have wished, as she forced herself on us boys.

I always associated Norma Greensit with the colour green. She had green eyes and green clothes. She went to a school which had an all-green uniform. Later, when she showed me them, I learned that she wore green knickers.

Her brother was called Kenneth and he was a year younger than me. Kenneth was a nice enough lad, but he had a hard time of it from Norma, who tied him up and hit him. She liked to make him hold skipping ropes in each hand, and to gallop around in front of her pretending to be her horse, while she held the reins and shouted, "Giddyup Horsey!"

If he didn't go fast enough she would kick him hard up the backside and call him names. She had a colourful vocabulary for a girl and knew a lot of words which would get me into trouble if I ever used them.

Kenneth also had a hard time of it from his father, who shouted at him most of the time. His father had a very red face and was altogether a very brown man: brown suit, brown hat, brown hair, brown moustache. I felt sorry for Kenneth.

Mrs Greensit was never seen outside the house. She sat inside all day behind closed curtains.

O'BRIEN'S SHEDS

My brother Eck and I soon explored our new surroundings. Our house was the last house to be built in Chestnut Grove. In front was a huge open field and at the side of this were some old abandoned farm buildings. One of these was a very large shed, built of blackened wood, which shimmered in the summer sun and gave off a strong scent of resin. This shed had tall double doors, rickety on broken hinges, doors which could easily be prised open. Inside were stacked wooden building materials which O'Briens the builders had stored there for safe keeping.

We quickly found that it was risky to play there during the weekdays as men from the building site were in and out of the shed collecting wood, as they were still building new houses, up at the top of Elmwood Avenue. But in the evenings and at weekends, then the shed was ours to play in. When their work was done the builders just dropped the padlock over the lock, without doing anything to improve the rickety doors. It was easy to squeeze through the gap and get inside. This wooden shack was therefore ours.

Outside this shed there was a grassy overgrown path, leading to a stone building, the door of which was securely locked. This building had however, two other entrances – one a hole in the roof, the other a lifted slat in a wooden extension. Both were simple for small boys to squeeze through. Once inside, we found there were stacks of pink-painted window frames and doors. There was glass too, stacked against the whitewashed walls.

And finally, among this wonderful adventure playground, there was a large metal storage tank, a tall rusty drum about fifteen feet high. It was empty and disused. It was possible to shin up the side of the tank, using the stone wall of the building to lever yourself up, and once there, there was more fun to be had.

The tank had a circular opening on top, with a long drop inside down to the bottom. You always had a scary feeling that if you were unfortunate enough to fall down inside, then you would never be able to climb out. We liked to bang on the tank with sticks and bits of metal, as it made a very satisfying noise, one which could be heard for hundreds of yards.

These three structures were known to us all as O'Brien's sheds and as they were firmly in the middle of our territory, we regarded them as ours. No other kids from outside Chestnut Grove ever came to play in them, so we were safe. The only danger was that O'Brien's workmen would catch us there. They were a constant threat, as there was always the danger of being caught inside the sheds, and this made our trespassing all the more exciting.

O'Brien's sheds were to be the site of many adventures, some exciting, some amusing, and one almost tragic.

KENNETH

O'Brien's workmen kept their tools in a little shed on wheels, which was parked permanently right opposite our house. It had a door which was always locked at night, and a window. Everything around us was dusty with sand and cement, which blew in from the piles they mixed on the road. There were always piles of sand and mountains of pebbles. We pinched the pebbles and threw them at the roofs of O'Brien's sheds in the nearby field.

One day I wandered over to the shed, hoping they had left it open. Just then I heard the noise of car tyres spinning on gravel and I looked up to see the green Ford Zephyr of the Greensits turning into their drive. Greensits were taken to their school by their dad in his car. They were the only kids that did this. The rest of us walked.

Even at this distance I disliked Norma. I waved to Kenneth and he smiled and waved back. Norma was sitting up straight in the back seat. She thought she was the Queen. I bet her dad would give her Queen if he heard some of the words she came out with. My dad would belt me if I said any of them, and I was a boy.

The Greensits went to a different school from the rest of us. Their school made them wear a green uniform, with green hats, green blazers and for Norma, a green skirt. We didn't have a uniform at all. In fact, some of the kids at our school wore just a jumper and thin little black pumps all year round, even in winter.

Norma had a funny nose. Her top lip joined onto it without the indentation people usually had. It made her look like a sheep. She had very light green eyes, which had very, very black pupils. They looked like hard, shiny black beads. Norma had hard hands too.

Once Kenneth was out of the car, he opened the side gate and started running away from his dad, towards me.

"Where do you think you're going?" Mr Greensit shouted at him. Mr Greensit had a face which got very red very easily. He wore brown suits and had a bristly brown moustache.

Kenneth, head bowed, trudged back to face his father's wrath.

At this distance I couldn't hear what was being said, but I could tell by the way his father was speaking down at his son, that Kenneth was once again in trouble. Mr Greensit glanced up at me, sitting in the grass at the side of O'Brien's shed, but he didn't wave or say hello. I didn't expect him to. I didn't like him.

I could hear what he said next, because he pointed his finger at his house and was shaking Kenneth by the shoulders.

"Get changed!" he shouted. "Get changed NOW!"

I was glad my dad was not like Kenneth's dad. Our dad didn't shout and if he ever did, we knew we deserved it. Kenneth's dad shouted all the time.

The car doors slammed. Mr Greensit opened the front door of their house. This door was very dark and made of heavy wood. It had black metal studs on it, and a tiny diamond-shaped window. The window had a metal cross on it and it reminded me of the window of a prison cell.

Mr Greensit had gone inside, but had left the door open behind him. I could him swearing at somebody inside. "Bloody useless!" he shouted. "Absolutely totally bloody useless!"

Even at this distance I could hear Mr Greensit quite clearly. He was such a loud person. This was probably why he had such a red face.

He hadn't finished yet. "Waste of bloody time! Why don't you get up off your arse and DO something woman?"

Then a door slammed with a bang. Someone was crying.

***

My Ma had already decided not to have anything to do with the Greensits, even though Eck and I played with their kids nearly every day.

I picked up a pebble. The kids in Ravenscroft called them Clemmies, a word I'd never heard before. My clemmie was oval and smooth and white. It looked like the almonds we had in a dish at Christmas. O'Brien's used mountains of them. Their little yellow digger went up and down the road, with a scoopful of them in its jaws, dribbling them out when it turned quickly or went round a corner.

In the field next to our house there were the old farm buildings which O'Briens used to store their building materials. They had corrugated tin roofs, which we regularly bombarded with clemmies. They made a great metallic noise when hit.

I loved throwing. I stood tall and curled my first finger round my clemmie. It was a perfect fit and I knew I could throw it a long way. So what should I aim at? I didn't want to waste it just on an ordinary shot onto the tin roof. Then I noticed there was a chimney stack on the furthest building. It was a long way off, about as far as I could throw. It had a single pot chimney, which stuck up invitingly. It looked as if it might break if I could hit it. I smiled to myself in delighted anticipation, and cocked my arm back.

I am right handed, so I took careful aim with my left arm first as a target indicator. I threw overarm, curving the missile upwards to gain distance. Then I followed through with my right, letting my body arch smoothly over in line with the target chimney.

It hit the side of the chimney, a perfect shot. The sound rolled down our street in the hot still air.

I turned, wishing someone else could have seen it. I could sense that I was growing and was getting stronger. I wasn't sure I could throw that far with any accuracy, but I'd done it. Now my ambition was to hit the top of the chimneypot, so that with any luck I would be able to knock chunks out of it. The rim would look like a row of broken teeth when I'd finished with it.

A door banged at Greensits and out galloped Kenneth. Even when he was not wearing the bridle and reins that his sister inflicted upon him, he galloped like a horse. Force of habit I suppose. He didn't run like a normal kid, he skipped. But he grinned and waved his arms at me, glad to have escaped. I was glad to see him too. I wanted to show him how I had hit the distant chimneypot.

But before he'd gone five yards, the door of his house opened and a bristly red face appeared. "KENNETH!"

Kenneth stopped in mid gallop and turned reluctantly to face his father. I noticed that his head automatically drooped and the smile had disappeared. He trudged back to receive his instructions.

"Don't go wandering off and DON'T get into any trouble! Is that clear?"

Kenneth nodded and nodded. He looked like a robot. He was obviously not taking it in.

"Oh and Kenneth .... don't you DARE be late for tea!"

Then finally he was free to start galloping and the door was closed. The prison door was shut. Poor old Kenneth.

***

We didn't speak. We didn't need to. I felt sorry for him; he felt humiliated at what I'd witnessed. He just joined me, where I was again sitting on the edge of the pavement, kicking my feet into the dusty holes in the road.

I always thought it was so fake in books where it always says "he said" or "she said" or "'Hello' she said." Even in *Jennings and Darbishire*, my favourite books. Kenneth and I were friends, but we never said much at all, certainly not "'Hello,' he said."

Kenneth sat down beside me and looked at my shoes. I'd been kicking my heels into the dry and dusty road, trying to unearth some more good clemmies to have another shot at the chimney. They were my black school shoes. Now they were white with cement dust.

Kenneth grinned mischievously at me. I understood. He was embarrassed about what I'd heard happening at their house and he wanted to banish the feeling.

I only had one pair of shoes, and I had wellies for winter. My dad polished my shoes for me each night and put them out for me to find in the morning.

My Ma always said, "I don't know what you do with them. How do you get them in such a state?"

And my Dad would reply, "They're only boys," and wink at us.

***

Kenneth had started to copy what I was doing, hacking with his shoes at the hard rocky ground. I dug too, getting faster and faster. Kenneth dug harder and faster. I squirmed my heels into the dusty hole I'd made, rooting out loose clemmies. Kenneth did the same. I grinned. He laughed. His shoes were filthy dirty.

I knew what Kenneth was thinking. He scraped and scraped at the stony earth, so that his shoes were scratched and damaged. He went mad at it, laughing more and more. Kenneth's dad was not going to be pleased with him, and the prospect of this made Kenneth go hacking the earth even more madly.

I nudged him to stop. I stood up. "Come on, Kenny. Let's throw some clemmies. Watch me first."

I sifted through the clemmies I'd found, and selected the best ones for throwing. Kenneth copied me. I set my feet apart and steadied myself to take aim at the distant chimney. I was going to hit it and this time I was going to knock a chip out of it.

I put my left arm up and right arm back. I checked that the all-important first finger hadn't slipped off the clemmy's rim, checked and aimed on the target once more, and over we went! Beautifully smooth and curling out and across the road and the field and the shed roof and it hit the chimney. A lovely sound of stone hitting chimney cracked the air.

"Got it!"

Kenneth prepared to do the same. Well, he tried to. The trouble with Kenneth was that he was very awkward and unco-ordinated. When I said he galloped he really did gallop, his arms and legs whirring all over the place so that he was more like a young horse than a young boy.

Throwing accurately wasn't easy, it was a skill. It was all about balance and timing and aim.

When Kenneth threw, he didn't take aim. He rushed things and all his movements were jerky and hurried, so even though he was quite strong and tall for his age, his throws were a danger to the public.

His clemmy, released too soon and too fast, flew off to the left and I knew, I just knew as soon as he'd thrown it, that it was going to hit glass and that we were in trouble, so I shouted, "Run!" - even while it was still in flight.

There was the awful sound of smashing glass, and we were off the pavement, running round the side of our house and out of sight.

His father really would kill him this time.

BREEDING

As my brother and I were of mixed Irish and Yorkshire descent, we naturally thought we had the best of both worlds. From our Dad we had the Yorkshireman's toughness and tenacity.

"God's Own People, us Yorkshiremen!" Dad would say.

To which Ma would respond, "He's welcome to them!"

From Ma we had Irish fighting spirit and physical strength - all her male relatives were six footers – as well as the Irish race's love of literature and storytelling. The first thing she did was to get us enrolled in the local library and we were both avid readers from a very early age. Yet the oddest thing was, I never once saw my Ma read a book.

As she would say, "Ach, where would I find the time to read? I've got you lot to look after!"

So, to put it mildly, things were never peaceful in our house. If things were too quiet, my dad might start it off in the dining room with a wink to his boys.

"You know boys, Yorkshire is the biggest county. It has the best cricket team, the biggest Town Hall (Leeds), the best cathedral (York), the greatest scenery......"

This would bring Ma storming in from the kitchen. "And the biggest heads!" She would never fail to rise to his bait. I wished the fish I tried to catch were as easy to hook as poor Ma.

***

Life at Ravenscroft was heavily dependent on their moods and the current state of warfare between them. Our mixed ancestry was always blamed by each parent for any misbehaviour. For instance, if I lost my temper with our Eck, my dad would shake his head and say, "Look at him, bad-tempered. Just like the Irish."

"Hark at him!" she would roar. "Bad tempered! I'll show you what bad tempered looks like!"

And Dad would flee from her wrath. She was fond of waving as a weapon whatever implement she happened to be holding at the time. It might be a ladle, a wooden spoon, a cooking pot. Once she chased him with the large clothes brush. It was harmless fun.

If either of us boys ever swore, Dad would mutter, "Wicked tongues on them, the Irish."

But if either of us boys was mean or cautious, Ma would start the battle. "Tight as a duck's arse, just like his father!"

There was little time for rest and recovery from this constant warfare. Even if we were merely sitting down, seeking a respite, Ma would burst in. "Look at them - the lazy articles! Lying there just like their father. Might as well have married a corpse for all the life that's in him!"

One night when our dad fell asleep in front of the fire, she kicked him and said, "Sure, he'd be dead himself, if only he had the sense to stiffen!"

It wasn't easy living in our house.

RATFEVER

It was a hot sunny Saturday, the best day of the week. Our bedroom door banged open. It was Ma.

"Get up out of those pits and get yourselves some fresh air!" she shouted, and just to emphasise how fresh the air was, she opened both windows wide.

The sun burst into the room. The sky was blue. There wasn't a cloud in the sky. We both jumped out of bed.

***

After breakfast we wondered what to do on this exciting bright blue day.

"Let's go down to town and see what's there," I suggested. I had a desire to explore in the other direction, away from the fields and O'Brien's sheds, down Chestnut Grove towards town.

As we passed Greensits, Kenneth stuck his head up above the wall. He'd been lying on the lawn.

"What are you up to?" he asked hopefully.

I waved towards town. The great Norman Keep of the castle was visible in the distance. "We're going exploring! Want to come with us Kenny?"

"Yeah!"

"What about your dad?"

"What about him?"

"Will he let you come?"

Kenneth grinned wickedly. "Yeah, course he will!"

He wouldn't but obviously Kenneth wasn't going to tell him. He carefully opened the black wrought-iron gate, quietly holding the latch so that it wouldn't click and alert his dad. Once it was open he slipped through and closed it silently behind him.

***

Chestnut Grove joined onto Elmwood Avenue for a short steep descent to the wasteland that we knew as The Tip. This was used constantly by O'Briens to dump rubble, so it often had new hillocks of rocks and all sorts of interesting junk. Amongst it grew dark green patches of giant nettles.

The three of us stood and looked at it. At the far end was a stone wall, and beyond that we could see into an interesting green valley. This was the Ghyll.

The Ghyll looked exciting, with its very steep sides and empty spaces, but we were too scared of the Green Howards kids to venture into it. We stood for a minute or two daring ourselves, but in the end, common sense prevailed. We would play on the Tip, then go into town.

"Let's go then!" I shouted, and led the way into the Tip. There was only one narrow path through the rubble so it was a dangerous Tip. The rubble was full of broken bits of old iron and splintered wood. There were broken sheets of glass to avoid, which would cut your foot in two if you fell on them. Then there were the beds of giant nettles.

I picked up a long wooden shaft and started to swipe a way through the nettles which blocked our way.

Kenneth, following behind me, called, "Hey cut it out!"

I'd accidentally swished nettles back over him.

"Sorry Kenny."

***

We continued. Then my heart stopped. In the clear patch in front of me, sitting where I'd cleared away the nettles, was a rat. A huge grey rat. I stood still. It stood still. It just sat there, looking at me. It looked at me, and I looked at it and I knew which one of us was the most scared.

"Get a move on!" called Kenneth, who was behind me and hadn't seen why I had stopped. "What's the hold up?"

I pointed at the rat.

"Jesus Christ!" said Kenneth, turning instantly to run.

"Run Eck!" I yelled.

We turned and ran back over the Tip, terrified that the rat was in pursuit.

***

We didn't stop until we reached the safety of the tarmac road. Only then did we stand, hugging our sides, trying to get our breath back.

Our kid said, "What are we running for?"

"A rat!" I panted. "A giant rat! Didn't you see it?"

Kenneth looked like he was going to cry.

"Bah," scoffed our Eck, "Is that all?"

"All? Are you kidding? It was big as a cat!"

He was a very pugnacious boy was our Eck, scared of nothing, so I decided to add some extra detail.

"Yeah it was big as a cat, and what's even worse, it had Rat Fever. All rats have rat fever."

Kenneth began to sob.

Eck asked, rather less confidently than before, "What's rat fever?"

"It's a terrible disease. All rats carry it."

Kenneth began moaning softly to himself.

Getting rather carried away, I added with relish. "Yes, if you catch rat fever, you'll die."

Kenneth let out a loud wail. "Noooooooooooooo!" and set off running for home, stumbling and skidding his way up the hill.

Eck and I stood and laughed.

"It's in their wee!" I called after him. "If you've touched any nettles that they've weed on, you'll catch it for certain!"

Kenny knew that he had touched nettles, the ones I carelessly swished over him. He ran and ran, his arms flailing and his legs stumbling.

***

Eck and I set off walking back together, still laughing at Kenny's departure. By now Kenneth would be home.

"Is it true?" said our Eck. "Is there Rat Fever really?"

"Yeah. Course it's true."

"I don't believe you."

"True, absolutely true. If you catch Rat Fever your stomach swells up and you burst. Cross my heart and hope to die."

Unimpressed, he said, "Right then, we'd better go wash our hands."

It was true! There was such a thing as rat fever. I had heard about it on the radio. That's why I was so scared of rats.

We had an angry visit from Kenneth's father that night. Kenneth was banned from playing out with us.

CLIVE LAWSON

O'Briens the builders were erecting new houses at the top of Elmwood Avenue. They were continuing the street up from the houses that had already been built, completing them one at a time. Naturally, this made an excellent playground for us kids, as the site was left open on evenings and at weekends. There were several buildings with scaffolding up and we would shin up this and run around the first floors of the new houses, playing chase.

Then, one evening, just as Eck, Kenneth and I were finishing and getting down from the building prior to going home, a large furniture removal lorry arrived. We scrambled down to ground level to watch what might emerge. There were three removal men in brown coats. This looked interesting.

A smart new Austin Cambridge arrived and out of it came a family. There was a father, a mother and a boy. The father saw us and waved.

"Hello!" he said. He had a different accent from us but seemed a friendly type.

The mother ignored us and started directing the removal men. We all watched the boy to see what he would do.

He was about my age, with a round face and eyes that were too close together. His black hair was like a Brillo pad. He was not a good-looking boy. Seeing us staring at him, he advanced towards us. He seemed very confident.

"Hello," he said. "My name is Clive Lawson and I am nine years old."

We all stared. Nine years old? He sounded like a grown-up! Then he did the most amazing thing - he held out his hand towards me. I looked at it in disbelief. Boys in Ravenscroft didn't shake hands. They were much more likely to give you some fist!

He came and took hold of my hand, shaking it vigorously. "Pleased to meet you. Jolly nice to make friends so quickly."

Eck, Kenneth and I looked at each other. This was a creature from another world.

"What are your names?" asked the strange boy.

"I'm David," I said. "That's Kenneth."

He shook Kenneth's hand and advanced to our kid. "And you, my little friend?"

"He's Eck."

Clive Lawson laughed loudly. "My goodness, what an odd name! I've never met anyone called Eck."

"Well you have now," said our Eck, scowling furiously. He was clearly not impressed by our newcomer. Clive Lawson was apparently a very posh boy indeed.

***

"Where are you from?" I asked.

"Abingdon."

I'd never heard of it. I looked at the lorry. "Near Oxford," I said, reading the address of the removal firm. I wasn't going to be talked down to by this new kid.

"Yes," he said. "Near Oxford."

There was a moment of silence while he sized me up and I sized him up. I could take him easily, I thought. He'd probably never been in a fight in his life. Here it was a daily occurrence.

The inspection over, Clive Lawson continued. "Daddy's been posted to the North."

'Daddy?' What kind of boy was this Clive? No-one used the word 'Daddy.' If he spoke like that at our school he'd get his head filled in.

"Well," he said with a dramatic flourish of his hands. "Must dash. Got to help the pater."

I nearly fell over. Pater? PATER?? No-one ever, ever called their dad a Pater. This kid did.

I happened to know what a Pater was, because I had read it in some of the *Billy Bunter* books. A Pater was a dad. But you did not, not ever, not if you wanted to escape with your life, use the word 'Pater' for your dad in Ravenscroft.

This kid was going to have fun living here. From now on he would be known as Clive Lawson, the Pater's son. If he survived.

THE CLEVELANDS

One evening, not long before bed time, I was sitting in the grass of the field next to our house. I was watching a little crawly creature trying to climb up a stalk of a plant. He kept falling off and having to start again. He was a very persistent creature and wouldn't give up. I wondered why he wanted to keep going. What was it about the plant that made him so determined?

There was a shout from my Dad. "David!" He was busy extracting lumps of builder's rubble from our back garden, trying to turn it into something he could grow vegetables in.

"Here Dad!" I called back.

He waved, glad of an excuse to take a break. Standing up, he put his hands to his sides. "Oh my aching back," he sighed. "That woman'll be the death of me!"

Ma, ever alert and ready for battle, called from the house, "That'll be the day!"

When he was twenty my Dad had broken his back in a motorbike accident, so I thought Ma was being a bit harsh on him, but then logic played no part in her battles.

***

Far in the distance I would see hills. They were many miles away, on the other side of the great flat plain I knew was called the Vale of York.

"What do you call those hills Dad?"

"They're the Cleveland Hills," he said, coming over to join me. "That one with the pointy top is Roseberry Topping, and just about there," he directed me, "that's Sutton Bank, the steepest hill in Yorkshire."

"How far off are they?"

"Must be, oh, thirty miles away or more. All of it God's Own County. All the way up to Middlesbrough." He took my hand and pointed it. "Middlesbrough is called Ironopolis, because it's the iron-making capital of the world. They made the Sydney Harbour Bridge there."

He lay down beside me, easing himself down slowly because of his bad back. "Aaah," he said contentedly. "Peace and quiet at last."

A moment later our Ma appeared at the back door. "Where is he?" she called. "Harry? Where are you? I want this useless article mending!" She held up the electric kettle and waved it at us.

Our Dad lay low until she gave up looking for him and went back inside.

"Heh heh heh," he laughed. "She's bust the kettle now."

Ma and technology just did not get on together.

We lay together and watched the light fade over the Cleveland hills. It was great to be in God's Own County.

MARCHAMS

The field opposite our house had long juicy grass and was full of dozens of different plants. I had tried to learn the names of some of them, but there were so many it was difficult to remember them all. There were the ordinary ones which I knew already: Dandelions, Buttercups, Primroses, Thistles and Cowslips. But I liked the exotic sound of Birds' Foot Trefoil, Purple Vetch and what about Snakes' Head Fritillary!

I plucked a blade of grass and checked its length, straightness and strength. I wanted to use it to make a blower. A blower was a piece of grass used to make a fantastically loud noise.

Satisfied it was good enough, I stretched it taut between my thumbs, making sure it formed a tight reed in the gap between my two parallel thumbs. It had to be perfectly vertical, perfectly straight and very tight, or it wouldn't work.

Pursing my lips, I put it to my mouth and blew hard. A tremendous rasping shriek tore the air. I drew it out, raising its pitch until it became a scream. You could hear it miles away.

My brother Eck, playing in our garden, turned and looked around. I waved. He waved back.

Suddenly, I was aware of movement behind me. I turned and saw a boy of about my own age, standing watching me.

"That was good that," he said. "How d'you do it?"

"Easy," I replied. "I'll show you."

He came and sat down next to me and I demonstrated how to make a successful blower out of a blade of grass, the way my Dad had taught me. The boy blew the one he'd made successfully and grinned at me. This was Alex Marcham.

***

I took him home with me and Ma gave him a drink.

"Where do you live Alex?" she asked.

"Over there." He pointed across the main road to Hubberholme. "Do you want to come and play?"

"Can I Ma?"

She nodded and collected the glass from Alex. "Don't be late for tea though."

Alex's house was a big detached one on the other side of Hubberholme Road. It had a drive and a large front lawn. Alex took me round the side of the house. I noticed a blue racing bike parked against the wall, and stared at it in awe.

He stopped, seeing that I was looking at it with such interest. "Do you want a go on it?"

Did I? I could only dream of having a bike like this. I hadn't got a bike at all. I had had a trike when I was little which I had ridden until we'd left Knaresborough. We used to ride around on it with two and sometimes three kids all piled on top, screaming and laughing and falling off. I hadn't had a bike since then.

"You can come and play any time," he said. "I've got a sister called Sandra."

I didn't get to meet Sandra, but I did get a ride up and down his drive on a proper racing bike, one with gears and drop handlebars. I told Dad when I got home.

He said, "I'm glad you're making friends."

GULLIVER TOWER

So far we'd only explored the field and the Tip and the outside of O'Brien's sheds and I wanted to see what was beyond them. Alex Marcham came round to our house, so there was Alex, myself and our kid in our gang. When we went out onto the road Kenneth Greensit came running over to join us (his dad was out at work, so he would never know.)

He begged to come with us, so we let him. As soon as he came I guessed his sheep-faced sister Norma would want to come as well. She wouldn't want her tame horse to escape from her that easily. I was right.

"Kenneth!" she called.

He winced. His simple happy smile vanished.

"Come back here. I want you!" Above her head she waved the skipping ropes that she used to tie him up.

Kenneth shuddered.

To save his misery, I relented. Reluctantly I said to her, "Do you want to come with us Norma?"

She galloped over to us, arms and legs flapping in the wind.

I studied her closely. Norma really did have a face like a sheep. Her nose and mouth were both sheep-shaped, and, quite remarkably, her green eyes had that light colouration and animal quality that sheep have, but humans lack.

Unfortunately, I had confided to my brother Eck that Norma was in reality a complete sheep and not a human being at all. As he had a good sense of humour, he now started going, "Baaa!" to her.

Norma didn't understand this, but she recognised it as an insult, especially when Kenneth and our Eck started to snigger. She stamped her feet angrily. "Stop doing that!"

Eck didn't stop. Kenneth was giggling.

"Why are you doing it anyway, you stupid baby?"

Our kid just laughed and went, "Baaaaaaaaaaaa!" in her face. She guessed it was some mockery aimed at her and chased him. He ran off into the field. The rest of us followed, laughing and swishing at thistle heads.

We had a whole day to spend together. What adventures would happen to us, I wondered?

***

The field had big thick hedges, so we had to wait as one after another we queued to get through a hole in the hedge, before we could get into the next field. The hedge was mostly hawthorn, which was sharp and thorny, but which had gaps which were quite easy to get through. Hawthorn grows quite tall but it curves over, leaving sheltered and secret little bays inside it, where you can hide and not be seen.

Beyond the next field we came to a stone wall. This was quite high, over four feet tall, and made of dry stones, without cement to hold the stones together. The stones were heavy and loose and could quite easily come away in your hands, so if you were using one to lever yourself up you had to be very careful you didn't pull one down on top of your head. You had to feel carefully how safe and solid the rock you were holding was, or you could brain yourself.

I watched carefully as our Eck, who was only four, clambered up without an accident. Inevitably, the accident happened to Kenneth, who pulled a stone down onto himself, and only just managed to jump back out of the way before the large heavy stone landed on his foot.

Norma thumped him hard. "Kenneth, you're such a stupid little bastard!" she said viciously.

***

At the end of the next field we reached the top of the hill. We stood panting, looking around us. It was stunning. We could see for miles and miles. Right across to the Cleveland Hills. Ironopolis. Roseberry Topping.

For a few moments all was quiet, then our Eck shouted out. "Hey look at that!" He pointed over the fields to our right. "It's a castle!"

There, standing isolated a couple of fields away, there was indeed a genuine, ancient stone castle. It had battlements and a castellated tower on top of high walls. It looked like something out of King Arthur and the Knights of the Round Table. Whooping and cheering at our discovery, we ran yelling over the fields to explore it.

The little castle stood majestically in the field, all on its own. There was nothing else near, nothing modern, nothing human. There was no sign on it. Nothing. No-one seemed to own it or look after it.

It was quite a small castle, perhaps twenty feet wide. We marched round and round it. "From now on it's our castle!" I announced.

Everyone cheered. We marched round and round it again in proud ownership.

Then Alex discovered a slight problem of ownership. "There's no way in."

We walked round and round it again, searching for a way in. We were in for a disappointment.

There was a doorway, but it was closed and made of solid wood and obviously sealed tight from the inside. We kicked at it and shoulder charged it, but achieved nothing except sore shoulders. We were defeated.

Looking for another way in, we studied the walls. These were smooth grey stone, with no handholds. There was no chance of scaling the walls. Defeated and dejected, we slumped down on the grass.

"I knew we wouldn't be able to get in," said Norma irritatingly.

That spurred me into action. I stood up and walked round the castle walls. Alright, so the door was impenetrable. But there was a farmer's stone wall in the field at the back, and by climbing up on top of that, it might be possible, if someone stretched high enough, it might just be possible to reach the bottom ledge of the window hole and for one of us, the tallest, to get inside and maybe let the rest of us inside.

"Norma," I said seductively. "You're the tallest."

"Get lost!"

"You're the best climber and you're the tallest."

"Yes, but I'm not the dumbest."

I tried to sound helpful even though she annoyed me so much I wanted to scream. "I'll give you a bunk up."

"Bunk up yourself!"

There was nothing for it but to try myself. I was next tallest. I climbed up onto the stone wall, then waved to Alex.

"Give us a bunk up."

He cupped his hands together to make a stirrup. I put one foot in this and slid myself up the wall of the castle. My fingers scrabbled along until I found the window ledge.

"Now Alex. Push me up!"

The others groaned in unison, "Up he goes!"

I was easily able to get a good handhold on the ledge. In seconds I was levering myself up and through the window hole. I stood, panting for breath but very excited, inside the castle. I had done it. I was inside our very own castle.

I stuck my head out of the opening and shouted, "Hey everybody!" and waved.

Everyone except Norma cheered. They seemed a very long way down.

How to get the rest of the gang inside was the next problem. There was no way we could repeat the entry trick for the smaller kids, so I looked round for another way of getting them in.

The castle was of two storeys. There was a circular central tower which formed the second storey. Round it ran a parapet, which I could walk along quite easily. Inside the tower there were steps leading up to the top and down to the ground floor. Even though I couldn't find a way for the rest of the gang to get inside, I kept smiling to myself at our discovery. It was unbelievable – a real live stone castle of our very own!

On the ground floor were a lot of loose stones. Picking my footsteps carefully over these, I made my way to the wooden door that had so easily defeated us. I had no hope of this opening as it was a stout door in good condition. It hadn't flinched when we had tried to shoulder charge our way in.

I checked the door, just in case, and lo and behold, miracle of miracles, it had a simple sliding bolt, which miraculously slid back quite easily when I tried it. The door opened with a creak.

I sneaked out. The others were round the other side of the castle, so I crept up on them.

"Yah!" I yelled, jumping out at them and waving my hands.

They all screamed.

"I'll kill you!" shouted Norma.

The rest quickly got over their fright and followed me round to the open door.

"Welcome to my lair," I said in a low, spooky voice.

Whooping and cheering, the gang charged inside.

***

We played there for hours. It was one of the best days of my life. When it was time to leave I had an idea.

"This is our castle. It's our secret. From now on don't tell anyone else about it. No-one at all. Promise."

We all promised. Even Norma seemed for once agreeable. I was pleased.

I thought of making it really serious by making it a pact signed in blood, but we were late for tea, so that idea would have to wait.

"You lot go out the way you got in. I'll lock the door and go back out the window."

It was a scratched but happy band of warriors who charged back down the fields, scrambled through the gap by O'Brien's sheds, and ran into their own houses.

The following day I went to the town library and asked to look at old maps of Ravenscroft. There it was. It had a name. Gulliver Tower. Marked with a little castle sign. Gulliver Tower. Our own little castle.

***

In Gulliver Tower we were kings. We fought battles, we held each other to ransom, we poured imaginary boiling oil on invading Scotsmen. We stood on the battlements and watched the Viking armies marching down the Vale toward York, where they were beaten in battle at Stamford Bridge by King Harold in 1066.

In Gulliver Tower we hoarded food stolen from biscuit tins at home. We lit fires among the dry stones of the ground floor and we roasted spuds we had stolen from our larders. We had feasts and forgot our mealtimes.

In Gulliver Tower we piled stones called Clemmies and we locked Norma Greensit out for being Norma Greensit. We wished we could live in Gulliver Tower.

And finally, one day I succeeded in making a flag from an old sheet and we hoisted it up on wooden stick, declaring ourselves Kings of Gulliver Tower and forever independent of the rest of the world.

MA'S CANADIAN

I knew very little of Ma's life before she married. I knew about Grandad and Uncle Jack and Aunt Peggy and our all our cousins back in Ireland, but almost nothing about Ma herself. Then, one evening, not long after we'd moved in, our kid and I were reading downstairs in the dining room. Our dad was still out at work.

Ma came quietly into the room, carrying a small wooden box. She sat down, without speaking, at the dining room table. This was most unusual, and I sensed that something way out of the ordinary was about to take place. I'd only seen the box once before, buried at the bottom of her wardrobe. I'd found it when I was searching for our Christmas presents. I guessed it was her secrets box.

Our kid was immersed in his comics. I was trying to read *Jennings and Darbishire*. I didn't look up because she was so quiet. I suspected she'd been crying.

I peeped up over the top of the book. She had opened the wooden box and was riffling through some letters and photos. I put down the book and went over to her. Without saying anything, she put her hand on mine. Then she held out one of the photos and showed it to me. It was a soldier in army uniform, smiling, standing in front of a tank.

"My Canadian," she said.

There were other photos, one a close-up. He was in battledress with the flash CANADA on the shoulder. She turned it over and written in pencil was the date March 1944.

"He was my fiancé," she said.

FIANCÉ? FIANCÉ!!! What was she saying? Fiancé? This was the first I'd ever heard about a fiancé. Did Dad know?

"This is his crew." She passed another photo over to me. This one showed five young soldiers sitting on the tank, all of them smiling and laughing for the camera.

"I came up from London to York to see them once, in 1944."

She took the photo from me and peered closely at it. I couldn't see her face.

"May 12th 1944. Thirteen years ago."

She was very quiet and thoughtful and was obviously back in the world of the photograph.

I didn't know what to say. We never talked like this. I looked for help to our kid but he kept his head in his comics; whether he understood or not I couldn't be sure.

Suddenly she seemed to brighten and, smiling at me, said. "Want to see what I looked like then?"

I nodded. She flicked through the box and selected a photo.

"That was me."

I was stunned, speechless. Ma was beautiful! She looked like a film star.

She laughed. "Oh I had them all running after me then." She put her hand on my arm. "Long before I met your father. He wouldn't have got a look in then."

I held the photograph of Ma as she had been then, aged 23. I was shocked. I had never thought of Ma as being anything other than our Ma. Here she was, with long black hair swept up in the style of the time, dressed in an elegant coat and high heels.

"Hey our kid, look at this!" I yelled, holding the photo out to him. "This was Ma when she was young."

He leaned forward and looked closely at it. "Cor," he said in surprise. "What happened to you?"

Laughing, Ma swatted at him and retrieved the precious photo.

The laughter seemed to change her mood again. Her expression was distant, her eyes focussed on something that had happened long ago.

"I came up from London to York to see him. It wasn't easy in wartime. The trains were a terror. I stayed at the Royal Station Hotel in York. He was in training for the invasion, based somewhere near York. It was just before D Day. I've often wondered where it was. I've looked for it on maps but never been able to find it. I wish I could."

I didn't know what to say, so I said nothing.

"I came to see my Canadian. We'd met in London. He took me to meet his crew. Lovely boys they were. They gave me a ride in the tank. It was so noisy and hot I felt sick." She stopped suddenly. She was back with us.

"What happened to him Ma?"

She paused. It took her some time before she answered. "All those boys were killed. Just after D Day."

"What about him – your Canadian?"

"Oh, yes. Him too. He was killed."

Then there was the sound of my dad undoing the back door and she quickly shovelled the photos back into the box.

"He could have been your dad," she whispered, just as the door was opening. "He was my Canadian."

NETTLES

As kids, at weekends and holidays we roamed absolutely wild. We had breakfast and would then disappear until lunchtime, out into the fields. It was just paradise to us.

One day we built a tent there in the field out of Ma's old wooden clothes horse and an old sheet. We planned on sleeping in it, and had to be dragged out, protesting violently, by our dad.

I liked flowers and insects and was interested in all the dozens of different plants you could find in the fields and hedges. I would collect flowers and bring them home, pressing them in a big fat book called the *Encyclopaedia of British History*.

In the field we played games like the one where you picked a buttercup and held it close under someone's chin.

"Hold still," we'd say. "We can tell if you like butter."

And if yellow reflected off your friend's chin you would shout, "Yes you do!"

I never knew what the point of it was, but it was fun.

***

The only enemy I had in the world was nettles. Nettles lurked over every wall and hedge, thick, dark green nettles that grew as high as our heads, nettles which were vicious and which stung bare skin. We always wore shorts and we were forever getting stung. I always hated nettles with their hairy leaves and hairy stems and nasty long-lasting stings.

After I found the rat in the nettles I hated them even more, and took every opportunity I could to find a swishing stick and to cut them down. Even then, the nettles weren't dead, they could still sting you. If you weren't careful they would slip down the stick you were swishing them with, and slide onto your hand. Or they would fly over your shoulder and land on a friend.

Under the nettles there were dark, dry places, where lurked nasty creatures. Nice creatures like rabbits don't like nettles, but rats do, so even when I'd spent ages beating down a nettle patch, I still hadn't won. The space I'd cleared was just as threatening as one with standing nettles. There might be a rat skulking there, waiting to leap out at me.

One day, after being particularly badly stung by nettles, I exclaimed bitterly to my Ma, "I don't believe there is a God!"

"Why ever not?" she asked, horrified at my sudden outburst.

"If there is a God, why did he create nettles?"

She laughed, but she couldn't answer my question.

***

Later, when she'd covered my stings in that smelly pink calamine lotion, she put her arm round me. "When we were children in Ireland the poor people used to eat nettles."

"You're kidding!"

"No. They used to collect the young green nettles and boil them and eat them, just like cabbage."

I didn't really get the point of the story at the time, but later, in bed, I thought more about it.

I decided that she was trying to tell me that even something as nasty and hurtful as nettles might have its uses. Maybe she meant that being stung by nettles might hurt for a bit, but being hungry all the time hurt for a lot longer.

FLASH HARRY

Our Eck was mad on comics. The *Beano, Dandy, Topper and Beezer*. His favourites though were the *Lion* and the *Tiger*, though he was also mad on *Victor, Hornet, Hotspur* and *Valiant*! He didn't just read them, he studied them, absorbed them and became so deeply involved that he was completely oblivious to everything going on around him. Once he had read a comic he would file it away carefully, keeping every comic in neat little sequential piles in his cupboard. On this particular evening he was reading the *Hotspur*.

Ma was busy baking buns in the kitchen. I was trying to draw a map of our territory, seated at the dining table. Our Dad was also at the table, once again trying to fix the electric kettle. This had, according to Ma, exploded on her without warning.

"Those oul Morphy Richards aren't worth the money," she alleged.

"Hmm," Dad said, holding up the blackened remains of the heating element. "Seems to have burnt itself out. Must be a fault in the design. Bit of a mystery." He glanced towards the kitchen.

It was about the third time the kettle had burned out in a month. He quietly nudged the kitchen door closed so Ma couldn't hear him. "Your mother and machinery don't get on too well."

This seemed an ideal opening to ask him some questions. Ever since that night Ma had told us about her Canadian I had wanted to know more about their relationship.

"Where did you meet Ma?" I asked.

"Stone, in Staffordshire." He didn't seem surprised by the question coming out of nowhere.

"I was on an Army course there - telecoms. I had a beautiful motorbike, an AJS, the pride of my life. My pals and I all had bikes, Geoff King, Ken Harrison – we all had big bikes."

I thought we were getting off the topic a bit, so I steered him back. "Ma," I said. "Ma. How did you meet Ma?"

Just then the door was pushed open and Ma came into the room, carrying a baking tray to put by the fire. "What are you two yammering about?" I could tell she was in a good mood.

"Just telling the lad how I swept you off your feet."

She snorted derisively. "Swept me off my feet? I never even noticed you. A wee Yorkshire runt!"

Dad stood up and modelled himself in front of the mirror, half-mocking, half-serious. He was hardly a runt, being five foot ten.

He posed like a film star, which drew a snort of derision from Ma.

"Would you just look at him! Doesn't he just love himself?"

Dad preened himself. "Oh, I was a very snappy dresser in those days. Flash Harry they used to call me."

"Flash Harry cos he wasted all his money on clothes!"

"Very snappy."

"Very vain!"

He tried to cuddle her, but she dodged his outstretched arm.

"Then I met your mum. One look at her and I was hooked."

"Oh yes!"

"I knew she couldn't resist me. One look at Old Flash Harry and she was mine."

"What a load of oul nonsense!"

"The best-looking girl out of thousands."

I was excited to hear this. "Is that right Ma, were you?"

"Don't be listening to that oul eejit," she laughed, blushing.

"She was expensive mind you. I spent a fortune taking her out."

"I'd be lucky to get a glass of shandy out of him."

"Expensive tastes she had."

"And look where that got me!" She folded her arms and looked defiant. Dad snuggled up to her and this time she let him put his arm around her shoulders.

"Anyway, I couldn't keep on spending all my money on her, so I thought I'd better pop the question."

"That's more like the truth. He married me to save money."

Dad put both his arms round her and kissed her cheek.

"And she said Yes. Made me the happiest man in the world."

"Is that true Ma?"

"Well, some of it is…. He could be a real oul charmer when he wanted to be."

"What happened then?"

"I thought it was time to take her home to Yorkshire to meet my parents."

"A great honour I'm sure."

Ma remembered something and gave him a dig in the ribs.

"I wanted to show her off to my Mum."

She smiled proudly. "I was the first girl he ever took home, or so he said."

"It's true," protested Dad. "I didn't let my Mum see any of the others."

Ma sniffed. "They probably had more sense than I did, taken in by him. If I'd have known how he was going to turn out, I'd have run a mile!"

But she was pleased, I could tell.

I didn't need to ask about her Canadian. Three years after he'd been killed she'd made the decision to marry Flash Harry.

GREENSIT'S TV

One afternoon I was playing in Greensit's front garden. Kenneth and I were catching insects off the thick purple catmint bushes they had growing alongside the path. It was really good fun and we were totally engrossed in it. You waited and you watched as the insects congregated on a particular flower. You edged yourself into position to strike. You quietly picked up a jam jar and put it around the flower heads, then slid the lid over the top of the jar, hopefully trapping the insects inside.

We collected them all in a giant Kilner jar I'd borrowed from Ma's store cupboard. She used them to make homemade raspberry jam. I think the insects must have been able to detect the smell of the raspberries, as they seemed happy enough in our collection jar.

Catching bees was tricky, as you had to watch the bee carefully to see where it would alight on the flower. Then you had to sneak up with the jam jar's mouth open ready. You had to be quick because the bee would see you, as they have very good eyesight, so you had to capture it before it took off. You could only catch them when they were absorbed in gathering pollen. Once they were in flight you had no chance, not even with a fat old bumblebee.

Bees were such brilliantly clever creatures that I'd always liked them. Unlike nasty old wasps, they wouldn't sting you. We didn't harm them, we just kept them for a while so we could study them, then we let them go.

There were several different types: proper honey bees from a hive, domesticated bees that belonged to someone, and fat bumble bees, which were wild. All the bees had little saddlebags on their legs, which they filled with pollen to take back to their hive. I thought they were just wonderful.

Among the other insects on the catmint were striped hoverflies, which were very difficult to catch. These too were amazingly clever creatures. They zapped about, changing direction instantly while in flight. They'd zip off away as soon as they saw us coming. I thought about what a great invention it would be if we could make a plane which could zip about in flight like the hoverflies did.

"Hey Kenny. Imagine if you could make a plane that would do that." I zapped my hand in different directions.

He shook his head. "No chance."

We watched the hoverflies from close range, to see if we could get any clues as to how they did it. They could change flight through 45 degrees, even 90 degrees. They could go upwards, downwards, sideways, backwards, any direction they wanted, without ever pausing in flight. They were stunning, incredible insects.

"I wonder if they've got a brain," Kenneth said.

"Course they have! Think they could fly like that without a brain?"

I was thinking how cruel people are. They kill flies without a second thought, yet flies could do things we would never be able to do. They could fly backwards!

Just then a tall shadow darkened the path. Norma was standing above us, hands on hips.

"What are you silly little boys doing?"

"Ignore her Kenny."

She bent down close and saw the jam jars full of insects.

"Catching flies?" she sneered.

"Go away."

"What are you going to do with them – kill them?"

"No we aren't!"

"I can think of better things to do than catch flies."

"I'm sure you can Norma. Why don't you just go away?"

"I'm going," she said, turning, and then stopping. "Oh, by the way, we've got a TV."

I knew what a TV was, even though we didn't have one of our own. When I was little, my mum and dad had taken me round to Mrs Day's house to see the Coronation of the Queen.

"Well," she snapped. "Do you want to see it or don't you?"

***

I didn't want to see it. I wasn't in the least interested, but I thought that if we went along with her she'd stay inside and leave us in the garden in peace. We stood up. My legs ached from kneeling so long. I looked at my knees. I had patterns of grass etched deep into my kneecaps. I laughed and pointed at Kenneth's knees. He looked down, saw he had the patterns and laughed too.

Norma barked, "What are you stupid creatures laughing at now?" She thumped Kenneth hard, causing him to start whimpering.

Their front door was heavy and solid and made of very dark wood. It had only a little window, and the window had lead strips in the form of a cross. It looked like the window of a prison cell.

Inside the hall, their house smelled strange and very different from ours, which always smelled of baking. Theirs smelled of varnish and cigarettes.

Norma led us into their lounge. Mrs Greensit was sitting there in the dark, behind drawn curtains. She didn't say anything, just exhaled a cloud of blue smoke. I could barely make out her shape, let alone her features. She was on a settee, a haze of cigarette smoke lingering about her.

Norma pulled us both into the room. "There!" she said, pointing proudly at a greyish flickering screen. "What do you think of that?"

I didn't think anything of it.

Kenneth was rubbing his arm in pain. "Mum?"

"What?"

"Norma hit me."

"Ssssh!" hissed the hunched figure on the settee.

On the TV screen a series of geometrical shapes appeared, of various shades of grey. We watched this for some moments.

"Is that it? I asked, bored already.

"It hasn't started yet," snapped Mrs Greensit, taking the fag briefly out of her mouth, and replacing it when she'd finished speaking.

We waited for several interminable minutes longer.

"I need the toilet!" I lied, and rushed from the room.

***

Later, I told my mum about it. I described how dreadful it was in Greensits, about the horrible mother, about the stupid and pointless television and about how I wanted to be outside with the bees and hoverflies.

I don't think she understood what I was trying to say, because later still, when my dad was home, she said, "I'd like a television. It'd be company for me."

THE BOX OF TRICKS

Our Dad worked for the Army at Catterick Camp. Unfortunately he wasn't anything exciting – he didn't get to shoot a rifle or drive a tank. He didn't bring bullets home for us to play with. We couldn't go and see him load a shell into a 25 pounder. What he did do was something to do with electronics.

He'd been mad keen on electronics ever since he was a little kid, when he made something called a crystal set and spent his time listening to radio stations on it. Then later, at the beginning of the war, he'd gone to work on the RAF stations of Bomber Command.

He never talked about it, but had been something to do with communications. All he ever said about the war was that it was a terrible thing and that he hoped we would be spared having to live through another one. He said that the young men who flew the bombers were only lads straight out of school and that it was all wrong. So we didn't learn anything useful out of dad's wartime experiences.

Our Dad had a large wooden box, in reality just an old drawer out of a wardrobe, which he had filled with electrical bits. This box he used to bring out on an evening.

He'd put it on the dining room table, and would then happily sit and make things.

Inside Dad's box were all sorts of exciting gadgets and bits of metal. There were valves. These were made of glass and had metal pins for feet. They were transparent and delicate and interesting, but I was always afraid of breaking them.

Then there were transformers, big heavy metal square shapes wrapped in unpleasantly sticky tape, but which contained powerful magnets. These could be used in all sorts of inventions.

There was also a clever device called an oscillator, which consisted of very neatly-manufactured blades of aluminium, which interlocked when wound with the control knob. I think it was used in a radio to tune in to the different stations.

Best of all in Dad's box were the resisters. These were little things shaped like toffees, stuck on wire. Their bodies were dark, but they had brightly coloured stripes painted round them, which, Dad told us, indicated their resistance value. He tried to teach us the codes, but I could never remember which was which. I disliked the ones with brown waxy paper wrappings, they felt to me like fly paper – a substance I loathed.

I liked the dark brown ones with red and yellow stripes best. Dad asked me why and I said the colours went so well together. It was at this point that he realised I would never make an electrical engineer.

***

Now by far the best part of Dad's box was that it gave us an opportunity to use a device called a soldering iron. To make anything you had to solder the ingredients together, by melting solder – a soft piece of wire – and join the bits so that when the solder cooled, it formed a permanent joint.

The soldering iron was shaped like a poker, with a wooden handle and a rectangular iron point. The soldering iron was placed in the embers of the fire, to heat it until it became glowing red. Then out from the box would come the solder, which was in the form of thick wire, wound round a spool.

Dad would hold the hot iron, I would hold the solder and together we would melt it onto the joint we needed to make. I loved it. Clouds of smoke came off it. Even the smell was intoxicating.

When we'd finished making whatever Dad was making, I was allowed to play with the soldering iron by myself. I used the solder and applied the hot iron to the bare end of the solder wire. This would melt and fall onto the fireplace, forming wonderful silvery drops of molten metal. These would cool on the fireplace and leave starry-edged circles of silver, which I could peel off and collect. I used to save them in a match box. I thought they were valuable.

A BIG SURPRISE

Every afternoon about five o' clock Eck and I would start looking forward to Dad coming home from work. We sat outside by the sheds, looking down Chestnut Grove for the familiar figure plodding tiredly up the hill. As we had no car (and probably to save money) our Dad used to walk to and from Ravenscroft town centre, up and down the steep hill where we lived.

Tonight, as usual, he appeared round the corner of Elmwood Avenue and as usual he carried his battered old briefcase in one hand. Tonight, however, there was something obviously different about him. He was carrying a large cardboard box under his left arm.

"Must be a surprise!" I yelled, running off down the dusty road to meet Dad.

Although to all intents and purposes our Dad was a completely normal man, wearing a shirt and tie and sports jacket or suit like other men, having his hair cut short and wearing glasses which looked just like other men's glasses, in actual fact he had a streak of complete insanity about him. What he was carrying now was proof of that streak.

"What is it? What is it? What is it?" Eck and I chanted all the way up Chestnut Grove as we pulled and tugged at his side.

"Go on Dad, tell us! Tell us!" But he wouldn't tell us until we'd got home.

Only when we were inside the kitchen and Ma had appeared to discover what all the noise was about, did he put the cardboard box down.

We had absolutely no idea what the surprise might be. There had been no discussions, no hint of anything out of the ordinary, so it was a complete surprise when he opened the lid.

There was a moment of utter silence, no-one breathing. Nobody could imagine what might be inside, then Dad opened the flaps and as we all craned forward to look as he revealed - a tiny, trembling kitten.

Ma screamed (she didn't like cats.)

Eck and I shouted, "A cat!"

Dad shouted, "It's a present for the boys!" and ducked as Ma tried to hit him with the colander she was holding.

The cat, no doubt terrified by this sudden exposure to lunatics, let out a yowl, leapt vertically in the air and sunk its little teeth firmly into Dad's hand.

Pandemonium followed, Dad running around shouting, "Get it off! Get it off!" the cat spitting, hissing and clinging on with all its might, Eck and I shouting, "Let me see it! Let's keep it! Aw Dad, can we, can we, can we?" and Ma shouting, "He's mad! Stark staring bonkers! He knows I don't like cats! I can't stand cats, and what does he do, he brings home a cat!"

The noise only ceased when the poor kitten, tired of being swung round on the back of Dad's hand, let go and dropped from a great height to the floor. The way it landed so neatly on all four paws amazed us all and we stopped shouting.

There it stood, six inches of frightened fur, mewing plaintively - and we all instantly felt sorry for it.

Even Ma said, "Aw, look at the poor wee thing!"

Then it did a puddle on the floor and set Ma off shouting again.

***

We named the cat Frisky.

"You'll hardly notice him at all," said Dad, to placate her. He kept well out of range of her missiles.

"If it makes ONE mess on the carpet, it's out that door!"

"Isn't he luvly," said our Eck. "He's going to sleep in my bed."

And so Frisky the cat joined the family.

WASHDAY

Our Ma strongly resented having to do housework.

"I wasn't born to cook and clean up after a load of lazy oul men!" she would announce periodically, and we all knew it was time to get out of her way as soon as possible. Ma could be very fierce when she was in the mood and she really was in the mood on washdays.

First of all, she would go round the bedrooms collecting all the soiled clothes we were too lazy to put in the washing basket. This was guaranteed to get her fired up. She would dangle a pair of dirty underpants in the face of the embarrassed owner. "Look what I found under your bed!"

Then she would get out the washing machine. I don't know where this came from but it was unlike any other washing machine I'd ever seen - a huge yellow monster of a machine, made of heavy cast iron.

Although it had four wheels, it was impossible to steer and it would take Ma ten minutes of lugging and heaving to drag it from its lair in the larder, and deposit it in the middle of the kitchen floor. It was not, quite apparently, anything like the washing machines other homes had.

"Too mean to buy me a proper machine!" she would shout at Dad, even though he was out at work.

After that, Ma needed a fag to recover.

***

When she'd revived, she would gather up armfuls of clothes and ladle them inside. The monster may not have been at the forefront of technological developments, but it had immense capacity. There was a great wide lid, which lifted off so clothes could be top-loaded.

Being Irish and being impatient to get the hated job over and done with, Ma didn't bother to sort the clothes into coloureds and whites, she just bunged the whole lot in together. This often led to interesting results.

Once the maw of the beast was full to overflowing (and I do mean full – she hated washing so much she only did it when we'd used up all our clothes!) - once the beast was full, she'd ram in a few extras, aiming to get the whole hated job done in one go.

Now inside the chest of the beast there was a solid pillar, obviously there for a purpose. This was an impeller, to swirl the wet clothes about in the water, and it was a vital part of the process.

Ma, however, had taken a violent dislike to this pillar. To her it was an unnecessary obstruction which merely prevented her from jamming more clothes inside the machine. She cursed at it, she forced more clothes tight round it, she even took the fag out of her mouth so she was freed up to wrap even more clothes round it. Finally she would hit it with her set of wooden tongs, which were her favourite weapon on washday.

"There!" she would announce triumphantly, having completely overloaded the machine, regardless of weight restrictions or the need to balance the load.

Then she would light up another fag, climb up on top of the machine and sit on the lid. With a hefty drag on the old fag, she would jab at the starter switch, grip the lid tight under her thighs, and away we would go.

It's the Great Washday Ride! A free trip round the kitchen.

The motor starts up, whirrs and judders unhappily when it finds it is grossly overloaded, then bucks and kicks and jumps when it finds the impeller is jammed, while Ma sits on top, gripping the bucking bronco tight as it starts to jump around the kitchen floor.

There she perches, face grimly determined, sitting tight and holding on for dear life, keeping the lid locked on and all the while sucking nervously on her fag.

"These new machines," she pants. "They're not a patch on the oul ones!"

FISHING WITH DAD

Our Eck wasn't bothered about going fishing, being instead totally obsessed with *The Tough of the Track*, *The Wolf of Kabul* and the antics of *Desperate Dan*. So he would stay at home with our Ma, while I would go fishing with my Dad.

Dad wasn't exactly an expert fisherman, as I had recognised from the start. There was a clue in the fact that he never caught any fish. He was very enthusiastic, but absolutely totally unskilled.

He certainly put everything into his fishing, calling out excitedly, "I've got a bite!" at regular intervals. Somehow the bites never seemed to result in a fish being on the end of his hook. This constant failure never seemed to dull his enthusiasm however, or his desire to go fishing.

When I was little, back in Knaresborough, Dad had taken me every week to fish in the River Nidd at Conyngham Hall, which was just a short walk away from our house. The place we fished was called Cherry Tree Deep, and with good reason. The water was extremely deep and dark. My Dad had once found the body of a drowned woman there. It was rumoured to hold monster trout in its mysterious depths. We never caught any.

Our tackle was crude. I had a rod made out of bamboo – emphatically not one of those beautifully-made split cane rods you could see in the window of Metcalf's fishing tackle shop. It was a rough knobbly old thing that looked like a giant garden cane. I was embarrassed to be seen with it.

My reel wasn't one of those clever fixed-spool reels which made it easy to cast long distances. No, my reel was a nasty little centre pin reel which made it impossible to cast further than the length of the rod. It was so difficult to use that I usually ended up casting my worm into my own hair, or, sometimes, into Dad's.

Tangles were frequent with this tackle, so that my line was full of knots, which made it even more difficult to cast. A knot would stick in one of the rings, causing the line to pull up short, and the worm once again to impale itself in the back of my neck.

This disastrous rig was topped out by my float, the one bit of modern tackle I possessed. Unfortunately however, it was a great big red perch bung, which my Grandad had given me on our last holiday in Ireland. It was fine with the Irish perch, who were voracious eaters and very easy to catch. It was useless with the finicky and aristocratic trout of the Yorkshire rivers.

Trout were our quarry, both at Knaresborough and now at Ravenscroft. Clever, subtle fish, with delicate palates and suspicious natures. The merest whiff of my worm, the merest sight of my bamboo rod, seemed to send the crafty trout shooting off downstream, never to be seen again that day.

So, dream as I might of catching trout, all I ever caught were gudgeon, small, stupid little fish who lived in the mud at the bottom of Cherry Tree Deep, and whose appetite for worms seemed undiminished no matter how crude the tackle.

***

When we moved to Ravenscroft and saw the beautiful River Swale, I realised immediately that my tackle was useless and that I would never catch a trout. Unlike the dark and muddy River Nidd back in Knaresborough, the Swale was fast-flowing and clear. You could see the trout lying in great shoals, but equally, the trout could see you, and would quickly vanish. My garden cane, my centre pin reel, my knots and my big red perch bung, stood absolutely no chance of catching the wily trout of the River Swale.

Nevertheless, we tried. Below the road bridge at Ravenscroft station, where the road crossed the river on its way to Catterick Camp, there, at a big bend in the river, was a wide, deep pool. The river turned sharply on the bend, and a steep cliff on the far shore prevented the river from widening out. On the near shore there was a stony beach. The water was deeper than in most places on the Swale, and here, we thought, we might have at least a chance of catching a trout.

Dad and I pitched camp on the stony beach, and started to tackle up. Some urchins appeared from the bushes, and gathered round to watch us. As the river at this point was virtually in the centre of town, there were always going to be spectators.

I unfurled my rod. Derisive laughter erupted. I ignored it and began to thread my knotty old line through the rings of my rod. My Dad, in his usual leisurely manner, sat down and started to daydream.

"Aren't you going to tackle up Dad?"

"In good time son, in good time."

Eventually he took out his rod, a totally unsuitable spinning rod he had bought in Ireland for pike fishing with Grandad.

There was more derisive laughter, bringing more and more urchins out of the undergrowth to watch the entertainment.

"Yer'll catch nowt wi that!" advised one, spitting heartily to emphasise his point.

"Aye," chirped up another, all of five years old. "Bugger all!"

***

I was ready. I fitted a nice juicy worm (dug that morning in our garden) onto the hook.

"Phew!" whistled one of the urchins, clearly impressed by the size of my worm. "Eez after sharks!"

I ignored them. I steadied myself and prepared to cast. The water, though deep, was very fast-flowing. I hurled the rod out and released the line. For once, I hadn't lassoed myself with the worm.

The big red perch bung sailed off into the water, only to disappear off downstream at great speed with my hook and worm. The line had snapped.

"Did 'e just say 'Bollocks'?" quipped one of the urchins.

I re-set my tackle and tried again, but each time with the same result. There was no chance I would catch a trout doing this. Still, we caused great hilarity among our audience.

***

For an hour or more we persevered. Dad even left his daydreams and had a go, but was no more successful than I had been.

Finally, our watchers, tiring of our incompetence, decided to start throwing stones into the pool.

This was the final straw. Any trout who may have fancied a taste of our worms would certainly disappear off downstream, frightened off by the noise of the stones. By now they would be nearing Masham Abbey, two miles downriver.

Pulling in our tackle, Dad said, "Let's call it a day eh?"

I nodded in glum agreement.

Then he added brightly, "Let's have a go at skimming stones."

So we ended up our fishing trip with the urchins, throwing skimming stones across the pool, emulating them and causing one to say, "Yer want to stick to chucking rocks, cos yer crap at fishin!"

OUR TELLY

Ever since I'd told Ma about Mrs Greensit getting a telly, she had been unsettled. I had made a big mistake, I realised. Ma was going on and on about getting a telly. None of us wanted one, but she did, and she wasn't going to let us forget it.

Her mood was fine if it was a sunny evening and we'd all be out in the garden. She liked to sit there watching our Dad sift through the rubble that the builders had left us instead of a lawn. She was content then and peace would reign, but on wet nights when she was stuck inside, her fire would start to simmer.

"It's alright for you men," she'd scoff, as she watched our Dad sitting down with us to play with his box of electrical bits. "You've got something to do with your time, playing with your oul bits of wire."

Dad would smile to himself and make no reply.

Our Eck would be sitting in his corner reading his comics and wouldn't even notice what was going on. I would often be reading too. I had just discovered *Biggles*.

The fuse, however, had been lit.

"Look at the lot of you. Dead from the neck up! I might as well be dead meself for all the conversation I get round here."

Dad made the mistake of responding. "You should try reading."

It was well-meant, but he might as well have thrown a bucket of petrol on the fire. Ma snorted, a snort so indicative of disgust no words could have done a better job.

Dad elaborated on his bright idea. "Why don't you get yourself down to the library and find yourself a good read."

I despaired of my Dad sometimes.

Ma was on her feet, raging. "Think I have the time to go gallivanting off to the library? I'm too busy here cooking and slaving after you lot! 'Get yourself down to the library' – what a bloody cheek!"

He was right in a sense. Ma didn't read books. She sometimes bought magazines called *Woman* or *Woman and Home*, but even these she dismissed as 'a load of oul rubbish.' Except for the knitting patterns they contained. She used these to embark on ambitious knitting programmes, which always ended up with our Eck or me being presented with some spectacularly horrible jumper, which she would insist we wore.

I had once been given a bright yellow jumper the colour of daffodils, and sent off to school wearing it. The kids called me Custard. I had more fights in one day than I had in the rest of my school career, and refused ever to wear it again.

In the end she gave it to some Hungarian refugees who had fled their country with no possessions. Even they refused to wear it.

Once, after reading *Woman and Home* she was enthused enough to try some of the cooking recipes she found there, but these somehow always failed to live up to expectations. When she produced some buns so rocklike they could have been used to fill holes in the road, she declared, "Ach, they must have got the ingredients all wrong!"

Ma wasn't a great one for the reading.

***

Back to the simmering row about the television…

Dad, having got both feet firmly wedged in a faux pas, decided to follow up with a real gem. "Why don't you try a Romance?"

"Romance?!! Romance!!! What would you know about Romance?"

Dad, somewhat baffled by the violence of her reaction, put down his soldering iron.

The iron wasn't the only thing that was getting heated.

"'Try a Romance', he says. 'Try a Romance'! Do you boys know what he bought me last Christmas? A pair of slippers!"

She glowered menacingly at us, daring anyone to contradict her. "True as I'm standing here, slippers. Yes, you can laugh. I slave for the lot of you all year and what do I get for my thanks? A pair of old slippers. I told him what he could do with his slippers." (She threw them at him and cried intermittently all Christmas Day.)

I knew where this was going. I wondered if my Dad did however.

"WELL HE'D BETTER GET ME SOMETHING DECENT THIS CHRISTMAS OR HE'LL KNOW ABOUT IT!"

***

I felt sorry for Ma. She'd been uprooted from her family in Ireland and had come to England to work. She'd lived and worked in London for years. She'd been a firewatcher in the City of London throughout the Blitz. She'd lived through danger and excitement and now she was stuck here in the wilds of the North Riding, without friends or any family except her own. It must have been difficult for her.

"Of course," she said, her voice full of menace. "Some people have a husband they can talk to. Some people aren't stuck at home all day slaving for a bunch of lazy men."

This was true. Dad worked hard and when he came home he was tired. He would often fall asleep.

"Some people wouldn't mind so much - (and then came the punchline)- if only they had a television for company."

Dad pushed his box of electrical bits away. He suddenly looked tired. It was the first time I had ever seen him look like this – resigned.

"I'd get you one tomorrow love," he said with a sigh. "If I could afford one, I'd get you one tomorrow."

***

I went to bed that night feeling oddly sad. I understood that life wasn't easy for our Mum or our Dad. He worked all the time and we had no money for extras. We didn't have a car, a vacuum cleaner, a transistor radio, a spin dryer or even a fridge. The only household goods we had were the monster washing machine and the mains radio, which had been their wedding present. We didn't go on holidays except to Grandad in Ireland.

As kids we didn't miss or want any of these things, but we kids had millions of things to do with our time. I realised that Ma and Dad must have had moments when they wished life was a bit easier for them both.

I wished Ma could have her telly.

DAD MAKES A START

The long summer was over and it was getting dark soon after we got home from school. We still didn't have a telly and there was no more talk of getting one, so we settled back into our old routine. Eck and I would play outside until it got dark and Ma would call us both in. Sometimes I had homework to do, so I did that on the dining room table. Our kid would be immersed in the *Topper* or the *Dandy*. His current favourite story was Black Bob, about a Scottish sheepdog.

Ma had found herself a hobby. She had taken to making rugs. These were bought as bare skeletons. She then bought bundles of coloured wool, and, sitting with the skeleton on her lap, she would pull the bits of wool through it with a metal hook. She found this restful and the evenings were pleasantly quiet as the autumn nights grew dark.

I liked the round bundles of wool. I liked the bright colours and the feel of the packed wool lengths. I liked the smell of the wool. Funnily enough, I never liked the finished rug as much. Suddenly our house was filled with shaggy rugs with faces and shapes that no-one liked.

Our dad would do the washing up and then come and join us round the fire. There were only two seats, so there was usually a fight to have the best one, the one next to the fire. If no-one was around (Eck having gone to bed, Ma busy doing her rug, Dad playing with his box of bits) I would pull the chair from its usual position at the side of the fire and place it right in the middle, up close to the middle of the fire.

Then I would stretch my legs out and put them up on the mantelpiece, or rest them up against the fireplace. The heat of the fire rapidly warmed the back of my legs.

If I was wearing long trousers the heat would scorch them, so I was careful not to let the hot material touch my skin. If my dad caught me doing this he would move up to me quickly and run his hands down the back of my legs, bringing the hot material into contact with my bare skin.

"Ow! I'm burning!" I'd howl.

"Serves you right!" he would laugh.

"It wasn't funny Dad!"

"It'll teach you a lesson."

I'm not sure exactly what sort of a lesson it taught me, other than that my dad had a very odd sense of humour. I still put my legs up on the mantelpiece whenever I got the chance.

As I have said, Dad would get his favourite box of bits out and sit silently with them. Our Dad loved to play with the thousands of electrical gadgets he had collected over the years. He never threw anything out.

Ma would retort, "Because he's a wicked oul miser, that's why!"

Dad would grin and ignore Ma. He was very patient and very skilled at mending anything that was broken. I thought he must be a good instructor to all the soldiers, though I wasn't ever sure what it was he instructed them in. He said it was something called AC Theory, which didn't sound very interesting, but if it had had anything to do with his drawer full of magical bits, it must have been good fun.

"Harry, don't tire the boy out," said Ma, looking up from her latest rug, a fetching little number in bright orange, green and purple.

Dad winked at me and spread out something in his hand.

"Look at this." It was a large valve, one I hadn't seen before. "Look inside." He held it up to the light.

I bent close, and inside there was a whole little world of metallic shapes all carefully contrived and designed to fit inside this small glass tube. I wondered how they got it all in there.

He let me hold it. I liked valves. They were such a clever invention. You had to hold them carefully because the spiny feet were fragile and easily bent, and when you tried to fit them into the holes made for them in the chassis, you had to gently feel your way in with the little spines, or they would bend or break.

Dad watched closely as I slowly eased the valve into position in the chassis.

I liked the word 'chassis'. The way my Dad pronounced the word it sounded like Shassy. I couldn't think of any other words in English that were spelled or sounded like it.

The chassis was the base plate of whatever it was Dad was making. It was made of aluminium and was a kind of rectangular box, though there were lots of holes in it, presumably to take things like the valves. The chassis was the structure of the device.

My Dad got out his soldering iron and heated it up in the fire. Then he undid the solder from its spool, which was the bit I liked best. The solder was soft and when he touched it with the hot iron it melted and made a blob of silver, which he skilfully applied to the chassis. He was joining up the various components of whatever it was he was making.

Once he'd finished, Dad let me play with the soldering iron, just for fun, and I dropped blobs of silver onto the top of a metal box, so they burst into brilliant metal stars.

"Look at this Ma!" I said excitedly, holding out my handful of silver stars.

"Don't you drop them on my carpet," she said threateningly.

I said nothing.

I had guessed something.

Dad was making a TV.

MISCHIEF NIGHT

Mischief Night was the 30th of October, and was the highlight of the year for us kids. For weeks we had been hearing tales from the kids at school of the wonderful things that went on at Mischief Night. Kids were let out on their own and roamed the streets in gangs, causing mischief to the adult world, mischief which was so exciting that no other day in the year, not even Bonfire Night, could compete with it. This was because it was purely a kids' night. The adults stayed locked up in their houses, and for once, the kids ruled the streets.

Our kid and I had never done it before. Last year our Eck had been too young to be let out, so this was to be our first Mischief Night. Other kids told us stories of knocking on windows and running away before you could be caught; of knocking on doors and running away; worse still, of putting treacle on door handles (imagine what fun that would be!)

Really tough kids like Kevin Batty told us how last year he had tied door handles together, which action apparently caused complete chaos to an entire neighbourhood. He told of lifting garden gates off their hinges and even swapping them round with other houses' gates. This sounded just unbelievable fun, so it was with a mixture of fear and fright and excitement that we went out together for the first time at night.

Of course, I was sure that nothing really bad was ever done – it was mischief – harmless fun. No-one would ever dream of doing anything that might harm a person or an animal - the main excitement was being allowed out after dark with your friends.

***

We all met up outside Greensits – me, our Eck, Kenneth and Norma, Clive Lawson the Pater's son and Alex Marcham and his sister Sandra. It was dark. We had torches. We shone them in each other's faces and made spooky noises to frighten each other. The streetlights were lit on Elmwood Avenue. There were no streetlights on Chestnut Grove. We set off down the hill towards the Tip.

We jostled each other, we boasted of the brave things we were going to do. Then, as we neared the Tip, everyone suddenly slowed down.

"What about the rats?" asked our Eck.

Without another word, we all changed direction, hurrying quickly away from the Tip. The rats which infested the Tip would certainly be out in force at night. In our excited state we had forgotten about the rats.

We stopped halfway up Elmwood Avenue.

"Let's bang on a door and run away!" suggested Clive Lawson.

Kenneth opened the nearest gate.

Clive stopped him. "Not that one you idiot! That's my house!"

We moved a hundred yards up the road.

***

"Okay, now let's knock on a door and run away," said Clive.

"Ooo – big deal," sneered Norma, who clearly hadn't really entered into the spirit of Mischief Night and was determined to spoil it for the rest of us.

"Just shut up Norma!" everyone chorused.

We moved another hundred yards up Elmwood Avenue, still arguing about who should be the first to do some mischief.

Our Eck, though the smallest of the Mischief Makers, was probably the bravest, and tiring of all the idle talk, volunteered to knock on the next house we came to.

The rest of us crouched down behind the stone garden wall. The chosen house was in darkness.

"Go on then!" hissed Norma loudly.

Eck marched confidently off down the path to the front door. He knocked loudly. There was no reply. He knocked again. No reply.

"Give it a right bang!" called Norma.

Eck turned at looked back at her, glowering fiercely, and hammered loudly on the door. Instantly a light came on.

"Run! I called. We all ran.

I waited until our Eck had got out of the garden, before pulling his arm and helping him along. Fifty yards or more we scampered, before ducking down behind another wall. We'd all got away, and we sat there panting, holding our sides and giggling.

"Oh it was so funny… the way he banged on the door! I bet they wondered what on earth it was!"

It was then we noticed Kenneth was missing. We'd left him behind.

"What a twat!" said Norma.

Alex peeked up above the wall to see where he'd got to. The rest of us remained hidden.

"What is it Alex? What's happening?"

An angry man, obviously the householder, had Kenneth by the shoulders and was shaking Kenneth and shouting at him.

We could hear it quite clearly.

"What's your name?" the man demanded.

Kenneth just stood there, saying nothing, but obviously terrified.

"Name!"

"Kenneth Greensit," blurted Kenneth.

An angry Norma exclaimed, "God! He's too bleeding stupid even to give a false name!"

"Address?"

We all listened in horror as Kenneth gave the man his full address.

"Right," said the angry man. "Let's go meet your dad."

Off marched the man, leading Kenneth by the collar, in the direction of Kenneth's house.

"Oh my God!" wailed Norma. "His dad will kill him."

***

It was a very chastened and unsuccessful band of Mischief Makers that trooped sadly back home to face retribution.

BONFIRE NIGHT

For weeks we had been preparing for Bonfire Night. Every kid in Ravenscroft was out in the fields, keenly scouring the trees and hedges for branches of dead wood for the bonfires. This was part of the excitement, for we were all very competitive kids. We all wanted a bigger and better bonfire than the other gangs and to that end we traipsed for miles, dragging branches home and building our own fire.

Our bonfire was on the waste ground at the front of our house. It started slowly at the beginning of October, with just a few bits of old wood we'd found lying around, and waste left by O'Briens the builders. Next we looted the hedges in the nearby fields, and soon the fire was three, four, five feet high.

Next we were going beyond the top of Hubberholme hill, to the woods on the other side, and to the Plantation and over the road to the wood near Gulliver Tower, in our search for more and more wood. It became an obsession! I would lie in bed awake at night, visualising a huge bonfire made of giant dead branches we'd hauled all the way from

.

Masham Abbey (where there were some massive ancient trees.)

Adults seemed to take no notice of swarms of kids everywhere in Ravenscroft, lugging dead branches along the streets and pavements. We didn't mind. Adults belonged to another world, one in which we had no interest.

Soon our fire was eight, nine, ten feet tall. We found some discarded builders' planks and brought the huge fire to a tall, volcanic point. Surveying this creation, we felt proud of our achievements.

It was time to enter the next phase of Bonfire Night preparations, which, according to Alex Marcham, was to attack other kids' bonfires. The aim of this, I was told in very forceful terms, was to sabotage other kids' bonfires by setting fire to them prematurely. This was the height of bonfire rivalry, to destroy someone else's bonfire.

I had my doubts about the morality of this, but all the other kids agreed with Alex's idea, so there was no point in avoiding the subject. Other gangs were going to burn our bonfire anyway, whether we attacked theirs or not. All the Chestnut Grove kids therefore had to take turns in protecting our own bonfire from alien saboteurs bent on arson.

Ma, ever the detective, noticed something strange was going on. She spotted me sneaking into our sacred front room.

"What're you up to?"

"Nothing Ma," I lied.

She didn't believe me, but, short of evidence, let me go. There I would sit, staring out of the front window to where our bonfire stood tall as Mount Etna.

Ma knew that we never went into our sacred front room (I don't even know why it was sacred, it only had a settee and an empty fireplace) so she was suspicious.

"Whatever are you doing in here?" she'd say. "You'll catch your death of cold."

I didn't reply. There was no point. She wouldn't understand. However, by my vigilance and that of the other Chestnut Grove kids, our bonfire was kept safe from attack.

Naturally, again according to Alex, we had to attack other kids' bonfires. This was the bit I wasn't keen on, aware just how much our bonfire meant to us, and how much of a personal disaster its destruction would be. Surely the kids in other gangs would feel the same?

Luckily for me, there wasn't much opportunity to set fire to the other kids' bonfires. There was an enormous one in the Ghyll, built by the great gangs of Army kids from the Green Howards barracks and its neighbouring estate. There was no way any of us was going to be stupid enough to set that one on fire, as the army kids numbered in their hundreds and if we'd even tried, they would have captured us and in all probability, put us on top of their bonfire and burned us alive (or so we feared.)

Lord Lovat's no doubt had a huge bonfire. We sometimes saw them pushing old settees along Hubberholme Road and once I'd seen a gang of them struggling along in a long line with a complete telegraph pole on their shoulders. God only knew where they had found that. Anyway, there was no way we would ever venture into the Lord Lovat's estate – it was like the Wild West down there.

So, night after night, we sat there in Chestnut Grove, watching and waiting and protecting our bonfire from attack, which luckily never came.

***

Ever since we'd moved to Ravenscroft in the summer, our Eck and I had been saving for fireworks. We didn't get regular pocket money (the household budget was tight) – but if ever our Dad or Ma had some spare change, they might slip a few coppers into our hands, with a quiet, "Put it towards your fireworks – but don't tell your Mum/Dad."

Even adults realised that Bonfire Night was something special - the best, the most adventurous and the most exciting night of the year as far as kids were concerned.

Every big heavy penny, every halfpenny went towards our collection, which Eck, ever the hoarder, would keep in an old biscuit tin under his bed. Occasionally we would get a twelve-sided threepenny bit, or even more occasionally, a lovely shiny sixpence. It all went in the tin under the bed.

On Saturday mornings throughout October Ma would get her coat on, Dad would be dragged out of his garage and off we would all go down into Ravenscroft town. There, in the marketplace opposite the Cross, was the most magical shop, a shop which sold fireworks.

Standard Fireworks, it said on a brilliantly-coloured poster in the shop window.

We bought them individually, one at a time. None of those big Standard firework boxes for us. We couldn't afford them and anyway, it was much more interesting to buy the fireworks one by one. We only bought the small fireworks – big ones like Roman Candles were out of our reach. But we didn't mind.

There we would stand, staring big-eyed into the glass display case in which they had spread out all the goodies of the firework world: Jumping Jacks, Golden Fountains, Diamond Cascades, Silver Zodiac Fountains, dangerous looking ones with a bright red spike, even Catherine wheels - what a magical world for us kids to choose from.

One week I would buy a bright blue Volcano, shaped just like a real volcano - while our kid would choose the long thin stick of a Golden Rain. Another day I might get a Jumping Jack while our kid would plump for a short fat Snow Storm.

All the fireworks carried that wonderful refrain: "Light the blue touch paper and retire."

We couldn't wait to light the blue touch paper and retire.

***

We loved those fireworks. We cherished them. We could hardly wait to get home to take them out of their brown paper bags so we could admire them. We stored them carefully in our bedroom and displayed them proudly along the top of the cupboard. There were Brock's, Standard, Pains, each one a different shape and size, each one promising untold fiery delights.

There were bangers too, dangerous little red cardboard tubes with a thin blue spout and a twisty blue paper fuse. Bangers were intimidating and always handled with great reverence and care, just in case they should explode.

As Bonfire Night drew near, we were each treated to a rocket, a long wooden stick with a missile on top. Mine was blue, with a shower of white stars. Our Eck's was red, with a shower of yellow stars. I preferred mine.

***

Finally, of course, there was the Guy himself. We had to have a Guy to burn on the fire.

The tradition apparently was that we would go out onto the streets of Ravenscroft and collect a Penny for the Guy, so we could raise money for fireworks.

First we had to make a Guy. Ma had given us a pair of Dad's old trousers and a shirt. Alex Marcham had provided an old jacket and Kenneth Greensit had very generously donated one of his Dad's hats (he wore brown trilby hats!) These we had taken to our Dad's garage and stuffed with old rags and anything else that wouldn't be missed.

In a short time our Guy was finished.

The four of us stood and surveyed our creation. Our Guy was, to be frank, not very impressive. "What do you think?" I asked.

"It hasn't got a face."

"It hasn't got any hands."

"Apart from that, what do you think?"

Together they all chorused, "I think it's rubbish!"

We all agreed. It was rubbish.

Nevertheless, it was an important part of preparations for Bonfire Night to have a Guy, so we loaded him into our Eck's old pram and scrawled on a piece of cardboard the legend PENNY FOR THE GUY.

This we trundled round the streets of Ravenscroft for a whole chilly Saturday afternoon. The residents of Ravenscroft, were, unfortunately, of the same opinion as us. The Guy was rubbish. We got threepence. We nearly got four pence, but one old man who had at first given us a penny, on closer scrutiny of the Guy, delved into our penny tin and retrieved his penny. Not a great success.

∗∗∗

As Bonfire Night drew ever closer, the question of the wretched Guy still hung over me. Our Guy was rubbish. It was going to ruin our Bonfire Night. Three days to go and our Guy was going to ruin the whole thing.

Ma, ever the detective, knew something was wrong and cornered me. "What are you looking so glum about?"

"We haven't got a Guy."

"I thought you'd made one."

"No, it's absolute rubbish."

"Oh dear." She patted my arm. "Never mind, no one'll notice."

No one'll notice? No one'll notice? The main attraction, the whole point of the bonfire, was the Guy sitting up on top of the fire. No one'll notice!!

She just didn't understand. She didn't even seem concerned; if anything she was smiling as if nothing was going to go wrong.

***

Bonfire Night arrived. Eck and I got all our fireworks laid out on the kitchen table.

Ma brought us two shoeboxes to keep them in. "And mind you keep the lid on them!" she warned.

We took a last loving look at our wonderful fireworks, and packed them into the boxes.

It was dark outside and other families were starting to gather round the fire. We were ready to go but there was no sign of our Dad.

"Where is he?"

"What's he doing?"

"They're going to start without us!"

"Come on Dad, come on! Where are you?"

In the kitchen Ma had a whole load of biscuit tins and trays full of food she'd made. There was Treacle Parkin, Ginger biscuits, Bonfire Toffee, and best of all, big shiny brown Toffee Apples, rows of them glistening golden and treacly, their heads stuck down on a baking tray.

"Do you want a hand carrying them?" I volunteered.

Ma was too crafty for me.

"Yes, but keep your hands off those Toffee Apples."

I lifted a tray of Treacle Parkin and just then Dad appeared.

"Come on, come on!" he said briskly.

"Dad! Where've you been? We've been waiting for you!"

"Never mind David, let's go." He ushered us out, each one of us carrying a box or a tray of food.

***

Outside was already exciting. The air smelled different, an ashy, smoky, sparky smell. In the distant sky we could see red glows where other bonfires had already started.

"Look at Lord Lovat's!"

There was a huge red glow in the sky over Lord Lovat's. Either they'd set a house on fire or they had one massive bonfire. Must have been all those settees they'd collected.

There was a crowd round the bonfire now. A circle of watchers formed - the Greensits (even the mysterious Mrs Greensit), the neighbours, all the people from our street. They were chatting, introducing themselves (for we were all new to Chestnut Grove and no-one knew anyone else.)

People were tense. It was time to light the fire.

"Dad?" I called. "Dad?"

Annoyingly, he had disappeared again.

"Mum, where's Dad gone?"

"I don't know."

The man from next door stepped forward to light the fire. The bonfire looked massive and impressive. If we'd only had a proper Guy it would have looked better still, but never mind. Our apology Guy looked down on us from under his hat, his faceless expression impressing no-one.

"Wey hey hey!" yelled Kenneth Greensit, clapping his hands together, pointing at the Guy and capering round in a wild war dance. His father was staring closely at our Guy. I think he had recognised the hat.

"Where's our Dad?" I called again.

Then Dad appeared. He and another man were carrying a chair between them.

He shouted, "Make way, make way! Let us through!"

"Dad!"

Dad grinned. Seated on the chair was Guy Fawkes! A brilliantly-realistic Guy Fawkes, with a proper face and hands. Dad must have been secretly making it all the time.

"Good old Dad!" I nearly cried. "Ma! You knew all along!"

She smiled and put her arms found Eck and me.

Dad and the other man carried Guy Fawkes in his chair and put him ceremonially on the top of the bonfire. Everyone applauded.

"There you are, Guy Fawkes himself!" said our Dad.

And with that the man put a light to the fire.

It was slow to take hold, and for a moment we feared the wood was too damp to catch light, but slowly it gained strength and started to spread.

We had fed bits of Tar (roofing felt) in between the branches, to make sure the fire would burn. Tar burned really well, so we were grateful to O'Briens the builders for their contribution.

Wooosh!

It went up suddenly and all at once the whole bonfire was ablaze. Everyone clapped and cheered. In the glowing orange light of the fire we all stood and marvelled.

Ma brought out all the food and served it herself. The Toffee Apples went first, a big hit. Then the Treacle Parkin and the Bonfire Toffee. Everyone stood chomping away, as the kids started to set off their fireworks.

What a night it was.

***

Guy Fawkes survived until the bonfire started to subside, then first his legs caught, then his jacket, and finally his hat. Slowly he toppled over, to a great cheer from the crowd.

Then I stepped backwards and fell headfirst three feet down the steps to our house, knocking myself out on the concrete path.

A night to remember.

FRISKY

Our cat was called Frisky. He had grown rapidly from a tiny kitten into a big beautiful cat. He was a tortoiseshell, striped and tigerish, and was exquisitely neat and tidy in appearance and manners. When he was in the house he would spend hours licking his paws, stroking his whiskers and washing his face. We all loved Frisky.

When he had first arrived as a kitten in a box Ma had been very much against him.

"Cats are smelly," she'd announced. "I don't like cats."

Eck and I had looked at the furry little face and prayed he wouldn't make a mess. Frisky must have understood English, because after that first day he never once 'disgraced himself' – as Ma called it. The kitten was allowed to stay.

Frisky had been born on a farm out in the wilds, way beyond Hubberholme, where cats were kept as working animals, expected to earn their keep by catching and destroying rodents. Frisky had been bred from a long line of fearsome warrior cats, cats bred to hunt all night, bred to rule the farmyard.

We didn't know this of course. We thought he was lovely to stroke and to pet and to curl up with at night. Well, he was. He used to sleep with a smile on his face, curled up in a tight little ball. We would curl up next to him and put our arms around him. I often used to go to sleep on the rug in front of the fire, with Frisky cradled in my arms.

As a kitten he quite happily played with us in the garden. He dug his little claws into balls of wool we held for him, and was swung off his feet, refusing to let go. Or he would doze in the sun in the garden or scratch Ma's stockings.

But as he grew older and bigger, we began to notice his increasing restlessness. We would find him sitting in the window-bay, looking curiously into the budgie-cage, testing out the strength of the bars with his claws. Then Eck's goldfish vanished in mysterious circumstances. Frisky was strongly suspected of supplementing his diet with a little extra protein.

Frisky tried. He resisted the call of the wild as long as he could, but it was no use. He wasn't bred to be a domestic dozer, a fat cat to sit on the mat. Frisky was a wild rover. He wanted to be off, out hunting the mice and voles in the fields, as his ancestors had always done.

He tried being domesticated, he really did. He sat obediently in the garden with us. He let his stomach be tickled, his nose stroked. But one day I watched him as he lurked among Dad's new spinach rows, ready to pounce out on the sparrows playing nearby, and I realised where his heart really belonged. Any self-respecting domestic cat could catch sparrows – they were beneath Frisky's dignity.

He hadn't been bred to be a tame cat, one whose only thrill was to kill such harmless creatures as sparrows.

He began to look at us with reproach in his eyes. He moped around the house all day. His whiskers drooped. And when night came and the fever was on him to be out, he prowled the hall, stalking up and down like a lion trapped in a cage.

***

Frisky was a good cat. He didn't howl or make a mess on the carpet. But he was a wild cat and it was cruel to keep him indoors.

Dad noticed it too. "He wants out," he said one evening. He glanced at Ma.

"I don't know…" said Ma.

"What do you think? Should we let him out?"

Ma looked at us boys. "If anything happened to him…" she trailed off.

We all knew what she meant. We would be heartbroken if he was hurt.

***

For a few nights more we kept him in, but eventually we knew we had to give in. Frisky was let out at night. He was overjoyed.

That night I said a prayer for his safe return. I wondered where he would go and what he would do. I need not have worried. In the morning Frisky was there when we went down to breakfast, sipping at a saucer of milk. He had visibly perked up. He looked sleek and glossy. He stalked once more as a King Cat.

A routine was soon established, whereby Frisky went out at night for his adventures, and returned at breakfast. At night he was once more a real wild cat, and by day he was a pet cat. At first I was concerned that he didn't need us any more, that he would no longer be satisfied sitting with us by the fire, but that wasn't what happened. He was happy in both worlds.

In the morning he would often return with a trophy from his night of hunting – a mouse, a vole, or once, a rat. These he would leave on the back doorstep so we would be sure to notice them. Ma noticed the rat alright, she trod on it. Frisky wisely kept out of her way for the following few days.

Frisky spent the daylight hours with us, doing whatever we wanted him to do – he was a very good-natured cat, but when our bedtime came and the sun went down, you could see him washing his face, stretching his claws and testing them out on the settee, and you knew his thoughts were turning to the fields and woods, to smells of vole and trails of mouse, to a fearsome battle with a cornered rat. For Frisky the cat was on the prowl!

CHRISTMAS

J ust after my birthday Ma made us sit down at the dining table and write our letters to Father Christmas. Now that I was eight I was just beginning to have certain doubts about the existence of this gentleman. I knew that we wrote letters to him and that he usually responded pretty well to these requests, but how on earth did he come down the chimney? Our fire was lit every night in winter and the chimney looked very sooty and black to me. I knew this because I looked up it and shone a torch inside one day. Still, our Eck was a firm believer and I wasn't going to say anything to spoil things for him. Anyway, I wanted a sledge.

"What are you asking for our kid?"

He held up a copy of the *Beano*. Then a *Dandy*. Then a *Topper*.

"Annuals," he said. "Annuals, annuals and more annuals."

He was easy to please, was our Eck.

"What do you want for Christmas, Ma?"

She looked up from her rug-making. "A telly."

I said nothing. She had no idea that Dad had been secretly building a television set out of his box of bits.

***

We had a Christmas party at school and then school broke up. At home we had a Christmas tree set up in the sacred front room. Ma brought out the set of six brightly-coloured glass baubles that we had each year, and we spent the evening trying to re-attach the little prongs that had come adrift, prongs which were needed to fix the baubles to the tree.

We made the paper streamers ourselves, gluing little strips of coloured paper together. Then there were some silver ribbons that came in a flat packet, which we draped over the branches of our Christmas tree. The Christmas cards that had been sent to us were put on a string and pinned to the wall. Excitement was building up.

Ma took us Christmas shopping and we bought a box of dates (we only ever had dates at Christmas.) No-one actually liked dates, but they were an important part of Christmas. Then there was also a box of edible sticks called Twiglets – I absolutely loathed these sour and arthritic fingers of food. There was a bottle of Stones Ginger wine and a bottle of QC sherry. I sipped it once and although QC was supposed to stand for Quality Counts, I had my doubts.

On Christmas Eve we were too excited to go to bed, trying to prolong the evening by making excuses to stay up.

"Isn't it time for your bed?" Ma would ask.

"No, we want to stay up to see Father Christmas," we'd reply.

This was repeated until Ma lost her patience with us.

"Come on, bed time."

"Yes," said Dad in support. "Up the apples and pears!"

"What if we don't?"

"Then Father Christmas might not come. He doesn't like disobedient children."

Hmm, I thought. That was a bit suspicious. How did he know we were being disobedient?

Eck and I shared a bedroom. We had single beds side by side, separated by a small bedside cabinet. Ma got us both into our beds and came to tuck us in.

"Say your prayers," she said.

I said a prayer. It was for a sledge for me and a TV for our Ma. I hoped she wouldn't ask me what I'd prayed for.

"Night night. Sleep tight."

"Night Ma. Night Dad."

"Night son."

Eck stirred. "Ma?"

"What is it now?"

"I can't get to sleep."

"I'm sure you can if you try. Now go on, get to sleep."

She tiptoed out of the room and switched the light off. I lay there in the dark, thinking about Christmas and what it all meant.

Our kid went quiet.

I looked down to the end of our beds. Ma had laid out a pillowcase on each bed. They lay there, flat and white and empty.

I thought of the sledge I'd asked Father Christmas to get me. I thought of Ma and her telly. Would there be enough money in Father Christmas's bank account to provide both of them? If not, I would prefer it if Ma got her telly. It would make her happy. It might even stop her making those dreadful rugs.

***

My eyes were open. Instantly I sat up. At the end of the bed was a big white bulge.

"Eck! He's been! Wake up!"

We were instantly out of our beds, pulling at the heavy white sacks, laughing, grinning, calling out, "Ma! Pa! He's been!"

He always wrapped his presents very neatly, did Father Christmas. I liked the wrapping paper, which this year had little white snowmen on a blue background. It always seemed a shame to me to tear open the paper and then throw it away.

I had a box of sweets called a Selection box, a whole trayful of different types of chocolates, including, to my great pleasure, a bar of Fry's Five Boys, which was my favourite.

Our Eck had been given his annuals. *The Topper. The Dandy* and *The Beano*. I had been given the only annual I really liked, an odd Scottish one called *Oor Wullie*. I loved

Oor Wullie. He was a boy who sat on a bucket and told stories about his adventures with his friends Fat Bob, Soapy Soutar and Wee Eck.

We ran through to our parents' bedroom, tugging at their eiderdown to wake them up.

"Look Ma!" I showed her my *Oor Wullie* annual. I didn't mention the sledge which I had so desperately wanted. Obviously Father Christmas's bank account had been emptied by all the annuals. Still, it was a great exciting moment, as we both piled onto our parents' bed to show them what Father Christmas had brought us.

***

Later, downstairs, when we'd had breakfast, Dad said, "Have you been in the sacred front room lately?"

I looked at Ma. She obviously knew nothing about it.

Eck stood up excitedly. "Let's go!" He had guessed something had happened.

I ran after him, Ma and Pa following.

There they were. Two sledges. A bright shiny black and red one, and a tall one with tubular metal runners.

"The tall one's yours David," said Dad.

I sat on it. It was just perfect. Just what I had dreamed about! I couldn't wait for it to snow so we could go sledging down the field.

Our Eck's sledge was very different, with wide flat runners. He sat on it, pulling on the steering ropes, grinning and grinning.

Our Dad wasn't finished. "And... "

He went behind the settee and bent to lift something heavy. "This is for Ma!"

It was a telly.

Ma hugged him in delight.

SLEDGING

I loved Winter. Spring would have us birds-nesting, Summer playing in the river and Autumn had conkering, Mischief Night and Bonfire Night – but to me Winter was best of all. I looked forward to those days when the sky was slate-grey and cloudless. I got bored with clouds in summer, but those grey skies meant only one thing – snow was on its way.

This year, we couldn't wait to see the snow start to fall. Our new Christmas sledges were stacked in the hall, ready to use.

Then there it was. I woke one day to find the world had turned white.

***

Our sledging run was in the field in front of our house, the same steep hill where I would launch my Dutch arrer, where Kevin Batty would shoot our Eck and where Norma Greensit lurked in the hedges trying to entice us in to join her.

Today it was a different world, a great white featureless land which had to be beaten down flat to form a sledging track. Snow fell deep here in Ravenscroft and already there was six inches or more. When it began to drift it would be over the top of the stone walls.

Eck was a great help. His sledge had big flat wooden runners, so we pulled it up and down the hill using it as a snowplough, to flatten and beat the snow and make it hard-packed.

The Greensits came out to join us, with expensive-looking sledges. It was quite safe to allow Norma to play with us, as not even Norma was foolish enough to want to show us her knickers in the sub-zero temperatures of O'Brien's field at eight in the morning. Later, perhaps, when it warmed up.

Soon there were lots of other kids in the field, the excitement of the snow banishing the usual animosities that existed. No-one could be bothered to fight or insult each other when there was sledging to be done. It was too exciting and too short-lived to waste.

Unfortunately our Eck's sledge proved to be a bit of a disaster. It flattened the snow alright, and it sailed down the slope at speed. The trouble was that it lacked metal runners to guide its path, so it was impossible to steer, and poor Eck would go flying off course into deep drifts, quite unable to do anything to prevent it happening.

"Hey!" he would yell, careering off into deep snow. "I can't steer it!" It was so funny to watch, and he was perfectly happy doing this, but it was dangerous. He was liable to vanish without trace into some of those drifts and he was my responsibility. So I let him share my sledge and abandon his own.

I guessed that my Dad had made my sledge out of thick shiny tubular steel, which he must have welded in the Army workshops. It had a seat long enough to take the two of us. It was a brilliant sledge, far outclassing the expensive bought sledges possessed by people like the Greensits and Clive Lawson the Pater's son. It rode high and could sledge even through unprepared snow. Its runners were naturally smooth and wouldn't block with packed snow as happened to the other sledges. It steered well and could take two passengers.

Its only drawback was that it was, if anything, a bit too fast. With two aboard it had a lot of weight and gained momentum rapidly, so that by the time it reached the bottom of the field it was racing uncontrollably and the only way of stopping it was by baling out. Otherwise you would hit whatever happened to be in the way. It was great fun, and the high-speed bale-outs were incredibly exciting.

***

We sledged all day and into the night and only came home when Ma dragged us inside. Red-faced from the snow and flushed with excitement, we didn't want to go to bed.

"Thanks Dad," I said, and gave him a hug.

HOSPITAL

Over a month later and the snow was still there. Ma was in a glum mood because she could hardly get out of the house. The snowdrift at the back of the house was almost at the top of the back door. We couldn't get out that way at all. A journey to town was slow and tiring.

I didn't feel well. It was definitely Winter outside. The skies were promisingly grey and there was that quietness about the world that foretold of imminent snowfall. But I wasn't enjoying it.

I sat in the dining room window bay, playing with the moisture on the glass, dabbing my finger and making the runnels coalesce into streams. I was waiting for the first faint white flakes that would mean more snow. I was looking forward to it as I liked to watch snowflakes falling.

Then I felt that pain in my throat again. Every year this happened. And every year I was taken to the doctor who told me I had tonsillitis and would have to stay off school. This year I was determined I would hide it.

An hour later and the snowflakes began. It was very cold, too cold for a heavy fall, which would only come when the temperature rose suddenly. But snow was definitely on its way. I wanted to be out with our sledges.

I stood up. Ma was watching me.

She had a very firm expression on her face. "Where do you think you're going to?" she asked.

"I'm going sledging."

"Oh no you're not," she said decisively. She should have been a detective, our Ma. She knew I was hiding something.

I had been trying to keep out of her way as much as possible, so she wouldn't notice the tonsillitis had started again.

"Go and get your coat on."

"But Ma, it's just starting to snow again. I want to go sledging."

She shook her head. "The snow will still be there when you get back. Now just you go and get your coat on, there's a good boy."

"Coat?" I asked, still trying to act the innocent.

"Coat. For the doctor's." There was no fooling our Ma, and little point in trying.

Worse was to follow. The doctor took a long look down my throat with a torch and announced, "They'll have to come out."

"What – now?"

He nodded. "He's a very bad case. You can go into the hospital at the end of the week."

He started filling in forms so I knew that to protest was useless. Ma squeezed my hand to reassure me, not realising that my reluctance to go to hospital was not out of fear, but out of regret. I would miss the sledging season, wouldn't I?

∗∗∗

On the Friday Ma and I caught the bus to Darlington, a long long way away. I was taken to the Memorial Hospital. It was to be my first night away from home. Ma was told she should leave, so she gave me a kiss and said goodbye.

I was made to change into my pyjamas and led into a great big cold room. It was lined with beds. All the other people there were grown-up men. It was very quiet. A nurse sat with her head bowed, at a desk in the middle of the room, writing notes.

After an hour a nurse came and gave me a plateful of watery goo to eat. I didn't know what it was. I left it. If hospital food was going to be as a bad as this, I would soon be really ill, I reasoned.

∗∗∗

Later than night my Dad came to see me. He brought me a *Jennings and Darbishire* and a *Biggles* book.

"Where's our kid?" I asked.

"Children aren't allowed to visit," he said. He wasn't allowed to stay long. The nurse came and told him his time was up. I wondered if mine was too.

"Don't worry," he said as he left. "It'll be a doddle."

I wasn't scared. My main worry was about going to the toilet. I was in this huge cold room with a lot of other people, all of them grown men. I was afraid of asking to go to the toilet. Nobody had said anything about where I was to go, so I hoped the need wouldn't arise. Working on this principle, I refused all the water the nurse offered me.

I wasn't worried about the operation itself, having no idea of what was in store for me. I trusted that it would be painless and successful, just as I had faith in everything my parents had ever said to me. They wouldn't have brought me here to this grim place if it wasn't for my own good. The doctor wouldn't have sent me here if it wasn't absolutely necessary, so I lay back quite happily and read my new *Jennings and Darbishire* book.

***

The first nasty shock was a big fat nurse. She came over and lifted my book out of my hands. She smiled a lot. As there was nothing for her to be smiling about, I knew she was up to something. She was. She put her hands under the sheets, fiddled about inside my bed, and suddenly pulled my pyjamas down. I was humiliated!

"Turn over," she commanded, which added insult to insult. I felt a cold draught of air as the sheets were lifted away, and could only pray that no-one else was looking at my bare bottom. Then I felt a sharp jab – that sneaky nurse had stuck something into me!

"That's better!" she said brightly, patting my bottom and tucking the thin sheet back over my body. It most certainly was not better and in future I would be much more careful in my dealings with these nurses, who had revealed themselves to be treacherous creatures, who liked to smile and stick needles in people's bottoms without warning.

I picked up *Jennings and Darbishire* and read fiercely.

∗∗∗

The next interruption was a man. He stood beside me and looked friendly. He was wearing pyjamas too. However, after the recent treacherous attack on my bottom I wasn't disposed to be too friendly.

"Now then son, what're you reading?"

I held the book up. He glanced at the cover.

"Oh," he said. "I don't read much meself. Which football team do you support?"

I wasn't used to talking to adults, but I didn't want to be rude so I said, "I don't support any football team." This was true, we just didn't bother with them.

The man looked stunned, and sat down on my bed. "You don't support a team! What kind of lad are you?"

I didn't know what kind of lad I was, but I could see that I was going to get no peace and that *Jennings and Darbishire* would have to wait, so I put the book down. I listened politely while he told me all about this football team that he was so keen on. They were called Manchester United.

I personally thought it all sounded pathetic, him being so mad on football, but as I had never been to a football match I thought it best to keep my thoughts to myself. Anyway, after a while he made it all sound very exciting when he told me all about the players' personalities and individual tricks.

He was interesting and in the end I was quite sad when the big fat nurse came over and whispered to him that it was time to go.

"Goodnight sonny," he said.

I thought he was a nice man and he had come to talk to me because I was alone.

The nurse escorted him back to his bed on the opposite side of the ward. He waved and smiled. Then she snapped loudly, "Lights out!"

What? Lights out? It was only about seven o clock in the evening.

But there was no arguing with her. The lights were turned out. I opened the book and tried to read it in the dim half-light, but it was no use, and shortly afterwards the big fat nurse came and quietly took the book from my hands.

***

The next day I wasn't allowed any breakfast. I started to read my book but within a few minutes that same shiftily-smiling nurse reappeared. She took the book from me and said, "Time to go," in a bright lively tone as if I was going to the funfair. I knew something was up.

I was lifted onto a metal trolley and wheeled into a white-tiled room. It smelled strongly of disinfectant. A man with a green cap on his head, wearing a green coat, came and bent over me. He put a smelly rubbery mask over my mouth and said, "Breathe deeply."

I did as I was told, but I remained conscious for some time, long enough to see a man with a silver horn strapped to his forehead bearing down on me. He had a mask over his mouth and although he said something, I didn't catch it as the words came out as evil grunting sounds. That was the last thing I remembered, that silver horn and those animal grunts.

***

I woke up back in my bed in the big cold room with all the men. I had a sore throat and wasn't allowed to eat or drink. I was very sad about this because my Dad had brought me a bunch of grapes and I had been looking forward to eating these. We never had grapes at home as they were viewed as an expensive luxury item. After a while the big fat nurse came and took them away and they were never seen again.

The man who had spoken to me about football waved and held up a thumb. I copied him. He slowly climbed out of his bed and for the first time I realised that he was in hospital because he had something wrong with him. He walked very carefully over to my bed.

"You alright sonny?"

I nodded. It was too painful to talk.

He sat down beside my bed and told me more stories about Manchester United and about his hero, Duncan Edwards.

I was glad of his company now as I was alone and there was nothing to do. I was hungry and cold and sore. He told me a good story about how he had taken his own son to a football match for the first time. He had been away for five years and had been a prisoner of war, captured by the Germans in North Africa in 1941. He hadn't seen his son from the age of three until he returned in 1946, when his son was nine. He took him to see Manchester United play.

"Come on you!"

It was the big fat grape-stealing nurse. "What are you doing out of bed?"

So I didn't hear any more stories, because the grape-stealer made him go back to his own bed. I wondered what was wrong with him and why he was in hospital. Then I was given another jab in the bottom, and drifted off to sleep.

***

When I awoke it was dark. The only light was a little lamp at the table where the nurse sat writing notes. There was a lot of coughing going on. Someone was shuffling about in slippers, as I could hear them slipping along on the cold shiny floor.

A little later, I ferreted out my secret torch from my bedside cupboard, sneaked my *Jennings and Darbishire* under the sheets and began to read. I managed to spend hours with Jennings and his pal Darbishire and their adventures with Mr Carter, my favourite teacher.

Then I was grabbed by the wrist, the torch and book removed by force. I was left to stare into the darkness until life returned to the hospital ward in the morning.

***

I wasn't allowed any visitors until the following evening when Ma and Dad arrived. I was glad to see them, but would have preferred it if they had brought our Eck, who I was missing badly.

"How are you David?" Ma asked anxiously.

"Alright." I was feeling a bit better. "It didn't hurt much. A man with a silver tube on his head sucked my tonsils out. That nurse pinched your grapes and she took my *Jennings and Darbishire*."

Mum put her hand on mine and stopped me. Looking warily around for the nurses, she put her hand in her shopping bag, and slipped something out of it and into my bed, under the sheets. Something book-shaped, hard-backed and very much in demand.

"Aw thanks Ma! I can finish the other one when I get it back, and how's our kid? Has it snowed yet? Tell him we'll go sledging next week. There's a nice man here who's been telling me about football. He supports Manchester United and he was a prisoner of the Germans. Can we go and see a football match some time?"

Dad grinned. "He's on the mend."

***

After they had gone I was given another dish of gruel. Then I was allowed up to stretch my legs. So I went across to the football man.

"How's it going young un?" he asked.

"Not bad. They say I can go home in two days."

The man lifted his eyebrows. "Wish I was off home. Going for the chop tomorrow morning. They've just told me."

Suddenly I realised that he was ill. It hadn't occurred to me before now as he'd been so completely normal. Of course he was normal, he hadn't had his operation yet. I wanted to ask him what was wrong with him, but I thought it would be rude to ask. Instead I tried to guess from his appearance.

He was quite old, with grizzled metallic black hair going grey. It was cut very short like a soldier and was bristly all over. He had deeply-scored lines on each side of his mouth when he smiled. He didn't seem to shave very well because he always had a snowfall of white stubble. His eyes were very deep-set and his skin was yellowy.

He hadn't spoken all the time I was studying him and I had the feeling he was worrying about his operation.

"Don't worry," I said. "It'll be a doddle."

This seemed to cheer him up because he laughed and ruffled my hair. Then the grape-gobbler marched across from her table and told him off.

"You," she said to me. "Back to bed!"

***

I never saw my friend again. They took him off next morning before I woke up and though I waited for him to reappear after having the chop, he never did. I presume they took him off to a quiet side ward to recover. I asked the big fat nurse where he was and she said, "Never you mind."

The following day there was great excitement. All the men on the ward were talking about it. There had been an air crash. An English plane had crashed in Germany. A place called Munich. It had been carrying a football team home. Lots of the players had been killed.

Then I heard someone say, "Duncan Edwards." And I knew it must be Manchester United.

***

I often thought of that bare green-painted ward in Darlington Memorial Hospital, and of a little boy with a sore throat and a stack of *Jennings and Darbishire* and of an old soldier with sunken cheeks, in to have his kidney removed.

FLYING

A couple of months later, when I'd recovered from the operation to remove my tonsils, I decided it was time I learned to fly. I had always been fascinated by the legend of Daedalus and Icarus – the father and son partnership who designed an early plane to fly them to the heavens. Of course, I knew that it ended in disaster, as Icarus flew too near the sun and the wax on his wings melted, sending him to his doom. But that didn't matter – what was important was that he had actually and successfully flown. And I wanted to fly. Not in a plane, but by myself, swooping and gliding just like a bird.

This was long before hang-gliding was developed, though it goes to show that other people were dreaming of flying under their own control, just as I was doing.

Now Daedalus and Icarus had achieved their dream by sticking feathers to a structure and flapping their arms a lot. Icarus had, unfortunately, died in the attempt, but I felt that that was through his own stupidity and pride in flying too near the sun. There was nothing intrinsically wrong with the idea of being able to fly like a bird – they just over-reached themselves. I wouldn't make the same mistake.

I knew that it wasn't possible to flap my arms to fly – our arm muscles aren't strong enough – but I reasoned that I might be able to glide if I could attach some supporting wing-like structure to my arms. Then I would be free of gravity and the pull of the boring old earth. So I determined that I would try it.

I thought it best to keep my ambition to fly well away from my parents, who might have objected to me flying in their front garden. Instead I built my wings in Alex Marcham's garage. With his assistance I found some bits of unwanted wood in O'Brien's shed. I made a lattice frame in the same sort of design I had seen used on the Wellington bomber. If it worked for them, I reasoned, it would work for me. I covered it in some cloth we borrowed from Mrs Marcham's airing cupboard. It was an old sheet, which Alex didn't think she would need any more.

Using screws to secure it to the frame proved difficult, so I had to bash nails in instead, though I realised that this wasn't exactly normal aviation practice. In the end I had two wings, big wide wooden frames in which I could insert my arms. It was with this that I set off for my first, and as it turned out, my only test flight.

Alex Marcham refused to have anything more to do with it and stayed at home, affecting to have discovered a sudden need to clean his bike. I went off with my wings in search of some high place from which to launch myself.

There was no way I could get my four foot wing span alone and unaided up the walls of Gulliver Tower, the most obvious launching site. (Our Eck was too small to give me bunkups.) Nor was it possible to get on top of O'Brien's shed. Trees were out, because the branches would play havoc with my finely-wrought workmanship, so in the end it would have to be the front bedroom window.

This was a far from ideal choice, not least because Ma and Dad were downstairs in the kitchen. Did Daedalus and Icarus, have similar problems with Mrs Daedalus, I wondered. "No, you're not going flying this morning, and you're certainly not taking young Iccy with you!"

Our Eck helped me to carry the wings round to the front door and let me in. I sneaked upstairs dragging my wings behind me. All that remained was to post Eck at the door to make sure that they didn't interrupt me, get my arms into the wings… and fly!

***

I opened the bedroom window and sat on the window ledge, my wings drooping down in front of me. Just then I experienced the same feelings those bold early aviators must have suffered – the ground looked an awful long way down. Not that there was for a moment the slightest fear. I was quite sure that once I launched myself out and stretched my wings, I would glide off safely. So there was no real need to examine the earth below my window. The fact that there was a horribly solid-looking stone wall in our front garden was irrelevant. I would fly!

"Right then our kid," I said confidently.

"Right then," he said. We weren't ones for wasting words.

I sucked in breath, held out my arms ready to glide, and jumped.

Foolishly, I had expected there to be enough time to get my arms outstretched to catch the upcurrents that were supposed to blow against tall buildings – but somehow there wasn't time.

One moment I was sitting on the window sill, the next I was desperately trying to flap my wings, and then I was thudding hard into the ground. I crashed straight into the stone wall, my knees shot into my chin, and as I was open-mouthed shouting 'Geronimo!' at the time, I bit clean though my tongue. Blood spurted everywhere.

I picked myself up, rapidly shed the remains of my ill-named and useless wings, and ran to the kitchen.

I tried to ask, "Is it bleeding Dad?" but all that came out was a shower of blood. I think I was hoping that my dad might say, no, it wasn't bleeding and that somehow he would be able to reverse my injury. It is amazing the faith that children have in their parents sometimes.

Dad took one look at me and jammed a towel into my mouth.

"Bite hard!" he said, marching me straight out of the house and round to Mrs Burton's. She was a nurse and she had the only nearby telephone, as well as a car.

I don't remember much of the rest of it. Mrs Burton kindly drove us to Darlington, where once again I was a guest of the Memorial Hospital. The doctor said that I had been lucky, though I didn't see why at the time. I hadn't completely severed my tongue. It was still held on by a bit of gristle, so the doctor was able to sew it back into one piece.

***

My parents were very good about the whole episode. They didn't beat me or berate me at all, but flying operations were suspended indefinitely.

I didn't mind. I'd gone off flying.

BIRDS' NESTING

There were other kids playing in our road now. There was Johnny Hopper, who came from far away on the other side of Ravenscroft. Johnny was very good-looking, as even us boys realised. All the girls at school were in love with him and wrote him love letters. I didn't either like or dislike Handsome Johnny Hopper, as he never said or did much. He was just good-looking and liked girls.

Teddy Sherman was his friend. Teddy was a very dark boy with very black, wiry hair. He was very tough and feared by everyone, but he was likeable and friendly. He too was from far away. Johnny and Teddy were best friends and were always together.

Kevin Batty was a very different character. He was the undoubted leader of the new boys and they came because of him. He lived across the Ghyll on the Green Howards estate. Kevin Batty was older than us. He was tough and scary. He had lots of ideas and was very clever in a malevolent sort of way. He attracted followers because he was always thinking of things to do, even though they usually involved something dangerous or illegal. He had a way of getting other people to do these things; he was very

147

persuasive and crafty, especially if it involved danger or risk. Somehow he had a way of avoiding trouble himself, but getting others into trouble.

Kevin Batty collected birds' eggs. This was then viewed very differently from the way it is seen today. Nowadays everyone knows it is wrong to take eggs because it is cruel and it harms the wildlife and kills birds and so on. But in the 1950s it was regarded as THE thing to do. Most kids collected birds' eggs, most kids went nesting, most kids boasted about their collections, and none more so than Kevin Batty. He reckoned he had the best egg collection in Ravenscroft. Not just the Spuggies, Blackbirds, Thrushes and Pigeons that everyone else had, but rare ones like Linnets, Lapwings and Curlews. Kevin Batty had eggs that were classified in the Observer's Book of Birds as 'RARE.'

I was the odd one out, though I wasn't stupid enough to admit it. I didn't collect birds' eggs and I didn't want to. I liked searching the hedges for birds' nests; I loved it when I discovered some secret hideaway in the middle of a gorse bush, where I had had to brave the prickles of the gorse to search. But I didn't take the eggs. I just didn't want to.

We had started to meet up with Kevin Batty and the others. They were older than us and somehow we were attracted to their gang.

One day Kevin Batty said, "I know where there's Sand Martins' nests."

The others were immediately interested and it was decided that we should go there straight away.

For some reason, I had misgivings and didn't want to go.

"You're coming aren't you David?" said Kevin Batty. It was a direct challenge.

I hated the way he called me David as if he was my friend. "Where are they?" I replied.

"At the Quarry."

Now the Quarry was a place that fascinated me, so I was interested. Though I'd never actually been inside it I'd seen it from a distance. It was a huge sandpit, with an excavated valley running between high cliffs of uncut rock. It looked like the Grand Canyon, a place I'd always dreamed of seeing. It was red and yellow, its cliffs high and unclimbable – and the rocky bluffs stood out in the valley like Mesas and Buttes. I had always loved the sound of those words – Mesas and Buttes – ever since I had read them in a cowboy story. The story was silly and pointless, but those two words had burned into my mind and had stayed there ever since.

"Yes," I said. "I'll come."

So the four of us set off to go birds' nesting in the Quarry.

***

I didn't really want to go with Kevin Batty and his gang, but I wanted to go to the Quarry, and that's how you get into trouble when you're a kid. I knew perfectly well that Kevin Batty was a nasty boy, that he was a thief and a liar and a bully. I knew that he liked to get people into trouble, and that he laughed when he himself escaped punishment. But I also knew that he could beat me up, and that I didn't want beating up, certainly not by Kevin Batty, who would sit on his victim, pinion his arms with his sharp bony knees and then dribble spit into his victim's face.

The Quarry was a long way away, miles away across fields, way beyond Gulliver Tower. I kept the other three very distant from our castle, not wanting to defile our secret and personal castle with Kevin Batty's polluted presence. Way past Gulliver Tower we travelled. We went further still, down a long lane and across a stretch of bright yellow gorse bushes. We paused here to search for Linnets' nests – Linnets love to nest in the protective prickles of gorse bushes– but we didn't find any.

Then Kevin Batty saw some seagulls and started throwing stones at them, which was typical of Kevin Batty. We waited until he had finished. We crept along a hedge on our bellies. Instinctively we could feel that we were very high up, and that somewhere unseen beneath us, on the other side of the hedge, was a huge open space.

Carefully, we edged forward until we could see what lay below. There it was. The Grand Canyon. As far as the eye could see, far below us there was a great scarred pit. Immense cliffs curved round the sides of the valley. In the distance, yellow earthmovers and diggers looked like Matchbox toys.

"Look! There they are!" Kevin Batty pointed into the distance on our left, where brown and white birds flashed in and out of the cliff face.

"Sand Martins," said Teddy Sherman.

You could tell they were Sand Martins by the white bob under their tails, and they were smaller than Swallows or

House Martins. They were making a loud cheeping noise all the time, as if they were talking to each other.

I watched fascinated. The best thing about Sand Martins is the way they fly, for Sand Martins are more skilful and delicate than any other birds at the art of aerobatics. I had once watched Sand Martins down at the river, where they zoomed down from hundreds of feet up to skim the water at the bottom of a full-speed dive, missing the water only by inches, then dipping their heads and taking a sip of refreshment, while still flying at speed.

Here at the quarry they were zooming straight into holes in a near-vertical cliff face, without even pausing. I wondered too how they knew which nest was theirs, among the many holes that pitted the cliffs like tiny black spots.

"It's no good, we can't get 'em," said Johnny Hopper, in one of his rare contributions.

We all looked hard at the nests, calculating how it might be possible to reach down to them. Three of us were afraid, and one of us very determined.

The holes in which the birds had their nests were near to the top of the cliffs, but even so, were several feet from the top. There was surely no way anyone could get down to them without a climbing rope. There was no chance of reaching them from below. Although the cliffs were not quite so vertical below the nests, they were still very steep. There was a lot of loose rock which would obviously give way if anyone was foolish enough to try to climb up, causing an avalanche of sand and rock. It must be a sixty or seventy foot drop to the bottom of the quarry.

Kevin Batty led the way to a spot vertically above the nests. "We can do it," he said urgently. "Course we can!" Then he turned to the three of us. "Who's going first?"

Johnny and Teddy both said, "No chance!" in unison.

Kevin Batty turned to me. Instantly I knew why he had been so keen for me to accompany them.

"I'll hold your legs for you," he said.

"Thanks a lot."

"No problem," he said, with a wicked grin.

$$***$$

So minutes later, there I was, doing something I did not want to do, something which looked suicidally dangerous, to please a boy I did not like. And I was supposed to be the bright one!

I lay down, inching forward on my belly, peering over the edge. In the distance, the world was a huge dusty bowl, which made my stomach sick. Down in front of me was the rock face. It wasn't even rocky, which might have been firm enough to provide good handholds and footholds. It was dry and sandy, which was obviously why the birds had chosen it in which to make their nests.

"Go on, you bugger!" Kevin Batty urged.

I played for time. "What do I do if there's eggs in the nest?"

Kevin Batty smirked and put his hand inside his jerkin. Out came a little box, which he opened to reveal a pad of cotton wool.

My stomach sank. "You've got it all worked out, haven't you?"

He nodded and grinned. Then, to show me he had had enough of my time-wasting, he showed me a close up of his big, dirty fist.

Johnny and Teddy stood back and amused themselves by throwing rocks towards the distant quarry bottom. Kevin knelt over me at the cliff edge.

Normally I liked climbing. I could shin up trees like a monkey. But not today. Today meant climbing downwards, feet first down a cliff. I don't like climbing downwards. It's alright going up something, where you can see a route and test its safety, but going downwards you can't see past your own body. You have to feel for holds with your feet, which are obviously much clumsier and less sensitive than your hands. Still, terrified though I was, I set off. I had no choice.

The valley bottom lay miles below me. All I could hear were the cries of the Sand Martins and the occasional yell from Johnny or Teddy as they hoicked rocks into the distance. Kevin stood grimly over me, giving encouragement as only he could.

I reached the first nest. The birds really began to scream. They had thought their nesting site was safe from marauding Man, and they were wrong. Nasty Kevin Batty had suckered someone into doing his dirty work for him, hadn't he?

I got my left arm into a hole to give me some extra support, and put my right arm inside the biggest nest hole I could find. It went in a long way. I scrabbled desperately with my fingers for the straw and feathers of a nest, but no nest did they find. Soon I was in as far as my elbow.

"What's up?"

"They're miles in," I hollered back. "I can't reach the nest."

"You'd better!"

I dug my feet into their frail holds and tried to work my way further inside the tunnel to the nest. It must have looked a comical sight, a boy glued to the face of the cliff, both arms stuck into holes as far as the elbows – but it wasn't funny for me.

My face was now pressed hard into the gritty wall. I searched and searched that long tunnel for that elusive Sand Martin's nest. I pressed into the holes as hard as I could, trying to force myself further in, but it was no use. The only way I could have got into that nest was to have excavated the tunnel and dug my way in.

"It's no use."

I had just said that when the fragile lip of earth that my toes had been standing on broke away.

Kevin Batty shouted, "Landslide!" and laughed.

Desperately I felt around with my feet for another hold, but there was none. I was stranded with both my hands stuck in holes, my feet in the air with nothing to stand on, and no way of getting either up or down.

"What's happening?" called Teddy.

"He says he's stuck."

I looked up and could see three faces peering over the lip of the cliff. Kevin Batty was grinning, the other two looked worried.

"We'll have to help him up," said Teddy.

"What are we going to do?" asked Johnny.

"I dunno. Nowt to do wi me," said Kevin Batty.

"What's it like below me?" I called.

"A bloody long way down!" said Kevin Batty, laughing again.

"Shut it Batty," said Teddy. Then he leaned over the clifftop towards me. "It's a straight drop for about ten feet or so. Then it's a long way down to the bottom."

"Think I should drop?"

There was a long pause. "You'll have to. After that it's all loose stuff. What're you going to do?"

I was near tears. "I don't know, do I? Ask Batty, it was his bright idea."

I don't know what Teddy said next, but I could clearly hear Kevin Batty protesting, "Not me! It's nowt to do wi me!"

Teddy's face reappeared. "I'll go get you a rope. You can't drop down there, you'll kill yourself."

Getting a rope would be no use. It would take too long. My arms were getting weaker.

"I can't hold on for much longer."

Johnny Hopper said, "Shit! He'll kill himself."

Kevin Batty said, "He'll be alright."

"Shut your mouth Batty!" retorted Teddy.

Then a fight must have broken out, because I could hear Johnny shouting, "Go on Ted, give him some fist!"

This was all very well, but I was getting weaker and weaker.

Johnny's face appeared. "Ted's belted Batty's mush in. He's gone home."

Great news indeed, but of little help to me. Teddy's face, bloody-nosed but smiling, joined Johnny.

"I'm dropping," I said.

"Good luck."

"Wrap your arms round your head."

"And keep rolling once you hit the ground."

I wriggled my arms out of the holes and let go.

***

I dropped straight down, then my feet hit earth. I tried to grab hold but it was no use, it was too slippery and too sloping. I fell over backwards and kept falling at speed, though the ground was soft and more like a huge pile of sand than the hard earth I'd landed on at first.

I remembered Teddy's advice and wrapped my hands round my head, bringing my knees up so that I was rolling over like a ball, with my head protected and my knees slowing me down. I was still going down at a hell of a lick and if I'd hit anything solid I would undoubtedly have smashed myself to pieces.

As it was, I rolled all the way down to the road at the bottom of the quarry.

∗∗∗

I was alive! I stood up, stretched and jumped to see if anything was broken - nothing was. I yelled my delight at my salvation to the other two. Up at the top of the cliff they looked miles away. They waved back.

I couldn't believe how far I had tumbled. I was bruised and battered and covered in mud and dust, but I had survived. I had jumped from near the top of the quarry! I must have been mad!

I tapped my body all over for signs of damage, and found something alien and nasty in my pockets. Kevin Batty's birds' egg box. All neat and prepared for its cargo of eggs. Nasty Kevin Batty.

I chucked the box into a muddy puddle and stamped hard on it. That was the end of Kevin Batty for me.

Then I made my way down the road and out of the quarry.

Oddly enough, for a day which had started out with such a near disaster, there was a great ending to it. I walked in the hot sunshine down the Grand Canyon, between the red Mesas and Buttes I'd always wanted to see – with no-one to bother me and no-one beside me. It was much better than birds' nesting with Kevin Batty.

HULA HOOPS

Hula hoops were a craze which arrived suddenly without any warning. One moment no-one had ever heard of them - the next moment every kid in the school had one. I don't even know where the craze came from – hula hoops sounded vaguely Hawaiian to me – but how Hawaii ever reached Ravenscroft was beyond me. Anyway, that didn't matter. Hula hoops were here and you had to be able to do the hula hoop properly, or you were nobody.

I was nobody. There just didn't seem to be any point to the game at all. You got a hula hoop, which was a ring made of red or blue plastic. You stepped inside it. You span it to get it started. Then you kept the momentum going by wiggling your hips. Big deal!

However, some kids were naturals at it, and some weren't. I was one of these.

When you're an adult you can sit on the sidelines and laugh at such things; after all, being able to hula hoop is pretty low on the scale of human accomplishments. But when you're eight years old and everyone else is wiggling away and laughing at you because you can't, well, that's hurtful.

It was no good me saying it was the height of idiocy to stand in the road wearing a red plastic hoop round my waist, grimacing and grunting and twisting furiously to stop it falling round my knees. Other kids thought differently; they spent hours wiggling away; they laughed at me. They called me rude names (yes, they had rude names in the 50s, not ones like they have nowadays, but hurtful ones nevertheless.)

Hula hoop gangs were formed based on your skill at hula hooping. Sinuous-waisted girls became playground heroines. Kids like me, who were useless, were ostracised. Kids who had been playground pariahs suddenly became stars.

Norma Greensit, of course, was very good at hula hooping. It didn't require much in the way of brainpower, just a whippy waist and a thrusting groin and she had those alright.

***

Luckily for me, hula hooping soon passed away into the tropical sunset from which it had first emerged. Soon there wasn't a hula hooper to be seen. The only reminder that the craze had ever existed was that somewhere, at the back of a garage, was a discarded and discoloured circle of red plastic.

Anyway, a new craze had come along, one which was much more to my liking. Dutch Arrers.

DUTCH ARRERS

Dutch Arrows, (pronounced Arrers) was another invention which came from nowhere, but which swept over the kids of Ravenscroft like a plague. I sometimes wondered if there was a mad inventor somewhere, who made it his job to invent crazes for kids, because they arrived so regularly, and each seemed so unlikely.

Who, for instance, would have ever thought of sawing garden canes in half, splitting one end into four pieces, inserting wings of cut cardboard and making a projectile? Not many, I'd bet, yet that's what Dutch arrers were. All that remained was for you to sharpen the other end with a knife and you had made yourself a lethal weapon.

The launching system was ingenious but simple. You laid a piece of string along the shaft of your missile. You carefully wound it in twists down its whole length. This left you with enough string to wrap around your wrist. Then you held the arrer between thumb and finger, pulled your arm back over your shoulder and hurled the arrer overarm, releasing the string at the end of the action. This would, with any luck, launch the arrer off into the distance (though it was quite easy to impale yourself if you held on too long.)

There was a lot of skill involved in Dutch arrers. Making the thing wasn't easy, launching it was downright dangerous, and wondering where it would go was an extra part of the fun. It was much better than standing disconsolately with a plastic hoop around my knees, being laughed at by Norma Greensit.

Soon the fields were full of kids throwing Dutch arrers at each other. It was great fun and an exclusively male operation. Girls when throwing were unable to make the necessary flex in the elbow to impart flight, thus, Norma Greensit was safely excluded from the game.

The gardens in Chestnut Grove and Elmwood Avenue were rapidly denuded of garden canes. (No-one ever bought a cane, they were 'acquired.') Kids roamed far and wide, going for walks among foreign gardens and estates, eyeing up the gardens as they went along. Adults must have wondered what on earth was going on when all their kids suddenly developed a passion for gardening. They never found out. Adults were for home and school and were never part of our world.

***

There were variations on the theme of Dutch arrers. Rapid technological developments were made. New refinements were constantly being introduced. Someone invented a double-tailer, in which two sets of tail feathers were used. These were difficult to make as the cane had to be split

161

carefully into eight pieces for the feathers to be inserted, but the result was worth it.

Double tailers flew with a loud whirr, to everyone's delight. Someone christened them 'Stukas' after the legendary German dive-bomber. However, Stukas, like their namesake, were slow in flight, so they rapidly became obsolete.

Someone else introduced painted tail feathers, though this did not interest me. I was after more radical improvements. So far all the arrers were virtually identical – a two to three foot length of garden cane and feathers about four inches across. What I was dreaming of was a much bigger Arrer, a Hindenburg of the Arrer world, a veritable V2 of an Arrer, with which I would stun the Arrer universe.

I tried using whole garden canes, instead of sawing them in half. No use. It was impossible to launch a four foot long arrer without impaling my private parts. Anyway, four foot long garden canes flew just like – well, just like garden canes.

I searched everywhere for especially fat garden canes, eventually finding one that was well over half an inch in diameter. This did produce a mighty arrer, enough to establish me in the forefront of arrer design, and enough to prove to me that I was thinking along the right lines. But what I was after wasn't just a minor revision of established practice, I wanted a whole new era, a quantum leap of arrer design. What I really wanted was a new material.

This was long before fibreglass or carbon fibre, so manmade materials were impossible dreams. What I decided on, and what I worked so secretly to perfect in our garage, was solid wood. More prosaically, it had formerly been known as a broom handle. I had to extract the nail which held it into my Ma's yard brush and hope that she wouldn't need it for a week or two.

The main difficulty was in cutting the cross-cuts for the tail pieces. I soon found that it is really hard to cut with the grain of the wood, and it took me hours to make the two accurate nicks in the smooth end of my giant arrer.

Then I made the sharp pointy end, using my Dad's prized Stanley wood plane, though I thought it best not to advise him of this useful service performed by his most cherished tool.

I used stiff thick card for the feathers, though feathers were a misnomer on my monster – I had wings, great thick wings, not delicate little feathers.

Finally, I painted it. This in itself was a quantum leap in technology, as normal bamboo arrers resisted paint, and had nasty knobbly bits which made them less aerodynamic. My specially-smooth arrer would fly through the air without disturbance.

I borrowed some red paint I found in Dad's garage, and boy did it look good!

***

The appearance of my monster arrer was greeted by cries of disbelief. No-one had ever seen such a huge arrer, no-one had ever seen a red arrer before, and no-one had seen an arrer with such big wings. Using a titchy bit of string to launch it was out of the question, so I borrowed my Ma's washing line and cut about four feet off the end. Armed with this, I was ready to launch.

I strutted up the field with my arrer over my shoulder, knowing how Barnes Wallis must have felt when he saw that his bomb really did bounce as he'd predicted. All the other kids trotted along behind. They wanted to touch it, to examine this wondrous new beast. Speculation was rife as to how far it would fly.

"A hundred yards at least," someone guessed.

There were admiring sighs. No arrer had ever flown more than forty or fifty yards, yet here we were talking of flying twice that distance. I slowed down, to bask in hero-worship. All my struggles in creating the arrer had been worthwhile.

There were dissenters or course, there always are.

Clive Lawson the Pater's son, for instance, who, having examined the arrer as closely as I would allow, announced, "It's far too heavy. Anyone can see that it'll never fly."

He was showered with abuse for his trouble, and passed to the back of the crowd. I said nothing, for he had raised the one minor doubt I had in my own mind – the arrer had not yet flown. Owing to unforeseen delays in its development programme, test flights had not been possible. So this, its first public showing, was also going to be its first test flight.

I wound the launch rope carefully round its body, and regretted being in such a hurry to show it off.

Clive Lawson the Pater's son said, "It's only a broom handle he's painted red," and was thumped.

We had gone way up to the top of the field just in case the arrer really did fly a long way. I didn't want it going through Greensit's precious television, did I? I also reckoned that launching from the top of the hill would make flight easier. The wind there blew straight off the moors in a harsh, unrelenting gale.

The kids backed off. I drew back my arm, measured out my runway, and set off. My arm was held behind me, as far as it would go, the heavy arrer lying flat along my straight arm like a javelin. Kids called encouragement.

"Let it go!"

"Now David!"

"Go!"

And off it went with a mighty crack, off off and up, caught in the wind. They all stood amazed as it soared into the distance.

"Christ!" they called. "Look at it go!"

I was sitting in agony on the ground, clutching my right arm and shoulder, both of which had made a loud crack at the moment of launch. Then the cries of alarm began.

"Bloody hell!"

"Where's it going?"

I sat up and stared in horror.

"It's off into Tessiman's!" they cried. "Tessiman will kill you!"

And with that they fled. I stood up instantly, watching petrified as my arrer veered off course, no longer flying safely down the field, but instead curving off right towards the back of the houses on Elmwood Avenue.

Already kids were running scared.

Straight into Tessiman's was exactly where it went. Tessiman, a great black-haired, black-moustached and fearsome figure, a man who wouldn't let his daughters play with us local kids, a man who had a greenhouse.

I put my one good hand over my eyes, unable to watch, just knowing what was going to happen next. There was a loud smashing of glass, and the delighted and terrified cries of the kids as they all scattered for safety.

"It's gone straight through Tessiman's greenhouse," said Norma Greensit with undisguised pleasure. "You'll be for it now."

There was a loud angry and very male bellow, and the kids vanished like flies.

***

A week or so later Ma couldn't find her yard brush. Then Dad discovered someone had been using his paint and hadn't put the brushes into turps after using them. He was surprised as to how blunt his beloved Stanley plane had become. Suspicion centred on me, the possessor of an arm in a sling.

Oddly enough, I was never punished. Mind you, I have suffered from a damaged right shoulder ever since. Who knows, I might have opened the bowling for Yorkshire if I hadn't launched that monster of an arrer that day.

Kids talked about it for months afterwards, even when the craze for Dutch arrers had finished.

"Did you ever see David's arrer?"
"Bloody hell, it was a monster!"

FRISKY

O ur Frisky sauntered out of our garden. He saw me and his tail went straight up in the air, the end curling over and back. He walked slowly towards me, pleased to see me, his tail flicking gently. I could hear him purring.

"Frisky, Frisky, here Frisky, here boy. Good cat. What've you been doing eh boy?"

He'd been hiding in the rows of spinach which my dad grew and tried unsuccessfully to get us to eat. It stayed green all the winter and looked tempting, but it still tasted like soggy green blotting paper when it was cooked.

Frisky hid there, watching the birds that came down onto the lawn for the bread that our Ma had thrown out for them.

"And then what do you do Frisky? You catch the little birds, don't you, you naughty, naughty cat."

Our Ma calls him a naughty cat, because he brings the birds to the back door and leaves them as a present for us, and she screams when she sees them.

Frisky knew I wasn't angry with him though, by the way I laughed. He was just a cat, doing normal cat things. Hunting, catching birds and mice, that's what cats do.

MRS BROOKS

My teacher was called Mrs Brooks. She was big and old-fashioned and smelled of mothballs, but I liked her because she was very keen on handwriting, something that interested me.

Mrs Brooks could write beautifully. She wrote wonderfully-curved letters on the board and said it was called Copperplate. Instantly, I loved the loops and the regularity of it all. More than anything, I wanted to write beautiful Copperplate like Mrs Brooks.

I had always liked writing and lettering and after one of her lessons I took a book out of the library which talked about all the different styles of lettering. Gill Sans, Times Roman and so on. I liked to whisper the names aloud to myself. Sans Serif was my favourite.

I remembered nothing else about Mrs Brooks's teaching, all I remembered was copying Copperplate off the board for her, over and over again.

I struggled with it at first. It wasn't easy. I liked the loops of the letters 'l' and 'p' best of all, and I would add great long poetic flowing loops to all my 'l's and 'p's.

She came and sat beside me at my desk and said, "No no no, that's no good. You've got restrain yourself!"

In the end she forced me to stop doing these extravagant flourishes. They were simply not Copperplate. I didn't like being made to control myself in this manner, but I could see that she meant well.

"The art of calligraphy is consistency," she said firmly. "Not the ability to write flourishes, no matter how stunning you might think they are."

I said, "Thank you," to her. I determined that from then on I would keep my curly 'l's and 'p's for home use only. At school my Copperplate would be faultless.

The next morning she died.

∗∗∗

She had just marked the register when it happened.

"Nicolette Goulding," she said and all faces turned to look at the beautiful Nicolette. She smiled and tossed her head, spinning her twin blonde plaits with their tartan ribbons.

"Present Miss," she said, while eighteen little boys looked at her with love in their hearts. Then Mrs Brooks slumped forward and banged her head on the desk.

No-one knew what to do. We were well-trained kids, not used to leaving our seats unless given permission to do so by Mrs Brooks. We sat in silence. From the other side of the glass partition came the sound of Miss Somerville marking the register of 4A.

I think we all expected Mrs Brooks to sit up, to smile and apologise and carry on with Copperplate. No-one said a word.

Miss Somerville continued next door. We could hear her say, "Now wipe the board please Geraldine."

Some of the boys at the back began to mess about. I was looking at Nicolette Goulding. She seemed as if she was about to burst into tears.

Stewart Aisbitt, who wanted to be teacher's pet (even though Mrs Brooks didn't have teacher's pets) and who sat at the front because of his asthma, short sight and fussy mother, called out.

"Miss!" he said, in a plaintive way. Receiving no reply, he began to cry.

I don't know what might have happened. We might have been there all day, had not Mr Morley, the Headmaster, passed by. He came in at the door behind me and I could hear his big booming voice call, "Mrs Brooks, could I have a word please?"

He hadn't noticed she was slumped over the teacher's desk.

Peter, his son, said, "She's passed out."

Mr Morley rushed to the teacher's desk and lifted Mrs Brooks's head.

"Class - leave the room!" he called. When the desk feet began to scrape, he shouted, "In an orderly manner!"

Miss Somerville came out of her room. We were all sent to the Hall, and Mrs Brooks was taken away.

***

At Assembly next day we were told that she had died, and we all had to say a prayer for her and for her family. I wondered what had killed her and asked everyone if they could tell me. No-one could, though I overheard Mr Morley say to Miss Somerville that they thought it was a 'stroke.' This sounded very strange to me. How could a stroke kill anyone? A stroke was a gentle movement. It certainly wasn't what had happened to Mrs Brooks when she clutched her throat and slumped forward that morning.

I missed her a lot. I never had another teacher who was interested in handwriting. If Mrs Brooks had lived we could have done lots more writing and I might have learned Copperplate to perfection. As it was, without her guidance, I was soon slipping back into my bad old ways, with ridiculously loopy 'l's and 'p's. People often said to me, "You write beautifully," but I knew better.

I knew Mrs Brooks would not have approved.

***

I often thought of her and wondered what it was like to be dead so suddenly and without warning. She must have left her family that morning, not realising that she would never see them again. It made me feel very sad to think of that happening.

SPITFIRE JACKETS

Poor Ma. She didn't have much money, but she was proud of us boys and always wanted us to look as smart as possible. One day she and Dad took us out on the train to Darlington. This was a big trip. We had never all been out shopping together.

We went to Binns, a great big department store. We were taken to the boys' clothing section and there we were fitted out with matching jackets. They were black and had fur collars and looked like the ones Spitfire pilots wore. We were oblivious to the fact that they were made of PVC rather than real leather, to us they were just great. We were very proud of them.

I felt really tough in mine. So thick and strong was it that I felt safe inside it and nothing could hurt me. This was to lead me into more trouble.

***

Some weeks later, we were out birds' nesting. Pigeons nested at the top of tall hawthorn trees, and so their nests were normally impregnable, because no-one could climb through the mass of thorns to reach them. Impregnable? Not any more! Not to me with my Spitfire Jacket!

Of course, I never gave a thought to the cost of it, that it was new and that I might damage it. I was determined to climb up to a pigeon's nest. No-one had ever managed it before, but now I was going to do it, in my scratchproof Spitfire Jacket.

Off we all marched, up the hedge at the back of O'Brien's sheds, to the trees where we knew there were pigeon's nests. Sure enough, we found one very quickly.

"Right then!" I declared. "I'm going up!"

I had to have my hands outside the jacket so I could climb, but apart from that I would be protected by the thick Spitfire Jacket. Oh, apart from my head. I searched around and was lucky enough to find a sheet of Tar, which I bent into a makeshift pointy hat and stuck on my head to protect it. I was ready.

My admiring gang, the Greensits, Alex Marcham, our Eck and Clive Lawson the Pater's son, stood open-mouthed as I charged up the tree. I told you I was invincible! No thorns could scratch me. I just shouldered them aside with my trusty Spitfire Jacket to protect me.

I raced up and was at the nest in no time.

"Nothing in it!" I shouted down.

There was a sigh of disappointment and they all started moving away, all except our kid.

He stood there alone, looking up at me. "Hey bruv, how are you going to get down?"

"Same way I got up!"

There was just one slight problem. The Spitfire Jacket had protected me on the way up, because I was going up. Now, on the way down, it would be of little use. I couldn't shoulder thorny branches out of the way. My unprotected legs would be cut to pieces. Pity I had never thought of that really.

So there I was, stuck about twenty feet up the tallest and thorniest hawthorn tree in the hedge. It looked a very long way down, a very long and thorny way down. I discarded the pointy hat as being useless, and pondered.

$$***$$

After I had pondered for some time, in a calm and logical manner, I decided there was only one thing to do.

"I'm going to jump!"

"Don't be stupid!"

"You'll kill yourself you idiot!"

There was no alternative. "Stand well back. I don't want to land on you."

I reasoned that if I fell quickly enough I might fall through the tree without getting scratched too badly. There was possibly a slight flaw in my logic, but I couldn't identify it at the time.

"Geronimo!" I shouted, and jumped. I didn't feel much on the way down. The branches snagged on my body a bit, but they weren't thick enough to stop my progress down to earth. I landed softly, rolled forward like parachutists do on landing, and stood up grinning.

"Easy!"

Our kid walked slowly up to me, bent his face close to mine, and examined me.

"Cor," he said. "You aren't half going to catch it from Ma!"

I had no idea what he was talking about. My Spitfire Jacket had a few scratches on it, but nothing too noticeable.

"Not your jacket. Your face!"

I rubbed my hand over my face. It came away smeared with blood.

"It's just a scratch."

He shook his head. "It's a lot of scratches."

Lacking a mirror, I was unable to find out how many. Still, I thought, there wasn't much I could do about it now.

On the way home our kid explained how I had hundreds of parallel scratches, so my face was covered in bleeding red lines, caused by my rapid descent through a hawthorn tree.

"It looks like someone has drawn all over you with a red pen," he decided. "Ma is gonna kill you."

***

When we arrived home, I had hoped that I might be able to sneak up to the bathroom to clear up my face, without being caught by Ma. But no chance. She was a born detective. She intercepted us at the bottom of the stairs.

"What are you two up to?" she asked.

I tried to keep my face hidden, but she stopped me and turned me round. By now my face was covered in a curtain of congealed blood.

She screamed. I looked like I'd been attacked by a mad axeman.

***

The wounds cleared up very nicely though and I was able to go back to school the following week.

I was a bit of an attraction. Kids kept coming up to me and gathering round to have a look. They were all impressed, I could tell.

"What a stupid bugger you are!" someone said.

It took about three weeks for the scratches to heal, though I still had lines down my face for some time after that.

Kids called me Biro for a time, but it didn't last.

MORE RATFEVER

In those days, long before AIDS and Multiple Sclerosis, Ebola and Motor Neurone, there were only two diseases to frighten us – Poliomyelitis and Ratfever. Nowadays there are so many more it gets confusing, you never know which one to worry about most. But in 1958 in Ravenscroft as kids we just had the two.

Both were, in our mythology, rampant diseases and both were easy to catch. You could get polio by going to the swimming baths, or to the cinema – the Goathland or the Odeon – it didn't matter which, though my money was always on the Odeon, as it was a seedy hole even then, and obviously chock full of polio germs just waiting to sink their fangs into unsuspecting small boys. Polio was only kept at bay by having a series of nasty jabs at the Medical centre on Reeth Road.

Ratfever on the other hand, was only to be caught in one place, the Tip, at the bottom of the Ghyll. This was where O'Briens the builders dumped all their loose rubble, plaster and laths. These must be conducive to the well-being of rats, because they absolutely thrived there.

There were rats as big as cats, rats with tails like hawsers, rats that would sit up on their back legs like kangaroos. Nor were they in the least intimidated by human beings. If you surprised a rat on the Tip by blundering into him, it wouldn't be the rat which would run – no fear. It would be you. The rat would stare you out, boldly and arrogantly, until you turned and ran.

Everyone was afraid of rats, there was no pretending we weren't. Even adults were scared of rats, even my dad was scared of rats. This was proved one day when we were fishing down at the river at Masham Abbey. Dad had found a good place to fish, but we would have to slide down a steep bank on our bottoms to reach this chosen place. It was a thick overgrown bank and at the bottom there was just a little muddy platform jutting out into the river. The water in front of this platform was lovely and deep and dark and just smelled of fish.

Dad said, "Follow me, brave men!" and slid off down the bank. Eck and I watched in amazement, as he got down onto the platform and found he was sharing it with a great big rat. You should have seen his face! Laugh? We nearly wet ourselves. Dad looked at the rat. The rat looked at Dad. The rat clearly wasn't going anywhere, but my dad was. There was no way he could go back up the bank, so he jumped straight into the water. It was way over his boots, so he just stood there, in water up to his chest. We were crying with laughter.

"Don't scare the fish Dad!"

He stormed off downstream to find somewhere to land, somewhere without a rat guarding it.

When he got back he was wet and muddy and had a big muddy streak down his trousers. He wasn't in the mood for witticisms like, "I usually take my wellies off when I go for a swim Dad."

Even adults were scared of rats.

✳✳✳

We certainly were, we were terrified of them. You might think, with the Tip being the only place where rats were common, that it would be easy for us to avoid them, but not so. The Tip was a great place to play. It was at the end of our territory, at the junction of the Ghyll and the main Hubberholme road. Across the road lived the Lord Lovat's tribe of runny-nosed nutters and across the Ghyll was the Army estate full of hard-cases with shaven heads, the sons of brutal Lance Corporals in the Green Howards, bred on a diet of brutality and beer and spells in Germany and Cyprus. The Tip was therefore a natural battleground.

It also provided the means of warfare. Being a dumping ground it was full of ammunition to throw, hurl, swish, swipe and lob at our enemies. There were clemmies for long distance throwing; bits of plaster (great for throwing against walls as they burst in a cloud of white dust, like real artillery shells); assorted planks, logs, boulders and bricks to be propelled by a variety of means in the general direction of the enemy.

Best of all these weapons was roofing felt, known as Tar. This dry, tarry substance was often discarded in sheets and could be torn into pieces the size of a plate. There was a special method of throwing Tar, which had to be perfected first.

Kenneth Greensit never managed it. He could only propel the Tar with great force straight into his foot. But once you had got the knack of holding the flat disc between thumb and forefinger, and of throwing it with a curved arm, you could send the Tar great distances. It always flew in a curving arc, was invisible in flight, and was very satisfying to use successfully. It wasn't particularly accurate, but it was my favourite missile.

If I had been given the choice of all the things I would most like to do when I was eight years old, I would without doubt have said, "Throw Tar." There was something so artistically satisfying about the way it flew if you got it right and had it sitting on the wind. It would go for miles.

There was something satisfying too about throwing a flat skimmer – James Bond latched onto the idea years later with his hat-throwing Chinaman. And didn't the Japanese throw flat star shapes in much the same manner as we threw Tar?

***

Back to the Tip. You only got Tar on the Tip. So if you wanted to do battle with the Lord Lovat's mob (or more likely HAD to do battle with the Lord Lovat's mob) then the Tip was the place to do it.

The other two gangs had the advantage of numbers. They seemed to do nothing but breed tribes of identically-demented kids in Lord Lovat's – but we had one big advantage. Because we lived at the top of the hill, we held the high ground. It wasn't easy for our enemies to throw missiles accurately uphill, whereas it was very easy for us to throw them downhill. Even feckless specimens like Kenneth Greensit could manage that simple task. We had the top of the Tip, while the other two tribes had to scramble over the rubble at the bottom of the Tip and cower behind piles of rubble as we pelted them with Tar and clemmies.

It is at this point that I have to boast. Not like me I know and I dislike most boasters intensely, but I have to be honest and admit that I was the best thrower on the Tip. Not even Kevin Batty of the Green Howards tribe, who was years older than me, who wore jeans and said 'fuck' every other word, not even Kevin Batty could throw as far or as accurately as I could.

I had a lot of practice. At every lull in our perpetual battles, I would put tin cans or milk bottles in a row on the wall at the far side of the Tip, where the tip ended and the Ghyll began. Then I would hurry back to my own side, and with a pile of clemmies at my feet, would knock the bottles and cans off one by one, each one smashing or falling in turn.

***

Back to the Ratfever. Ratfever was spread by rats. Just touching a rat was enough to give you it and a bite from a rat was reckoned by us kids to be fatal. None of us had ever touched or been bitten by a rat, but the mere sight of one was enough to send us shrieking for safety, yelling, "Ratfever! Ratfever!" at the tops of our voices.

We lived in mortal fear of this and yet no-one ever knew the origin of the fear. I do know that every kid on Hubberholme hill was scared of it, for there was no antidote. You just died a terrible death, slavering and screaming and sweating until you went into a coma and your brain burst.

Ratfever was such a common fear that it became part of our vocabulary, in use far beyond the territorial battle ground of the Tip. If there was a new kid at school, nasty-minded kids would gather round him at break and taunt him with cries of "Ratfever!" – pretending to run away from him as an infected being. God only knew what the newcomers must have thought – that all North Riding kids were mentally defective, I should imagine.

Now one night at home I said Ratfever in front of my dad. He told me off.

"Stop saying that! There's no such thing as Ratfever."

I did what I was told. I believed my dad. After that for weeks I never said Ratfever again, though I was still afraid of rats. I believed my dad.

Then, one day, I was reading *The Yorkshire Post*, which we sometimes had at our house. There was an article about some canoeists who had gone down the River Aire, through industrial Leeds. One of them had capsized, swallowed a lot of water and had contracted a terrible illness, from which he died in appalling agonies some days later.

He had died, the autopsy revealed, of Weill's disease, a terrible and horrific illness without antidote –

WHICH WAS SPREAD BY RATS.

I couldn't wait until Dad came home. The minute he got through the door I thrust the paper at him.

"Read that!" I said, pointing out the rat article to my Dad.

After reading it, he sat down in his chair.

"Ratfever," he said.

I nodded. "Ratfever."

ROBIN HOOD

There was a new craze among the kids. It was Robin Hood.

Robin Hood was a programme on television – well it was on some people's television. It wasn't on ours because we only had one channel – the BBC. Our telly wouldn't pick up a signal from the other channel, ITV.

Nevertheless, Robin Hood suddenly appeared one day. Hula hoops were long forgotten, lying discarded in sheds and garages. All the kids at school were talking about it, and I felt left out. I wanted to know what all the fuss was about. I had to go to Kenneth Greensit's house to watch it.

Robin Hood opened with a close-up of a tree trunk. Across it written in mediaeval script was the title

THE ADVENTURES OF ROBIN HOOD

Then there was a wonderful sound of an arrow in flight.

Sssshhhhhhhhhhhhhhhhhh THUNK! as it hit the tree trunk and stuck straight in. Wonderful!

Then the music...

Robin Hood Robin Hood
Marching through the glen.
Robin Hood Robin Hood
With his band of men.
Feared by the bad
Loved by the good
Robin Hood, Robin Hood!

***

Robin Hood was soon all the rage. It told the familiar story of the outlaw who lived in Sherwood Forest and stole from the rich to give to the poor. He had a girlfriend called Maid Marian and an enemy called the Sheriff of Nottingham. We all knew the story, but what we all wanted was a bow and arrow. We wanted to shoot arrows into tree trunks with that wonderful sound... Sssshhhhhhhhhhhhhhhhh THUNK!

No-one aspired to wear Robin Hood clothes. Green tights and little green smocks with castellated edges were a bit too theatrical for Ravenscroft kids and anyway, tights didn't exist then. No, what all the kids wanted was the bow and arrow. Oh, and the quiver. And the song.

Soon the hedges and trees of Ravenscroft were being stripped of likely branches. Swarms of kids scoured the district in search of wood for bows and arrows. Within days gangs of kids were to be found sporting bows and arrows.

Any visitor to Ravenscroft must have thought the entire town still lived in the Middle Ages, as armed gangs of kids roamed the streets joyfully singing:

Robin Hood Robin Hood
Marching through the glen.
Robin Hood Robin Hood
With his band of men.
Feared by the bad
Loved by the good
Robin Hood, Robin Hood!

It was a great craze.

ECK GETS SHOT

One of the most terrifying and nightmarish things that ever happened to our family occurred completely unexpectedly, in the way that these things do. The cause of it all was the Robin Hood craze.

Opposite our house was a huge grassy field, which sloped up the hillside from our house, up to the moors which stretched far beyond. This field was the scene of most of our games, cricket, football, sledging – we played there happily with the kids of Elmwood Avenue, Chestnut Grove and Hubberholme Road.

The main group would be our Eck, Kenneth and Norma Greensit, Alex Marcham, Clive Lawson the Pater's son and sometimes the delectable Sandra Marcham.

Kevin Batty was an occasional scary visitor. He would be three or four years older than me, and though he lived across the Ghyll on the Green Howards estate, he knew no territorial boundaries. He wasn't popular even among his own gang of Green Howards and was usually to be found wandering alone.

Kevin Batty was a dangerous boy, tough and hard and unpredictable. He was prone to thump you if he felt like it and no excuse was needed. He always wore a green jumper. Whenever you saw him you felt a sinking feeling in your stomach – oh no, not Kevin Batty - what's he going to do this time? And you'd hope he'd pass by and wander off somewhere without noticing you.

Anyway, the particular day of the dreadful accident, we were messing about quite happily in the field. Norma Greensit had tied her brother Kenneth up in her skipping rope and was trying to get him to gallop and be a horse. For some reason today he was reluctant to do this.

She held the reins and gave him occasional encouragement, like "Gee up Hossy!"

Poor Kenneth had had enough of this, and just slumped to the ground, a tired and discouraged horse.

Norma went mad. "You useless little bugger!" she yelled. Poor Kenneth just sat there, taking the abuse. We all thought it was hilarious, and felt very sorry indeed for poor old Kenneth.

Suddenly, everyone went quiet. Someone had seen Kevin Batty. We all turned to look and there he was, coming towards us. No-one spoke. On he came. It was too late to run for it.

"He's got a bow and arrow."

He had indeed.

We could all see by the cocky way he was holding it that it was new and that he was showing off. It was clearly not the usual sort of bow and arrow that we had all tried as Robin Hoods. Ours were made out of a bit of ash tree and were totally useless. This one was a real bow and arrow.

As he approached us, swaggering along, we could see that it was a proper genuine shop-bought bow and arrow. I couldn't help but be envious. My own bow and arrow was tied with a bit of old string. I'd made it myself. My arrows were bits of elder and they were no use, because when you tried to fit them to the string, the wood split and the string shot straight up the arrow. My bow and arrow had a maximum range of about two yards and was more of a danger to my feet than to my enemies.

Not Kevin Batty's though.

He had a real bow. It was beautifully curved, made out of varnished yew. The string was taut and striped and you just knew that it would make lovely twang if you pulled it and let go.

Kevin Batty didn't say anything. He didn't need to. From a sheath on his waist he drew out an arrow.

I gasped. I'd never seen a real arrow close up before today. It was perfectly straight with red and green striped feathers, and a shiny, sharp, pointed brass tip. You could really imagine you were Robin Hood with a bow and arrow like Kevin Batty's.

Open-mouthed we stared, full of envy as he fitted the arrow to the string, slowly pulled back the bow and aimed it skywards.

"God!"

"Wow!"

"Look at it go!"

Kevin Batty smirked as the arrow curved into the distance, paused for a second to let the enormity of his achievement sink in, then casually sauntered off to retrieve it.

He wasn't going to give us a go, no chance of that. He was Kevin Batty, Cock of the North. Never again in his life would he be the hero he was at that moment.

***

After watching him for a time, we started to drift back to our games, but the fun had gone out of them and we soon broke up. Eck and I began to walk back down the field towards our house.

"Wouldn't it be great!" I said, unable to contain my feelings.

"Yeah!"

That was all we needed to say. But there was no chance of ever owning a real bow and arrow like the one he had. We didn't have the money and it was far too dangerous for Ma and Dad ever to let us have one like that. We mooched back, heads down, depressed.

"He probably stole the money," was all I could manage, but it was a poor response and we both knew it.

***

We had just about reached the fence at the bottom of the field when we heard a shout. I was holding the fence wire for our kid to get through, so I was slower to react than our

Eck, who turned immediately to look at whoever was shouting.

I turned, just in time to see it coming. Our Eck obviously hadn't seen it.

There was a THUNK and the arrow hit him.

It went straight into his forehead, just above the eye. He didn't say anything, just turned to me for help and sank to his knees.

I picked him up, the arrow still sticking out of his head. I pulled it. It came out easily enough, but had left a perfectly-shaped hole deep in his head. Inside the wound it was red and layered. It wasn't bleeding too much, but it was a significant hole.

Kevin Batty came running up. I thought he was going to say sorry. No chance.

"Giz me arrer back!" he demanded.

I put it over my thigh and snapped it in two. He glowered at me, swore foully, but did nothing.

Then I picked up our Eck and pulled him over the fence to our house, half dragging him because he was too heavy to carry.

We fell in through the back door to our kitchen. Ma was busy doing some baking. I could tell by the nice sweet smell of apple pie. She turned and saw us and screamed.

***

Amazingly, our Eck survived, with no permanent damage, though it did mean a further series of trips to the Memorial hospital, which was a very long bus ride away in Darlington. They should have given our family free concessionary bus travel on that bus.

Kevin Batty. He never said sorry. Of course he didn't.

NORMA

We roamed wild, living as we did on the very edge of Ravenscroft, which was in itself very isolated. Our house was still the last one on the road, and beyond it stretched fields and moors for miles and miles, so that we always had a new place to explore. Each day we would go off together, secure in the knowledge that we wouldn't see an adult until we returned home at teatime.

Beyond O'Brien's sheds the fields began, fields full of flowers and animals like little voles and field mice. Most of the fields were surrounded by drystone walls, each of which was a severe hazard to our Eck, as he was only five. I was eight and there was no wall I couldn't climb, but he was so short he had to be helped over each one.

Yorkshire walls are very dangerous when you're only three feet tall because the stones are only loose-piled and are not held in place by any mortar. Many a time our Eck would reach up above his head, searching for a hand-hold, only to bring a heavy stone tumbling down on himself, so he had to be watched very carefully.

Rarely, only very rarely, were our wanderings through the fields a source of adult trouble. There seemed little sign of adult life and of authority. Only when we got out into the Vale of York, where the land was flatter and more intensively farmed, did we meet anyone.

It occasionally happened that a farmer or a farmworker might be out ploughing and might see us in the distance doing our balancing acts on the top of the walls (we played games dancing along the tops, as fast as we could go).

There would follow some angry bellowing, a panicky jump off the wall to the far side and a quick roll on landing. There might be a chase until they gave up – always with the fear that our Eck might have been left behind. Luckily our Eck, as everyone knew him, was quite fearless and would jump off any wall no matter how high, without a thought for the consequences.

Fields not bounded by stone walls were connected by hedges, of hawthorn or elderberry. These of course were always full of wildlife and always worth exploring. Hawthorns were favourite nesting places for a whole variety of birds, so they were always closely scanned for nests from March until June. In Autumn hawthorn bushes provided the red hawthorn pips which were the ammunition for many a catapult or fist, until they started to go soft in November.

Tall hawthorn hedges also provided us with good dens, as they would form a natural desert underneath, ideal for kids to hide in. Many was the time we sat there huddled together under the canopy of a hawthorn tree, dreaming of ways to reach that pigeon's nest fifteen feet above our heads.

Now elderberry hedges I hated. There was something about them that made my skin crawl. Perhaps it was that green furry skin that the mature elderberry branches always had. Perhaps it was just the ugly roughness of the bark itself. When you peeled the outside of an elderberry branch, the flesh inside was nasty and slimy and yellowish white. Perhaps it was the smell of the elderflowers, which always reminded me of cat pee. But far more likely, is the association I have of elderberry hedges with Norma Greensit.

***

It was under an elderberry tree, deep in the cave beneath, that Norma Greensit told an enthralled audience of me, our Eck, Clive Lawson the Pater's son and her brother Kenneth, about a fabled land.

"It's called Fuckarada," she said. She went on to tell us stories of life in Fuckarada.

Apparently all sorts of odd things went on in Fuckarada, things which fascinated Norma.

We all sat and listened intently. I was the eldest, apart from Norma herself, and I had absolutely no idea what she was talking about. I knew instinctively however, that what she was telling us was Forbidden. It was the sort of thing that would invariably result us getting into big trouble from our parents, if they were ever to hear of it. So I hated Norma Greensit for bringing this fear into our lives.

***

From now on I would have to be constantly alert at home in case our Eck blurted it out.

"Can we go on holiday to Fuckarada please Dad? Norma has been telling us all about it."

No.

Or when there were visitors. "What sort of games do you play Richard?"

"Oh, we listen to Norma and Fuckarada."

Or, even worse, at school. "Richard, can you tell us about what you did at the weekend please?"

"We went in the bushes with Norma and Fuckarada."

It was sad really. Elderberry hedges were useful in all sorts of ways. You could make a brilliant drink from the white flowers. You could make jelly and fruit and wine and cough mixture from the black fruit, and when you snapped the young branches you could scour out a whole inner tube of soft pith from its beautifully neat insides. But I still hated them.

Norma Greensit had a lot to answer for.

THE TANK AERIAL

There hadn't been any more fishing trips with Dad for some time. Firstly, because it was winter, and winter in Swaledale meant you did not go out unless you had to. You certainly didn't voluntarily go and sit out on a wet and windswept river bank. Secondly, we didn't go fishing because I just couldn't face the humiliation - at the hands of the riverbank urchins, and the trout. We waited until summer time.

Our next attempt at catching the wily trout of the River Swale was going to be more successful. Of this I was determined. We didn't have the money to buy proper tackle, but my Dad had had a bright idea. He would make me a rod!

He was always very clever with his hands, was our Dad. Hadn't he made a telly for Ma? Hadn't he made our brilliant Guy Fawkes? Well now, he promised, he was going to make me a proper fishing rod. And what was he going to make it out of? Split cane? Fibreglass? No, he was going to make it out of a tank aerial.

Somehow, from his army friends at Catterick Camp, he got hold of an aerial from a tank. It was about ten feet long, and made of steel. It would survive an attack by the Russians, so it was immensely strong and whippy. He lugged it home one evening, having travelled on the bus with it all the way from the camp. God knows what his fellow passengers must have thought.

He presented it to me with a flourish. "It'll make a wonderful rod!" he announced with confidence. I was sceptical. I could barely lift it. It was so long and so heavy I doubted if it would ever be a usable fishing rod. But Dad, as I have said, was clever with his hands.

He somehow cut it into two sections, so that we could transport it to the river in a rod bag. He created ferrules so that the two halves would fit together neatly. He found red silk and bought rod rings, and showed me how to whip the silk so that the rings were firmly attached to the rod. He bought cork in little rings, which he glued to the thick end of the tank aerial, creating a butt for the rod. Finally, he varnished it. In the end it looked great! I was very proud of it.

***

Down to the pool below the river bridge, one Saturday afternoon. The urchins quickly gathered, recognising us immediately from our previous trip, the news spreading quickly that the entertainers were back. The urchins were in buoyant mood, no doubt expecting more free entertainment.

"Ey up Sharky!" one called in happy greeting.

I ignored them. This time, I was confident. I had a beautiful new rod. I was going to catch a trout. I took the two pieces of my tank aerial rod from their bag, and slotted them together. They fitted perfectly. The urchins were stilled.

Next I tackled up. I still had the useless reel, but with a long rod I should be able to cast a long way. A nice big juicy worm completed the outfit.

I was ready. I hooked my finger over the line, ready to cast out. I turned round, holding my beautiful new tank aerial rod ready.

The urchins ducked and called, "Wooo!" in encouragement.

I cast out with all my might. The worm, hook and float flew out across the river. Majestically, and tragically, the top end of my tank aerial detached itself from the rest of the rod, leaving me holding on to the butt end, while the top section sailed off far across the river.

"Aww!" cried the urchins, hugging themselves in delight and rolling around with laughter.

We all stood and watched, fascinated as the tank aerial disappeared into the distance. With a splash, the top end of my lovely new rod landed in the deep fast-flowing water near the far bank. Lost for ever.

The urchins hooted.

"Eez chucked iz rod int river!"

"What a bloody idiot!"

Dad said philosophically, "Never mind son!"

I was inconsolable. I didn't want philosophy. I had lost my beautiful tank aerial rod.

And I wanted to catch a trout.

BABY OWLS

I was fascinated by the idea of taming a wild animal. I don't know where I got the idea from. I never liked Tarzan or that woman who talked to the lionesses, but I was obsessed with the dream that I might find a wild creature and somehow 'tame' it. I don't know why, but is there any explanation for the many of the things we want?

I never kept a pet rabbit, as other kids did. What was the point - they were already tame, they couldn't do anything. All they did was eat lettuce, and what could be more boring than sitting watching a rabbit eat lettuce?

I'd seen hamsters kept by other people and I definitely didn't like the way the hamsters were expected to run round and round inside those wheels. Instruments of torture, they seemed to me.

No, what I wanted was a real wild animal, not some pathetic domesticated specimen.

I tried telling people that our tortoiseshell cat, Frisky, was in fact a ferocious Scottish Wild Cat, which I had tamed, but no-one believed me. I even tried taming a sparrow I found, which had a broken leg, but it died.

Then one day in early summer we were out in the fields. There was me, our Eck, Norma Greensit, Kenneth on his first outing after he had had measles and Clive Lawson the Pater's son. We were miles from home, further than we'd ever been before. I exaggerate not when I say we were miles from home – we were way beyond Scriven Beck – in a wild and wooded area with a lot of old trees.

Suddenly our Eck shouted and pointed to the sky. "Look! It's a vulture!"

It wasn't a vulture, but he was only five and thought all big birds which circled high in the sky were vultures. He'd recently been to see a cowboy film at the Goathland.

It was in fact an owl. An owl which was clearly disturbed by our presence. That could only mean one thing.

"It's got a nest with young uns!" I yelled excitedly. If it hadn't had a nest it wouldn't have stayed, but would quickly have flown away from us. And if it had eggs in the nest it wouldn't be circling so angrily.

This was my big chance. I was straight up the tree it was circling. I was scared the mother owl might attack me and peck my eyes out, but luckily I had on my trusty Spitfire Jacket, which was immune to any branches, even thorns. All I had to do was tuck my head inside the collar and force my way up the tree trunk.

Kenneth Greensit ran away, shouting that he didn't want his eyes pecked out.

Norma Greensit shouted at me. "You'll get into trouble. They'll take you to court. You'll go to prison!"

Only our Eck kept watch.

I reached the nest and put my hand inside. It felt warm and fluffy. I pulled myself up higher, scrabbling to find a branch to stand on safely.

"Woh!"

There were two baby owls inside. Big balls of fluffy white feathers, beautiful owl faces in downy fluff, both staring with big eyes at this panting intruder to their nest.

"Two baby owls!" I shouted down to the others.

"Watch out!" called our Eck, and I could see the angry mother owl over my shoulder, screeching in rage.

Norma Greensit ran away screaming.

I tugged at the zip of my jacket with one hand, tore it open and grabbed for a baby owl. My foot slipped and I nearly fell from the tree. The mother was screeching and flapping at me, though strangely, the baby owls were sitting calmly watching me.

Desperately I reached into the nest, and grabbed a baby owl. I tucked it inside my jacket, got my hand round the other owl, and wondered what on earth I was going to do next. There was no way I could climb down the tree one-handed, as it was about fifteen feet down and difficult to climb. The mother owl was going mad at me, and I was scared. So I jumped off backwards, cradling the owls to my chest.

Miraculously I landed on my feet unhurt.

"Run!" I yelled.

Our Eck led the way, his legs pumping as fast as his wellies would allow him. The mother owl pursued us as we ran home, screaming with anger and hurt.

***

"What's that you've got there?" our Mam asked, when we arrived breathless in her kitchen.

"Owls," said our Eck.

"We're going to tame them," I added quickly, in case she disapproved of us bringing wild creatures into the house.

She looked at them and said something like, "Ooooh, whatever next?"

She didn't seem to understand what a magnificent opportunity this was. We were going to tame two owls… we would be famous.

"What do they eat?"

I didn't know. That was the start of our problems.

"Where did you get them?" she asked.

I caught a glimpse of the mother owl circling our garage.

"Found them," I lied.

"Hmm," she said doubtfully. "Anyway, get them out of my kitchen, I've got baking to do."

***

I put the owls in a cardboard box, and went to dig some worms for their dinner. Disappointingly, the worms proved not to their taste. I sneaked back into the kitchen and pinched two buns from my Ma's baking and gave them to the owls, who definitely preferred them to the worms.

I spent the afternoon making a hutch for my owls, from an old orange box and a piece of chicken wire. By the time my Dad arrived home from work I had finished the job and was all ready to begin taming the owls.

"I hear you've got some new pets," said my Dad, entering the garage quietly.

"Not pets Dad, wild owls!"

He came carefully into the garage and sat down beside me. I opened the lid of the cardboard box and he peeped inside.

"My," he said, "Aren't they beauties!"

I pulled out the hutch I had made. "I'm going to tame them. I've got it all worked out. They're eating already."

"Oh, yes, what do they eat?"

"They like Ma's buns."

He smiled. "So do I."

I lifted one owl out. It was a beautiful little thing – I've never forgotten it – everything about it was just perfect. And it was so soft. It just sat there and let me stroke it. Dad touched it with his finger.

He didn't need to speak. There was a long silence as we both admired the owl. I knew I had done a terrible thing taking it from its mum. I had hated to hear the mother owl's cries of distress, but I'd wanted those baby owls so much I'd been willing to shut my ears to her wailing.

I opened the box and took out the other owl. I gave this one to Dad. Together, Dad and I walked through the fields, carrying the two baby owls back to their nest. It was nearly dark when we got to the tree. I climbed up, and put them carefully back where they belonged. The mother flew in as soon I got down to the ground.

None of us who saw them ever forgot those baby owls. They are my favourite wild creature, but they are best left that way.

For years afterwards my Ma would suddenly stop what she was doing, look at me in an odd way and say softly, "Baby owls."

THE FRIDGE

There was great excitement in the house. We were getting a fridge! It is hard to conceive nowadays how people coped without a fridge, but we did. Of course, not having a fridge meant that we could not keep meat or anything perishable for more than a day or two. This in turn meant that Ma had to go all the way down Hubberholme hill into Ravenscroft town practically every day of the week to do shopping for fresh food. As nothing could be kept fresh, if we wanted to eat and survive without getting food poisoning, that was what she had to do. This was all very well in summer, when the roads were clear, but when Winter came to Ravenscroft, it hit hard. Snow fell frequently and it fell deep. Poor Ma had to struggle each day down into town to buy us the food to feed us. She didn't complain.

Well, she did. Frequently and bitterly. And eventually my Dad could stand it no longer. He wasn't able to make a fridge himself, so we would have to buy one.

I don't know how they could afford it, but for the first time we were buying a proper piece of modern household equipment and the money had to come from somewhere.

So it was to be, that for the first time in their lives, Ma and Dad bought something on what they called the Never Never.

***

The fridge arrived one day when Eck and I were out at school. We arrived home to find that the kitchen had shrunk considerably. A massive great yellow thing took up the whole of one wall. We had been expecting something modern, something American-looking. This great ugly beast had horns and looked like something Russian.

Nevertheless it was exciting.

Ma proudly demonstrated her expertise by opening and closing the front door of the fridge. It had shelves for food and one for milk bottles. We were very impressed.

Then I noticed there was a little compartment at the top of the fridge. I opened the door. It had a metal-walled cupboard inside.

"What's this for Ma?"

She shrugged. We had reached the limit of her technical ability. "I don't know do I? What do you keep asking me questions for?"

Clearly, she was embarrassed at her lack of knowledge.

This little cupboard, it turned out, was the freezer compartment. It made ice. We could make ice cubes! This suddenly seemed the height of sophistication and the object of our desires.

Now I have to be honest about our Ma, she was prone to doing odd things. Once, shortly after I had been born, she was so proud of me that she had entered me in a Beautiful Baby Competition (much to my embarrassment at the time and often since.)

I only came second, at which she was outraged. Marching up to the judges she had announced that the contest must have been fixed, that the winner was nothing but a "wee prune face" and a "horrible wee runt I'd be ashamed to look at."

Even years later she would see the child, by then grown big and tall and she would announce loudly, "That's the wee runt that robbed you of the First Prize!"

***

Back to the fridge.

The possession of a shiny new fridge was in some ways a pleasure to her – she no longer had to go out in rain and snow to walk all the way into Ravenscroft and back - but in other ways it unsettled her. She never actually came to terms with what a fridge could and could not do.

The freezer compartment was the main difficulty. Every few weeks it would fill up with white snow, and it had to be defrosted. This process took several hours and involved leaving the fridge door open, wedging the freezer compartment door open as well and allowing the snow to melt to water, which had to be collected in a bowl.

Ma was totally impatient with this. It drove her mad. It was far too slow for her. So, not long after the arrival of the new Fridge on the Never Never, what did she do to speed up the defrosting?

She brought the electric fire into the kitchen. She lugged the fridge over nearer to the sink and she stood the electric fire on top of the sink. Then she opened the freezer compartment, wedged the door open, and turned the two bar electric fire on to full heat, so that both bars glowed red.

"That'll defrost it in no time!" she announced proudly. "Isn't that just the job!" and off she went to have a smoke outside the back door.

When she came back, she found that something terrible had happened – thanks to the glowing electric fire, the freezer compartment door had melted in the heat, and was buckled beyond repair.

"Harry!" she wailed to our absent Dad. "What have I done?"

***

Poor Dad. When he came home he took one look at the wreckage of his new fridge and sighed. He was used to Ma after years of electronic disasters.

"Ach, I was only gone five minutes!" Ma said.

Dad had to cut off the twisted door of the freezer compartment in order to get the fridge to close. After that the freezer never worked properly, and persistently filled the rest of the fridge with snow.

"I was only hurrying it along," Ma said, in that winning way of hers.

No-one could be angry with her for long.

"We should never have bought it on the Never Never!" she concluded.

SAVAGES

When Summer came that year I had fully recovered from my Tonsillitis operation, my cut tongue had healed and I had even recovered from the effects of my stays in Darlington Memorial Hospital. However, ever since I spent that week in the care of the hospital, I have loathed such dishes as Frogs' Spawn, Prunes and Boiled Cabbage.

I soon forgot about all this, as I had a new craze and I was just dying to try it out.

Having finished the entire works of Anthony Buckeridge (*Jennings and Darbishire*) I had gone rooting along my dad's bookshelf to find something new. There I discovered a book called *Coral Island*, by RM Ballantyne. This was a wonderful book about boys living on a desert island, who spent their days catching fish and cooking them, finding fruit and eating it raw, or chopping down trees and making canoes. In other words, generally living an exciting life, a life which I was determined I should attempt at the first opportunity.

I realised of course that there wasn't quite the variety of fruits to be found in the Yorkshire Dales that you might find on a tropical island, but I was sure we could get round that difficulty. What was lacking in the way of fruit I would have to make up for in other ways – rabbits, pigeons, hares, pheasants, partridges and other game in the woods. There would be trout and grayling from the river. I was sure we could live wild and free for ever!

***

I gathered the gang together and told them all about *Coral Island*.

"So you see, we could live like savages quite easily," I concluded.

My assembled audience said nothing. I was very disappointed. Couldn't they see what great fun it was going to be?

Our Eck spoke up. "Sounds a great idea our kid, when can we start being savages?" Good old Eck.

But Alex Marcham, Norma Greensit and her brother Kenneth, and Clive Lawson the Pater's son, all looked less than enthusiastic. I could see that I would have to compromise to get my way.

"Alright then," I conceded. "We won't go off and live like savages completely. We'll just do it for a day."

This was obviously much more to their liking. Kenneth Greensit at least looked interested. Getting away from his parents appealed to him.

"You can come home at night," I added.

At this even Norma looked interested.

And when I said, "So you've no need to miss any of your telly programmes," I knew she at least was won over.

Clive Lawson the Pater's son said challengingly, "How are you going kill all these things you claim we can live off? The rabbits and so on."

"Easy. We can trap them."

"Oh yes, and how do we do that?"

"In snares."

He was going to ask next, "How do you suggest we do that?" I could tell. Clive Lawson the Pater's son was a friend, but he just had no imagination at all. I didn't know how we were going to snare them, did I? That was half the fun, finding out!

However, I managed to restrain myself from pouring the abuse on the head of Clive Lawson the Pater's son which he so richly deserved, and instead said placatingly, "Come on Clive, it'll be great fun!"

He grumbled, but because I'd called him Clive and begged him to come, he begrudgingly agreed.

I was to regret this later. I don't know why I'd bothered roping him in as he made a rotten savage when he got to the river. I think my main motive was to spread the blame in case anything went wrong. If he was there I wouldn't get into too much trouble. On the other hand, if he wasn't there, then I would be the undoubted leader in adult eyes, and if something disastrous did happen, like Kenneth Greensit stabbing himself or setting fire to himself, then I would be the one to take the blame. And let's face it, there was a strong chance that things would go wrong.

Anyway, the plan was agreed. We were going to go down to Masham Abbey and live there like savages. Masham Abbey, though not noted for its variety of tropical fruits, or even the prolific nature of its wild creatures, was far enough away to appear wild and near enough to the shops to provide Mars Bars in case things went wrong.

The others even started to get excited about it. Elaborate plans were made, survival kits assembled. There was wild talk of building tree houses, of swinging through the forest on jungle lianas, of sleeping out under the stars (this mainly led by Norma Greensit, who brightened considerably at the prospect.)

I privately hoped that this last would not come about, because of my fear of night predators. Mainly Norma Greensit, who had obviously got over her usual hatred of me, and was now to be found in devoted rapture feasting on my every word, her sheep-like eyes turned upwards in a most un-nerving manner.

Kenneth was a constant irritation, as I knew he would be.

He kept asking questions like, "What are we gonna eat? What are we gonna do all day? What are we gonna do if big kids come?"

I knew what I was going to do if big kids came. I was going to leave a sacrificial offering staked out on the ground. And run like hell.

∗∗∗

I decided it wouldn't be a good idea to tell our parents too much about our plans. They might object to us living like savages on creatures we had killed ourselves, going in more for meals like fish fingers and chips themselves. So I swore the others to secrecy.

The appointed day arrived. Actually, it was the next day, but appointed day sounded more dramatic. We all gathered at the back of O'Brien's shed on the appointed day. We compared survival kits, laying them out on the short grass in front of us.

"What've you got?" asked Clive Lawson the Pater's son. He proudly displayed a proper camping knife – one with devices for getting stones out of horse's hooves and suchlike ingenious gadgets.

While I brought my kit out of my pockets, he idly showed off how he could use a magnifying lens and the sun's rays to burn a hole in Kenneth Greensit's leg.

"Ow!" howled Kenneth, when the pain got through to his brain.

I brought out a large carving knife, more usually used in our house on the Sunday joint.

Clive Lawson laughed in derision. "What's that?"

"A machete for hacking our way through the forest."

He hooted with laughter. "Looks more like a kitchen knife to me!"

"It can be used for that as well," I conceded, feeling that Round One had gone to Clive Lawson the Pater's son.

Further comparison of survival equipment was abandoned. Anyway, I consoled myself, we'll see who is brave enough to kill a rabbit, much less skin it, cook it and eat it.

So we set off on our expedition to live like savages. Me leading the way, followed very closely by Norma Greensit, then Clive Lawson with his proper camping knife, Alex Marcham, our Eck a long way behind because he was only five, and finally Kenneth Greensit, who had got his wellies on the wrong way round and couldn't figure out why it was such agony to walk in them.

***

Masham Abbey was a ruin on the banks of the River Swale, a couple of miles away. The Abbey ruins themselves were not that interesting, as they consisted entirely of bare lawns and piles of dead rocks, and in addition it cost 6d to get in. So we never bothered.

However, around the Abbey were woods, an old mill and the River Swale, wide and shallow. It was here that one day Thomas Evans would drop the boulder on my head, here that my Dad always claimed Robin Hood had died, and here too that I would one day tickle my first trout.

As soon as we got there Clive Lawson the Pater's son said, "I suppose we're going to live off trout you've tickled."

This was a snide reference to my oft-repeated desire to catch a trout by tickling one, a skill I had not yet acquired. He could be infuriating, could Clive Lawson.

Alex Marcham chirped up with, "I'm hungry."

It was annoying, but there was nothing I could do about it now. As leader I would have to accommodate such minor difficulties and smooth them out, rather than beating them both up, which was what I really wanted to do.

"Right. First thing to do is to find somewhere to make camp."

Clive Lawson said, "You find one if you're so clever."

And Alex Marcham said,"I'm starving."

"Let's eat our survival rations," said Clive Lawson.

"Good idea!" said Alex.

I protested. "They're only for use in an emergency!"

"It is an emergency," said Alex. "I'm starving." And with that he took out his Crunchie bar and wuffed it down.

I left them to it. Faithful Eck followed me, as did Norma of course, and also Kenneth, who had finally, after four miles, located the source of his foot troubles and had taken off his wellies.

"I'm going barefoot like a savage!" he declared.

I commended his spirit, although it might not have been a great idea considering the large number of dogs who were taken for walks in these woods, but at least it was in the spirit of *Coral Island*.

***

We eventually chose as our campsite a clearing next to the river. It couldn't be approached by land because of thick hawthorn clumps, which forced the riverside path far into the woods and well away from our chosen site. We had flat shelving rocks on one side, which would be good and safe for lighting our cooking fire without burning down the woodlands. And it had soft grass so we could lie in the sun and daydream.

This we did for ten minutes before Kenneth Greensit decided he needed to go to the toilet.

"You should have gone before you came," said his sister.

I thought this was a pretty stupid thing to say. Could you imagine the characters of *Coral Island* saying, "You should have gone before you came."

"Do it in the woods," said our Eck sharply. I could see he was getting fed up of Kenneth Greensit.

"I can't," whined Kenneth. "I want a Number Two."

This was Kenneth Greensit's way of saying he wanted a shit.

Eck giggled. "Use a docken leaf."

Kenneth Greensit began looking around for a docken leaf, reducing our Eck to hysterics. Kenneth Greensit had no understanding of sarcasm.

When he'd finally gathered a fistful of docken leaves, he wandered off alone into the woods behind us.

I forgot all about him, until a few minutes later, when I could hear him crying.

"Stupid baby!" said his sister sympathetically.

As leader I thought I had better go and see what was the matter with him. I found him sitting on the ground, naked from the waist down, crying uncontrollably.

"What's wrong Kenny?"

"It's no good," he wailed. "My finger keeps going through the docken leaf."

Further activities were suspended indefinitely while we all collapsed with laughter.

There being no sign of Alex Marcham or Clive Lawson the Pater's son, it was left to the four of us to collect wood to build a fire. Norma Greensit soon proved herself useless at this, trying to break off branches from riverbank bushes.

"They're green," I pointed out in disgust.

"So what?"

"So they're still growing. They won't burn."

"Stupid branches," she snapped.

It was tough being the leader of novice savages.

***

We started gathering wood again, but this time I tried to direct her to pick only dry wood from dead branches. Eck, meanwhile, had found a complete dead tree, and was trying manfully to lug it into our clearing.

"This'll burn!" he said proudly. It certainly would. It was about twenty feet long and nine inches thick. It would last us a week.

Once the materials for a fire were gathered, it was time to go out hunting for food.

"I'll come with you David," volunteered Norma Greensit.

Here was another tricky problem for our leader. I appreciated her devotion to duty, but I didn't fancy having her dog my footsteps all the way through the jungle.

"You can do the cooking," I said. Her face fell instantly, so I had to add, "You're best at that" – to appease her and maintain the fragile peace.

Kenneth couldn't come hunting because he had a sore bottom and he found it difficult to walk. He had blisters on his feet caused by his odd wellingtons, and now the blisters were swelling into watery eggs, so Kenneth was left lying face down, sobbing quietly to himself.

In the continued absence of Clive Lawson and Alex Marcham it looked like the hunting party was going to be reduced to two members, Eck and myself. It didn't look as if we would be able to trap rabbits by surrounding them and running them down as I had hoped.

Eck and I gathered up our weapons and snares and got ready to leave. "We're off then," I said, which was a mistake.

Norma Greensit leapt to her feet, puckered her lips and lunged towards me.

"I'll try to bring you some food," I said, dodging her attack, though I knew perfectly well that it wasn't food she was after.

***

Rabbits proved even more elusive than I had feared. We didn't see a single one. However, we did set snares over likely rabbit-runs, so we would probably catch some during the day.

"We'll eat later," I said.

Eck looked unconvinced.

Snares, incidentally, were lengths of my dad's garden twine, laid in a lasso shape on the ground, and covered by leaves and moss. Any rabbit foolish enough to step into the lasso would be trapped instantly, (though I wasn't quite sure how) – and hoisted up into the air, there to be suspended until I came to collect it.

We did see some pheasants, but they flew away when we got within a hundred yards of them. And partridges weren't any more accommodating as food. A whole flock of them whirred into the air at our feet and were gone long before we could draw our weapons.

Our armoury consisted of a bow and arrow – only one arrow, as they were hard to find; a catapult of doubtful accuracy (so far I had only fired it once, propelling a steel ball-bearing with great force into the thumb with which I was holding the catapult); the aforementioned and somewhat dubious machete; a penknife and a big lump of wood to club them to death if all else failed.

"Sssh!" said our Eck, who was proving to be a surprisingly good stalker of wild game. He pointed ahead through the undergrowth. "Look! Pigeons."

They were indeed. Great big fat bluey-grey pigeons, happily cooing and pecking away in a clearing just ahead. We stood behind a big tree and watched them.

"It's a Baobab tree this," I said expertly. Eck seemed impressed.

"What weapon should we use?" he asked. I drew out the bow and our arrow.

Unfortunately this wasn't one of those lovely bows and arrows with which Kevin Batty had shot our kid. This was a home-made one, cut from an ash tree, with a length of my dad's famous garden twine tied tight between the two ends. The arrow was similarly home-made, by me, a nice straight hazel shoot that I'd trimmed and sharpened with a pen knife.

Carefully I loaded the weapon and took aim. The pigeons pecked on, regardless of our presence. Eck held his breath, close by my shoulder, his pen knife ready in case I should only wing one. I drew the bow back, though not very confidently. I squinted along the arrow, pulled the bow as far back as I could, and let go.

The arrow sailed among the pigeons and belly-flopped gently in their midst. One or two of them stopped eating long enough to eye the arrow suspiciously, but the majority took no notice at all.

"Fuckarada!" said our kid.

**

There was nothing now for it, but a frontal assault. Eck held his pen knife, I used the club like a savage, and we charged those bloody pigeons. They skittered away long before we got within ten yards of them, disappearing into the wood, and, I fancy, chuckling at our incompetence as savages.

We said nothing. Glumly, we retrieved our precious arrow and set off once more to hunt for food.

By now I was starving too, and was beginning to wish I'd let our party of savages stop by the chip shop on the way for sixpennorth with scraps, as they'd begged me to do. But I wasn't going to give up on my dream and start on my Mars bar just yet. We crept along the water's edge, in search of ducks.

There were flocks of mallard on the river, living there more or less permanently. In summer they settled on the grass in front of the Abbey and allowed silly tourists to feed them meat paste sandwiches, a diet on which they seemed to thrive (though I detested the stuff myself.) The ducks would at least have plenty of meat on them.

"There they are!"

Our Eck pointed them out. He hadn't let me down, becoming a really good tracker after only a day in the wild.

The ducks were lying and squatting on the bank just ahead of us. One or two were in the water looking wide-awake and ready for flight, but the others seemed nicely unaware of the presence of hungry savages. We checked our weapons.

"Forget the bow and arrow," advised Eck.

I decided on the lump of wood as a more effective, though undoubtedly less artistic method of catching our supper. Eck slotted in behind me, clutching the machete in a most piratical fashion, and we padded through the trees towards the unsuspecting ducks.

I kept thinking they would fly up like every other wild creature we had met that day, but they didn't. They just sat there, creaking their beaks contentedly at each other or preening themselves. They were a vain lot, those ducks.

I tried to count them, but lost the number at a dozen. They were mostly brown females, but with three or four gorgeous green-necked drakes and a great fat white thing that must have escaped from a farmyard.

"Ready?"

"Ready."

Eck nodded and fingered his knife. With a bloodthirsty yell, I lunged forward, bearing the lump of wood aloft like some pale-skinned Dervish.

The ducks came running. Yes! They ran towards us! They were so used to humans and so tame the stupid birds thought we were tourists bearing gifts of Shippams dreadful potted-meat sandwiches. They didn't realise we were bloody half-starved savages come to club them to death and to make them into sandwiches! I couldn't believe it.

I stopped yelling, with a dozen ducks gathered about my feet, all of them quacking plaintively away.

"Go on then!" yelled our Eck. "Belt 'em one!"

I wanted to. I should have done. But somehow they looked so trusting, so friendly, I just couldn't. Once I had seen those handsome green throats and those lovely little brown eyes, I knew I could no more kill a duck than I could kill Clive Lawson or Alex Marcham. In fact, I could have killed Clive Lawson or Alex Marcham with far less guilt. So I stood there, lump of wood absurdly poised.

"Go on!" yelled our Eck. "You can't miss!"

I knew I couldn't miss, that was why I lowered my lump of wood so carefully to the ground. Eck turned away in disgust. It was no use. They were such beautiful birds I just couldn't do it.

In the end I got my Mars Bar out and broke it into tiny pieces, which I fed to the ducks.

Eck sat on the riverbank, going, "Hmph, some savage!"

I couldn't help it. I just couldn't eat ducks.

***

"What are we going to do now? We can't go back with nothing."

This was true. To return empty-handed would be defeat on a massive scale, defeat which Clive Lawson would never let me live down.

"Should we try tickling a trout?"

Eck was aware of my fascination with this skill, and equally aware that I had no talent.

"Nah. Let's just try catching bullheads."

Bullheads we could definitely catch. They were small brown ugly fish that lived under flat stones in the river. We often caught them, kept them in a pool and then returned them alive to the river. Catching enough Bullheads to provide a meal for six hungry kids was a different proposition however. Bullheads were seldom more than two inches long. A three inch bullhead was a veritable record-breaker.

"I don't think there's much meat on 'em," said Eck, voicing my exact thoughts. "We'd need about a hundred to feed us all."

"Fifty," I corrected. "I'm not feeding Clive Lawson or Alex Marcham. They can starve."

We started fishing for bullheads.

***

We'd caught a couple when I called a halt. It was taking too long and bullheads were horribly ugly little creatures. I wasn't sure that I fancied eating one, let alone enough bullheads to satisfy my gnawing hunger. Instead we caught crayfish.

Back at camp things were exactly as we had left them. Norma had done nothing to get ready for cooking our meal. No-one had even started building our shelters or a tree house. The only change was in Kenneth Greensit. He was sitting half-naked, scratching his bum.

"What's wrong with him now?" I asked Norma.

"He wants to go home."

"Shit?" said Eck.

"No," said Norma. "He can't. He went again and nettled his bottom. He says he's in agony."

I didn't really want to inspect Kenneth Greensit's bottom just before a meal, but as leader I had little choice. It was covered in red nettle stings and great red scratch marks where he'd been rubbing them.

"Well?" he asked. "What's it look like?"

"Doesn't look too bad," I lied.

"Silly bugger," said our Eck.

I wasn't going to give up being a savage and go home defeated just because he'd nettled his bum. He would just have to suffer.

I handed Norma the spoils of our food hunt in a handkerchief.

She screamed.

"Ugh! Horrible things. What are they?" she howled, leaping about and knocking the crayfish to the ground.

"Crayfish."

She stopped screaming and bent down to look at them closely.

"They look like little lobsters."

I was delighted. "Lobsters! That's exactly what they are Norma. And when they're cooked they taste just like lobsters too!"

Eck and I got on with the fire, easily the best part of being a savage so far. We were experts at lighting fires, as we did it everywhere we went except in the Plantation, which being a dry wood, would have burned down. All we needed was some dry grass and a match. No paper or any of that civilisation stuff, a bit of dry grass, some dried up stalks and then a mass of bigger dry twigs and wait until they were flaring, then feed in real branches and you were away.

In five minutes we had a fire going, nice and crackly and blue-smoky. After the branches had been burning for a quarter of an hour we would add logs, and when they started to turn into red hot ashes, then we would drop our spuds into the ashes. Roast spud from an open fire is one of the best meals I have ever had, and nothing, not even Kenneth Greensit or the rest of my useless savages, could spoil that pleasure.

Eck and I brought up flat stones from the river and set them around the fire, to prevent any chance of the fire spreading. These were to double as our cooking oven, because they soon became hot enough to cook on. Norma had decided she didn't want to be chef when she had seen what was on the menu, so I had to do it, dropping the crayfish gently onto the hot rocks and letting them sizzle.

They smelled delicious and no doubt it was this which brought Clive Lawson and Alex Marcham crawling out of the undergrowth.

"Are you hungry?" I asked, casually flipping over a cooked crayfish.

Clive Lawson's eyes nearly popped out of his head. Eck backed me up by pushing spud after spud into the core of the fire. Alex Marcham edged in beside us both, trying to be friendly.

"I wouldn't eat them," declared Clive Lawson, pointing at the crayfish.

"Good. 'Cos you're not going to get the chance."

That shut him up. Well, he didn't deserve it. He'd played all afternoon, throwing stones at a bottle they'd found and floated down the river, while Eck and I had worn ourselves out trying to find food for them all. Norma sat down beside me, pushing her brother out of the way.

***

The spuds were delicious, burnt black and crisp on the outside just as they should be, but white and fluffy inside. With a generous coating of salt they were surely the best food you could eat.

The pair of loafers sat hungry while we ate our spuds. Even Kenneth Greensit perked up enough to forget his sore bottom for five minutes and eat a spud. The spuds were unforgettably good. They made us forget the previous debacles of our lives as savages. I relented and gave them both a spud.

The crayfish too were unforgettable, in their own muddy little way. They looked just like the prawns you can buy at the seaside, but unfortunately there the resemblance ended. They tasted just like mud, which was hardly surprising when you think about it. Mud was where they lived, mud was what they ate. Mud was what they tasted of.

I managed one and a bit. Eck claimed loyally to have eaten three, though I saw him throw two over his shoulder when he thought no-one was watching. Norma had one. Kenneth had one as well and then had to rush off into the bushes again.

Clive Lawson the Pater's son watched us with undisguised malice, and when we had finished the crayfish, announced, "I hope you get the shits!" and went off home in a huff.

Alex Marcham, having spotted that there were more spuds in the fire, stayed with us.

Kenneth Greensit came back from the bushes crying, with his pants around his ankles.

"I got stung!" he cried, holding out his widdler to show us the damage.

***

Despite Clive Lawson's departing curse, we suffered no after-effects from eating the crayfish, though I was never fond of prawns after that day.

That night we trudged home in the darkening evening, happy and tired, covered in ash from the fire, mud from the river, nettle stings and midge bites.

As we reached her house, Norma Greensit said, "Can I have a kiss?"

I suppose she hadn't been too bad as a savage, though I couldn't say I would like to be marooned on a desert island with her. I gave her a kiss.

Eck and I went inside our house, to sleep a night of wonderful dreams. Life as a savage wasn't too bad, provided you remembered to bring some spuds from home.

FRISKY

F risky was by now a beautiful, fully-grown tortoiseshell cat. I loved him and everything about him, from the way he licked his paws, to the way he curled his tail in curious little movements when he was watching the birds. Frisky liked to snuggle down with me on the rug in front of the fire. I would curl myself up and Frisky would come and lie inside my arms. There we would fall asleep.

Frisky liked me to stroke his nose with my forefinger, in gentle upward movements which would cause him to close his eyes in pleasure. Then he would start to purr.

After Frisky had been asleep he would wake up, stretch his legs out straight, then he would open his paws and he'd extend his claws. He was just practising being a cat. Frisky never hurt me or anyone else; he was just such a gentle, beautiful cat.

And so clean. Even Ma, not the greatest fan of cats, had to admit he was clean. He never, ever, did a wee or a poo in the house.

After tea, Ma would call him. "Frisky!" and he'd wake up, stretch himself and saunter off in his majestic way, off to the kitchen for his supper.

Frisky ate Top Cat. It came in a tin and was pinkish meat, with a strong and fairly unpleasant smell. Yet the odd thing was, that no matter how much Top Cat Frisky ate, he never ever smelled of it.

After his meal Frisky would come back to me to say goodnight. Then he would go and wait by the back door for Ma to let him out for the night. By now we had become used to this routine and we no longer worried about letting him out.

When morning came Frisky would be there outside the back door, waiting to be let in for his breakfast. Often he would bring us back a trophy as a present from his nocturnal hunting trips – a mouse, vole or, once, a rat.

***

One night Eck and I were in bed. Eck was asleep hours ago in his bed beside mine, but this night I just couldn't get to sleep. I didn't know why, but I just couldn't sleep. No matter what dreams I tried to make me sleep – thinking of the river, or of tickling trout, of trying to fly, or being a savage, nothing worked. Not even when I thought of Nicolette Goulding and what it might be like to kiss her.

Nothing worked. For hours I lay there twisting and turning from side to side. Something was wrong, I knew it.

Neither of us possessed a watch, but I could guess it was late, because it was by now very dark outside. Ma and Dad were still up, as I hadn't heard them come up to bed.

I climbed out of bed and went downstairs.

"Hello, who's this?" said my Dad.

Ma knew instinctively something was wrong. "What's the matter?"

"I can't sleep."

"Are you sickening for something?" asked Ma, coming to me and putting her hand on my forehead.

"No. I'm fine. It's Frisky."

Dad smiled in relief. "He'll be fine. Don't worry about him, he can look after himself."

"No Dad. Something's wrong. I can tell."

Dad looked at Ma. Ma looked at Dad. Dad shrugged.

"Get dressed then. We'll go and look for him."

***

Five minutes later Dad and I were in our back garden. Dad had a torch. Frisky wasn't there, so we headed over to the looming black shapes of O'Brien's sheds. It was very, very dark. I wasn't scared for myself. I was scared for Frisky. I knew Frisky was in trouble. He needed our help.

We searched all around the big wooden shed. He wasn't there. We went round the back, to the brick building. He wasn't there. Then I heard something.

"Dad!"

He stopped.

"Listen!"

"What is it?"

We stood still and strained to hear the faint noise.

"There! Can you hear it?"

It came again. An animal cry. Together we ran towards the sound. It got louder.

"What is it?"

"It's Frisky! I know it is!"

We searched among the rubble and stacked wood. He wasn't there.

The cry came again. It was a mystery. Where on earth was it coming from?

Dad flashed the torchlight over the wall of the building. There was nothing unusual there, just a tall drainpipe going all the way up to the roof. Dad stepped forward. He put his ear to the drainpipe.

"He's in here!"

"Where?"

"Inside the drainpipe!"

Frisky meowed. He was stuck inside the drainpipe.

"Frisky!" I called. He meowed loudly back, recognising my voice.

"How on earth did he get in there?"

Frisky was stuck firmly inside the vertical drainpipe. It was made of iron and seemed very solid. It reached all the way to the roof and all the way down to the ground. Dad could just about get his hand up inside it, but there seemed no way of getting Frisky out.

"Stay here!" said Dad. "Don't move." He ran off towards our house.

I got down on my knees and spoke into the drainpipe.

"It's alright Frisky," I whispered to him. "Dad'll get you out."

He was back in minutes. He was holding something in his hand.

"What's that?" I asked.

"Butter."

Dad scooped butter out with his hands. He rubbed it up and down his arm, and then inside the drainpipe. Then he put his hand inside.

Frisky went quiet.

Dad's arm disappeared further and further up the pipe. There was no sound from Frisky.

"Dad…"

"Sssh… I can feel him… if I can just get a hold of his fur…"

By now he had squeezed his whole arm up the drainpipe. His face was contorted against the pipe. I held the torch closer. Dad grimaced with the effort. Then…

"Got him!"

Out came Dad's slimy arm, and out came Frisky. He was dark and wet and covered in butter. He looked dead.

Then he meowed.

"Frisky!" I shouted, cuddling him close in my relief at hearing he was alive. "Cor, thanks Dad!"

"Let's get him home and clean him up."

***

After a hot bath and some milk, Frisky was wrapped in a blanket and we took him in by the fire. He was a bit shaken by his experience. We lay on the rug in front of the fire and I cuddled him close. Soon we were both asleep.

By the next day Frisky had licked himself clean and was back to his normal self.

"What I can't understand," said Ma, "is how the boy knew the cat was in trouble."

Dad just grinned. "We'll never know."

THE PLANTATION

The Plantation was our name for the wood at the top of Hubberholme Hill. It was a place that we sometimes went inside to explore, that is me, Kenneth Greensit, our Eck, Alex Marcham and perhaps Clive Lawson, the Pater's son.

The Plantation was a dense wood of pine trees, growing in symmetrical rows, close to and just behind a high stone wall. It was a gloomy rectangle of dark trees, planted artificially in very straight lines. We actually had to climb up this wall to get into the Plantation. You really had to want to get inside, you couldn't just wander in.

It was not a pleasant place to be, as there was always a sense of something dangerous about it, probably because it was so dark and so close-packed. All the trees had been planted equally spaced and now they had grown so big that there was very little room between them. They grew up tight-packed, right up to the surrounding wall, so that to get inside we had to slide in and drop down on our bellies, or turn around and drop down blindly.

The Plantation was also <u>Private,</u> with several signs to remind us of this, so that there was always an added danger of being caught there. If we were chased, there would be no chance of escape. It took ages to climb up and over the stone walls and there was a strand of barbed wire on top of the wall, so that you had to get someone to hold it while you clambered over, or crawled underneath it.

You might wonder why anyone would ever want to go to such a menacing place, and the answer was that inside the Plantation it was like nowhere else on earth. It was another world, a dark, soft world of musty smells, lurking danger and murky shadows. Nothing ever grew there, so the ground beneath the trees was a soft and forgiving brown carpet of dead pine needles, piling deeper and thicker with each passing year. This carpet tempted you to lie down, it was so soft and yielding. There were no birds, no animals, no noise, nothing but darkness and a kind of tempting naughtiness about being there.

It wasn't often that we ventured inside the Plantation. It frightened Kenneth Greensit. He went in only reluctantly and constantly complained that there were evil men lurking in the shadows. Usually we hurried past the Plantation towards our favourite places, like Masham Abbey or the river. If ever we did go inside the wood it was with a secret sense of something forbidden, a feeling of being near to something we did not like or understand, but which was nevertheless tempting to us.

Go on, said the voice. Go inside the Plantation.

***

On this particular evening there were five of us. Kenneth Greensit, our Eck, Clive Lawson the Pater's son, me, and unusually, Norma Greensit. Alex Marcham couldn't come. Norma had invited herself. Why she was with us no-one knew. No-one wanted her here with us, but no-one had the courage to say so.

"I'm coming with you," she said challengingly.

Our Eck said, "Does she have to?"

She took a swipe at him.

Norma, being the biggest, oldest and strongest, took the lead of our little gang. I usually liked to be leader, but I wasn't feeling well. I had a strange sense of something bad happening. I was unsettled and simply followed her quietly as she took us through the hedge at the side of O'Brien's sheds.

I stopped under the hedge. I had spotted a birds' nest, so I let the others walk ahead. The hedge was hawthorn, which was always good for birds to nest in, as it gave them some protection. Blackbirds made a nest of dead grass and don't bother to line it. Song Thrushes made a similar nest, but lined it with mud which dried and baked hard. They made a much nicer and neater nest. Blackbirds' eggs were dull mottled blue with brown freckles. They weren't very attractive eggs. Song Thrushes' eggs, on the other hand, were very attractive. They were bright sky blue with coloured whorls and swirls. They were beautiful eggs.

I never took birds' eggs. I just liked finding their nests and seeing what was inside them. Kenneth Greensit would have liked to collect birds' eggs, but as he was useless at finding nests, he had only two eggs in his collection. If I did find a nest I tried to keep it secret from him.

I looked at this nest and decided it was probably a blackbird's nest. I didn't tell the others.

***

At the top of the field I caught them up. They had stopped because there was a very high stone wall. They were all waiting because our Eck would have to climb on my back to get a bunk up over the wall. He was only five. Norma was waiting impatiently and getting irritable.

"What did you have to bring him for?" she snapped. "He's only a baby."

"Mind your own business Greenshit!" said our Eck. He had got one hand round my neck, and with the other was scrabbling for a secure hold on the stone wall. However, once he was up on top of the wall he stood and faced her, wobbling on the loose stones.

"You look like a sheep!" he crowed. "Baaaa! Greenshit!"

Norma let out a howl of rage and tried to reach his ankle to pull him off the wall.

I grabbed at her to stop him. "Don't you dare touch him Norma!"

If he fell off he would break an arm or a leg.

Norma shot out her bony fist and hit me straight in the chest. I knew it was called the Solar Plexus and if you got hit there, you were really winded. Norma had got me right in the Solar Plexus. All the air went out of me with a sudden shock and I gasped for breath, staggering around gulping for air, with my eyes full of tears.

Norma turned away from me in triumph, only to find that our Eck had lifted his arms, and was ready to jump down the other side of the wall and escape her wrath.

"Yaaa!" he called. "Norma the sheep face!"

Norma grabbed for his leg, but she was too late. Our Eck had jumped and landed safely out of her reach. He was already running away in the next field.

By the time she had pulled herself up on top of the wall he was twenty yards away in the long grass on the other side, laughing at her and tormenting her by going, "Baaaaaaaaaa!"

Everyone was laughing, even me, when I got my breath back.

Norma would thump him if she caught up with him, but luckily for our Eck, Kenneth had found something interesting, which distracted her attention.

It was a large cowpat. A fresh new sloppy one, round and about a foot across. It looked like a large apple pie, with a crust on top. What interested Kenneth was that it was a nice fresh pie and would be therefore full of nice juicy wet green cow muck. Kenneth had a stick which he poked through the crust, and stirred round and round.

Now one thing which I didn't mention about Kenneth was that he could be absolutely insane. For one thing, he loved cow muck and the other thing about Kenneth that we all knew and understood, was that as soon as he had managed to get a lump of juicy cow muck to stay on that stick of his, he was going to chase us with it and try to smear it onto us. That was the sort of person Kenneth Greensit was, a mad cow muck wiper.

Without needing to speak, we ran away from him, up that field.

Clive shouted, "No Kenneth!"

I warned, "You'd better not!"

Only Norma stood her ground. Norma wasn't scared.

"Kenneth, I'm warning you! If you come near me with that stick I'll kill you!"

She turned and faced him. "You'd better not Kenneth. I'm warning you!"

He grinned and flicked a bit in her direction to test her temper.

"If you hit me with that shit Kenneth I'll give you some fist!"

Kenneth flicked again.

"If you flick shit at me again, I'll tell Dad."

Bad mistake. Kenneth instantly took this as a sign of weakness by Norma. Kenneth stirred his green porridge and succeeded in getting a large moist bit to stay on his stick, which he flicked at her.

Norma screamed and ducked, ducking just in time as it flipped over her head. Then she too ran for safety.

We all ran, screaming and yelling, with Kenneth in gleeful pursuit. We ran all the way up to the wall at the top of the field, the wall into the Plantation. I grabbed at the wall, wondering where our Eck had got to, then saw Kenneth heading in my direction, still brandishing his stick above his head, still intent on wiping some of it onto whoever he caught.

I saw our Eck was safe, some distance away. Clive Lawson the Pater's son was with him and had got him to the Plantation wall. Eck was safe, so I thought it was time to save myself.

Climbing stone walls was easy if you were careful. There was always one rock that stuck out so you could get your foot up onto it to use as a step. I felt for one, tested that it was secure and wouldn't knock my brains out and swung up, trusting it with all my weight. Then I was up on top and sliding down inside the canopy of darkness that was the Plantation.

I dropped onto the soft floor, panting heavily.

Immediately, all sounds of the outside world were shut out. It was very dark. My eyes, used to the sunlight, could see nothing. All I could hear was my own breathing, all I could see was the soft ground in front of me, scattered with brown needles.

It wasn't frightening, but there was something about being there alone that made me want to look behind to check that no-one was near me, no-one was creeping up on me in the dark.

Then there was a sudden skittering noise. The pine branches above me parted. A bare leg kicked through and someone burst through, landing on top of me. It was all arms and legs and bones.

"Careful Norma!"

She blundered in, destroying the silence.

"I didn't see you there," she said. "It's your own fault!"

She crawled along on her knees, head down, and sprawled into my body. I could feel how hot she was.

"Sssh! He'll hear us!" she whispered.

She put her hand over my mouth to stop me talking. I could hardly breathe and tried to wriggle free. She held me even tighter. We lay there panting together in the darkness of the wood.

***

Eventually, she removed her hand. I spat at the earth. I sat up and deliberately moved away from her. I was still angry with her for hitting me. She didn't need to have done that, I was only looking after our Eck.

I struggled up onto one knee. The trees were so tight-packed I couldn't stand up. I had to edge forward on my knees, trying to get room to raise my body. As I did so, I felt her hand on my leg. Her strong bony fingers had grabbed me just above my ankle. I tried to kick free of her.

"Get off!"

She didn't let go.

"Norma! Get off me!"

She laughed. She knew she had me trapped. Her breath was hot in my ear.

I fought and wriggled but it was no use. She was stronger than I was, and there was no room for me to run.

Ahead of me I could see the trees were all spaced at exactly the same distance apart in lines. I looked at them as she slid her hand up my bare leg. There were no birds inside the Plantation, no sounds of animals.

Norma started to whisper to me. "I want to tell you a story."

"I don't want to hear your stories."

"You'll enjoy it," she cooed.

I had never been this scared before. I tried to think about our Eck, who was my responsibility. If I had lost our Eck I would be in big trouble with my dad. I tried not to think about what Norma was saying.

"No Norma. Don't! I don't want to hear."

She laughed. "I'll tell you anyway."

I turned and faced her, full of hate and anger and frustration because I knew she wouldn't shut up and there was nothing I could do to make her stop.

Then suddenly there was a shout, and there was Clive Lawson the Pater's son peering over the wall at us.

"What are you two doing?"

Norma started to laugh.

Clive Lawson put his head inside the darkness and looked closely down at us lying there together.

"Ooh!" he taunted. "Have you two been courting?"

Norma was smiling. I blushed redder and redder. Norma started to snigger. I kicked free of her and scrambled up to the wall. She made no attempt to stop me escaping.

I could hear her laughing to herself as I climbed out of the Plantation and into daylight. Our Eck and Kenneth

Greensit were waiting there, the cow muck forgotten amidst this new excitement.

"Where've you been?" our Eck asked accusingly.

Norma was emerging from the Plantation behind me.

Clive Lawson the Pater's son grinned knowingly.

"He's been in the wood with Norma."

"I haven't!"

"Yes you have! I saw you."

Norma's face appeared, grinning at us. Her normally pasty white cheeks were red.

"Yes he has," she said proudly.

✳✳✳

We all walked home separately and in silence. Our Eck didn't understand why.

When we neared our house I stopped and waited for him to catch up. "Eck. Don't tell Ma and Dad anything."

"Tell them about what?" he said, bewildered by my fear. Then he burst into tears and I had to try to cheer him up all the way home so Ma and Dad wouldn't start asking him questions about why he'd been crying.

Norma Greensit went off to her own house, singing to herself.

"Hello boys, where've you been – out playing?" Ma asked.

I glanced threateningly at our Eck.

Ma had sensed something was wrong. "You look tired, the both of you," she said. "Early to bed for you two tonight."

The night was a hot and humid one and I had to sleep with the bedroom windows open. I had nightmares of Norma Greensit climbing up the drainpipe and getting into my bed.

THE MILL RACE

O ne day we set off for Masham Abbey, which was our favourite place to play apart from Gulliver Tower.

At the top of Hubberholme Hill, past the house where Alex Marcham and his big sister Sandra lived, there was a stony lane. This led for a mile or more down to the main road that led from Ravenscroft to Scriven village. We crossed this road and went down a tarmac road which led to Thornton on Swale. Here we turned right and down past the cottage hospital, we came to the ruins of Masham Abbey.

I always thought of Robin Hood whenever I went to Masham Abbey. My Dad had told me that Robin Hood used to roam the woods around there, and that when he died he was buried secretly somewhere in the grounds of the Abbey.

"I thought he lived in Sherwood Forest," I had said.

To which my dad had replied, somewhat shiftily I thought, "He did but he lived here as well."

I was half-convinced because I had a little red book called *The Adventures of Robin Hood*, which I had won for getting high attendance marks at Sunday School, and in that

251

little red book there was a colour picture showing the death of Robin. It had always made me sad because I liked to think that Robin Hood would live for ever. However, what made me think of that picture was that the background in the picture, just behind the dying Robin, looked very like Masham Abbey. So maybe my dad had been telling me the truth after all.

We didn't actually play in the grounds of Masham Abbey because it cost money to get in and we never had any. We went past it to the river, which was free and a lot more exciting than a lot of old walls without any windows, which was all that remained of Masham Abbey.

We were already very hot after our walk. The sun was high in a blue cloudless sky. Kenneth Greensit had been crying because he had nettled himself in the face, despite everyone telling him to watch out for the nettles. We had had to stop several times to search for dock leaves to rub on his nettle stings and while we were looking he had been sitting crying sorrowfully to himself and all the time rubbing his stings so that they had swollen up into ugly white bumps across his cheeks. These turned red because of all the rubbing and then black because of the tears he'd rubbed away with dirty hands.

When our Eck saw Kenneth's face he said in disgust, "You're such a baby."

This was a bit of an insult as our Eck was only five and was tiny compared to Kenneth Greensit. Nettles towered over our Eck, but he never complained or said he was scared of them. He just whopped them with a stick.

Of course, now he had been insulted as well as nettled, Kenneth wanted to go home, so an argument broke out.

Clive Lawson the Pater's son, Eck and I wanted to go onto the river, but if Kenneth wanted to go back home then we would have to go with him, because the last time we had left him to go home on his own he had got lost and we all had a mighty telling off from our dads.

Mr Greensit, who had had to phone the police to report a missing son, hadn't been very pleased either. When Kenneth had finally turned up after getting himself lost, Mr Greensit took out his displeasure with Kenneth by using a slipper on his son's bottom.

To end the argument, I resorted to bribery.

"Kenny, if you shut up moaning and come with us, we'll buy you some sweets."

He stopped moaning. "Will you really?" He looked doubtfully into my face.

I assumed an honest expression. "Yes. Really."

"Promise?"

"Promise."

"Cross your heart and hope to die?"

"Yes."

"Alright then."

The expedition continued.

Our Eck whispered to me. "You haven't got any money to buy sweets, have you?"

"Of course I haven't."

"He'll go mad when he finds out."

"It'll be too late then, won't it?"

Our Eck laughed out loud.

Kenneth stopped. "What are you laughing at? If you're laughing at me I'll go home!"

So Eck stopped.

***

The river at Masham was wide and shallow and stony. We sat down on the soft grass and took our shoes and socks off so we could paddle in the cool clear water. We were all oddly elated, because Norma Greensit wasn't with us for once. Her dad wouldn't let her come out. We had heard him shout something about School Uniform, sounds which billowed out of their front door when Kenneth had escaped to join us. So we kept out of the way until Norma had been driven off in a hurry by her red-faced father.

The water was lovely and cold on our hot feet. Shoals of little minnows fled just out of range as we walked unsteadily around on the slippery rocks. It was better to stay in the water to walk than to try to step onto dry rocks with wet feet. You could easily slip off and fall in. This was the River Swale, the fastest flowing river in England, of which we were very proud. But it was also very dangerous.

We stayed in the shallows however, not going near the fast-flowing stream of the main current. Out in the main stream were fat speckled trout. We knew this because we had once seen a fisherman land one. That was the nearest any of had ever been to catching one.

For an hour or more we amused ourselves by catching stone loach and bullheads. We kept them in a stock pool we had created by damming some water with rocks.

It was easy to catch bullheads. All you had to do was slowly lift up as big and flat a rock as you could manage, and underneath would be lurking a bullhead. As long as you moved gently, you could wangle your fingers into position just behind and in front of the bullhead and ever so gently close your fingers in on him.

The bullhead would just sit there unmoving, those big eyes on the top of his head watching you, not suspecting what you were up to until you pounced!

Quick! You got two fingers round that slippery little body, so that he couldn't wriggle out of your grasp, then you cupped both hands together to make a trap for him, and you stumbled over to the stock pool and put him in with the rest of the day's catch.

Stone loach were a bit trickier as they moved more quickly and were much more suspicious than the old bullheads, who weren't exactly the brainiest of fish. Even so, with stone loach you could usually catch them once out of every three or four attempts.

Everyone that is except Kenneth. Kenneth started crying because he couldn't catch any and because we were catching loads.

***

After a while we came out of the water and up onto the grassy banks. There we lay back in the hot sunlight and let the heat of the sun dry and warm our feet.

Suddenly there was the whistle of a steam train leaving the station at Ravenscroft a couple of miles away. Clive

Lawson the Pater's son pointed into the distance at the plume of white smoke, which was rising above the tops of the trees on the far bank of the river.

The railway line wound its way down the valley of the River Swale, through the woods, all the way out onto the flat lands of the Vale of York, until it reached Darlington. We all stopped what we were doing and stood to watch the engine appear out of the trees.

There it was! A big black tank engine. We all waved and the driver waved back. The engine clanked slowly by, dragging its little line of red carriages.

I liked engines. I liked the railway. Somehow it always made people happy. I thought of the lovely station building in Ravenscroft. I began thinking that we had never been exploring through the riverbank woods as far up as Ravenscroft station.

Clive Lawson the Pater's son must have been thinking exactly the same thing, because he shouted, "Let's go exploring! See if we can get up to town!"

So we scrambled to our feet and hurried into our socks and shoes.

We set off on a path beside the Abbey, along a way we'd never been before, heading alongside the river, aiming for the general area of Ravenscroft. We could see the massive stone Keep of the castle in the distance, so we knew we were heading in the right direction.

We went through a farmyard, where a black and white dog came out and barked at us.

Kenneth hid behind Clive Lawson and shouted, "Go AWAY!" which the dog thought was a game.

The rest of us laughed and shooed the dog away.

Beyond the farm there was a gate into a grassy field. There were Friesian cows in it, some sitting, some standing and eating contentedly. We half-expected the farmer to shout at us and tell us to clear off, but as there was a gate and an obvious path it looked as though it might not be Private, so we went through and into the field. No-one shouted at us.

I started singing, "We love to go a-wandering," which is the only line I knew of a song I'd heard somewhere.

We had moved some distance away from the river now, although we could still see its position because of the line of trees to our left. The path we were on led us across the field of cows. Far more interesting however, were the old stone buildings we were approaching.

"Might be owl's nests in there," I said. I was still dreaming of finding an owls' nest and bringing up baby owls.

"Come on, let's go find out."

Kenneth protested, "No! We'll get in trouble."

But I had already jumped over the three-runged metal fence and the others were following me. Once over, we ran as fast as we could for the old stone building and the trees that surrounded it.

We slipped down a steep bank under the trees and were quickly out of sight of any farmers or passers-by.

Inside the wood the trees were thick and old and cut out most of the light, so we had to bend low to walk. It wasn't easy in the half-darkness. The earth was soft and covered in flowers - wood anemones with little white flowers like bells, and celandines, which were bright yellow stars. There was a sweet smell too. Instinctively I liked this place.

We skirted round the old stone buildings, which all seemed empty and unused, and headed off vaguely towards the river, still bending low under the branches. Our legs ached with the strain.

Suddenly I stopped. I could smell water, fresh clean cool water. I was in the lead and called back, "Ssssh!"

I waved them to be quiet. I liked doing that. I bet Red Indians did that when they were on the trail.

I edged forward very slowly, dropping onto my knees. In front of me in the dim light I could see a dark, mossy shape.

"What is it?" someone hissed from behind me.

"I don't know," I whispered back.

I crept forward on my knees, one little step at a time. I peered into the gloom. The mossy shape was made out of stone. It was part of a wall, part of something mechanical. I could see old iron machinery. There was a big iron lever. What was it?

I could hear that there was water running in a straight line from me, towards the river. I edged another couple of feet forward and I could make out a ledge. I put my hand forward and it rested on mossy stone.

Clive Lawson whispered, "What's the holdup?"

Eck said, "What is it?"

"I think it's a stream." I moved forward another foot. Yes, I could see what it was now. There was a kind of stone wall, and below, inside it, was running water. Not the river, but some sort of cutting for water, inside the mossy stone walls.

My eyes were getting used to the dark now and I could see that there was a deep channel. The water was running in a cutting, between the two mossy stone walls, from the river towards the old buildings. I guessed immediately what it was.

The building was a mill, the iron lever was to operate the sluice gates, so this was a Mill Race!

Clive Lawson shuffled up beside me and I pointed ahead.

"What are you looking at?" he asked.

"This. Have a look. It's a Mill Race."

He peered over the edge of the wall, and down to where the water was racing below us.

"Wow. It's really fast!"

Eck and Kenneth Greensit joined us and together the four us lay on the ground, peering over the stone parapet of the deep cutting. We'd discovered something exciting, something none of us knew existed.

Clive Lawson grabbed my arm in excitement. "Look! Look!"

"What?"

"Look there!" He was pointing his finger at the water. He was so excited. "Trout! Monster trout! Just look at 'em!"

"I can see them! There, just by that branch!"

Our eyes strained in the semi dark.

"Bloody hell! Just look at the size of 'em!"

"Monsters!"

Black shapes in the water. Torpedoes in echelon.

Kenneth started to stand up.

"Siddown Kenneth, they'll see you!"

The trout were in a shoal and miraculously hadn't seen us, probably because only our heads were peering over the top of the wall, but down there, down below us, were the biggest, fattest trout any of us had ever seen. And they were only feet away from us!

We had never been this close to trout before and it was so thrilling, so exciting that for some minutes we just lay there enthralled.

I was so excited I wanted to back away so I could think about what we'd discovered - this wonderful secret place full of monster trout. I tugged at Clive Lawson's arm and nudged him to move slowly backwards.

"Keep your heads down!"

We edged away without being seen.

**

Back from the Mill Race, we gathered together. There, in that stone channel, only about six feet wide, in a Mill Race about twenty yards long, in water only a foot deep, were trout we had dreamed of, trout that would haunt me for the rest of my fishing days.

The others were animated too.

"How are we gonna catch 'em?"

"We could chuck bricks at 'em," suggested Kenneth.

"Oh yes Greensit, as if that's going to work!"

I wanted to say, "Let's leave them undisturbed, let's just leave them as they are, leave them in peace" - because it was just such a magical place. But the others were full of schemes and dreams.

"There's dozens of 'em!"

"We'll get a sackful!"

"We could wade in with nets, catch 'em all!"

For a magnificent moment, we all dreamed of what this might be like, the water boiling with immense trout as we scooped them up in our arms, a gluttonous feast of fishing.

But as soon as we'd thought of it I knew it wouldn't work, and I was not sure that I'd want it to work anyway.

"This mill race is going to be our secret," I said firmly. "I think we should leave it like that."

But Kenneth had an idea. "We could bomb 'em with rocks!"

Our Eck thumped him.

Unlikely though it seemed, my suggestion had caught on.

Clive Lawson the Pater's son, said, "Yes. We'll keep quiet! We won't let anyone know about it!"

"No-one uses it, you can tell," said Eck.

"Right then, that's what we'll do. It's our secret. Swear on it!"

We each held out a fist and swore to keep the secret of the Mill Race.

We clambered back out of the little wood and emerged blinking into the bright sunlight.

Kenneth was still thinking. You could always tell because he frowned when he tried to think.

"We could drop an atom bomb on 'em," he said.

We all ran for home and left him behind.

THE BROWN FRIED EGG

Ma was not what you would call a practical person. She was always very attentive and kept us clean and tidy, but as she often said, "Ach! I was born for better things than scrubbing and cooking for a load of lazy men!"

She was a militant feminist long before they had been invented.

When the first 'plastic' cooking utensils came on the market, Dad bought her some. Being Irish, she was very fond of the old frying pan, using it as the basis of every meal. Every day we would have what she called 'An Ulster Fry' - a great pile of bacon and egg and fried bread and sometimes black pud or a tomato.

With her new plastic spatula she immediately started using it in the same manner as she had used a wood and steel spatula. She had always left the old wood and steel spatula in the pan while the bacon was frying, so she saw no reason to behave any differently with the new plastic one she'd been given. She left it in the pan, while the bacon cooked away and she went outside for a 'five minutes smoke.'

When she came back she was baffled to find that the new spatula had vanished. In its place was a short plastic stick at the side of the hotplate. She looked into the frying pan.

There was the bacon and there was a strange little puddle, looking like a brown fried egg. 'Isn't that a quare thing now', she thought, 'I don't remember putting an egg on to cook.'

She left it merrily sizzling away with the bacon.

***

When Dad came in for his breakfast she served him a plate, with the bacon and with the brown fried egg. Dad happily ate the bacon and then tried the egg.

"Agh!" he spluttered, clutching his jaw.

"Whatever's the matter?"

"What the hell's this? I nearly broke my tooth!" He fished out the brown fried egg for inspection. He tapped it with the knife. It was hard as, well, as hard as plastic.

"What have you been feeding me woman? Are you trying to kill me?" He flipped the hard plastic egg towards her.

Ma picked it up and inspected it. "Jesus!" Ma said. "So that's where my new spatula went!"

We all collapsed with laughter. The only one not to laugh was Ma. She was incensed to discover that the new plastic spatula had melted, half of it falling into the frying pan and forming the mysterious brown fried egg. She was so convinced that she had been sold shoddy goods that she wrote to the manufacturers to complain.

The biggest joke of all was that they sent her a replacement spatula, and their apologies.

THE POT LEG

A terrible thing happened to our family and it was all my fault.

O'Briens the builders had left their shed unused and unvisited for as long as I could remember, but one day a lorry arrived. Men got out, opened the big padlocked double door and started unloading materials from the back of the lorry and taking them into the shed. It was a good job Norma Greensit wasn't inside offering to expose her lower regions to us all, or there would have been trouble.

As it was, none of O'Brien's men had the slightest idea that we regularly used their shed as part of our territory. The men stacked everything inside, the double doors were shut and padlocked once more, and the lorry went away.

We kept away from the shed for a day or two in case the men returned, but soon it seemed safe to enter and anyway, our curiosity quickly conquered our fears. Alex Marcham, our Eck and I crept in through the hole in the roof.

Everything was very different now. It used to be that there was a long drop from the hole in the roof down onto a kind of wooden shelf. Now there was no drop at all, the space had been filled up completely. It took us some time to find out what it was, as the light was so bad – but by exploring on our hands and knees we came to the conclusion that was what now stored there was a stack of completed window frames, glass and all.

I didn't like it and said so. Glass was dangerous and frightened me and the recent visit by O'Brien's men had unnerved me. They could come back at any moment and catch us in there and then there'd be trouble.

"Let's go," I said and turned back.

Alex Marcham laughed, a sniggering sort of laugh that annoyed me.

"What's up with you?" I asked him.

"Nothing," he said.

I could tell he was sneering at me. He thought I was scared. At this point I should add that though he was my friend, there were times when I didn't really like Alex Marcham.

Angered by him, I hurried to get out into the fresh air. Unfortunately, this was what led to the disaster. Instead of picking my way carefully over the window frames, walking only on the most solid and thick pieces of wood, and avoiding the glass, in my hurry I took bigger steps and accidentally put my foot straight through a glass pane. I wasn't hurt, but the glass was broken, and I'd done something I'd never done before – damaged someone else's property.

I pulled my foot slowly and cautiously out of the hole I had made in the glass, and was about to leave, when the strangest thing happened. I realised that it felt good when I broke the glass. There was something exciting about it, something pleasing.

"Good fun eh?" grinned Alex Marcham.

It was. I wanted to do it again.

There was a crash. Alex had broken a pane.

I did it again, this time with cold deliberation. He was right. It was good fun breaking the glass. It was very wrong of me, I was quite aware of that – but at the same time it was very satisfying to feel that glass give way when I sunk my heel into it.

Our Eck called out. "What are you doing?"

He sounded half-afraid, half-excited, as if he had guessed we were breaking the law.

"Smashing glass!" I called, my voice high with excitement.

I instantly regretted saying this. Eck was only five and he would want to do the same as his big brother. Alex Marcham was putting his foot through pane after pane. This was getting out of control. I began to panic.

"Come on Eck! Let's get out of here!" I called. But it was too late. Eck had already taken his first swing at the glass.

What he didn't realise, because he couldn't see us in the dark, was that Alex Marcham and I were breaking the glass by jabbing hard at it with the heels of our shoes, and we were being very careful not to put our feet straight through the shattered panes.

Our Eck was only five and didn't realise the danger. I raced back across the stack of windows to get to him, but it was too late.

I arrived just in time to see his foot hack at the glass. The glass broke and the back of his heel went right into the jagged edge. We were near the hole in the roof and I could see him quite clearly. He caught the glass just above the leather of his shoe, which might have saved him. Instead, the glass edge sliced straight through his sock and into his Achilles tendon, which, being poised for another blow, was rigid and tense.

The glass cut into it like a sharp blade cutting bacon. Blood shot out and our Eck screamed. I grabbed his arm, pull-hauled him up through the hole in the roof, and yelled to Alex Marcham to give me a hand getting him down the back of the shed.

Alex Marcham ran away.

What was I to do?

I jumped down to the ground, leaving our Eck bleeding on the roof. "Jump down!" I said.

"No!"

"You'll have to!"

It was ten feet or more and I wasn't sure I could catch him, but there was no option. I knew I had to get him medical treatment as soon as possible. This was no minor cut, this was a serious injury. He could die!

"Jump kid!" I pleaded, as he hung back. His face was white and there was blood on his hands where he'd been holding his injured leg. He jumped.

He landed right on top of me. I'd had my hands outstretched in an attempt to catch him, but they weren't strong enough and he went clean through them, piled into me and knocked me to the ground. We both fell, but without further injury.

"Are you alright?"

He nodded, frightened and pale. I could see the inside of that awful cut – a deep slice right through the Achilles tendon on the back of his right foot. It was white inside. Blood was everywhere.

Surprisingly, Eck wasn't crying at all. "Is it bad?" he asked.

I said, to reassure him, "No, you'll be alright, but we'll have to get you to a doctor. Get on my back."

I got him aboard and piggybacked him the whole way home, over two hedges and across the rough ground beside our house and he never complained once, though he must have been in terrible pain.

I kept seeing the inside of the cut dancing wickedly before my eyes.

"It was an accident," he said.

What a brother! He was trying to protect me from blame, even when he was suffering. I redoubled my efforts, and got him down the back steps to our kitchen.

He had completely severed his Achilles tendon.

***

It was back to the Memorial Hospital in Darlington. There, they discovered that the two halves of the severed tendon had separated – one had shot up inside his leg and the other had shrunk into the stump in his ankle. He was put to bed and a screen was erected between him and his foot.

Dad stayed there while the doctors worked. They had explained what they were going to try to do – to pull the two halves of the tendon together and sew them together. If they failed, he would never walk again.

After the operation, Eck was put in a pot. The doctor said, "He's a grand little lad, isn't he?"

He was that.

He was in the pot, and then another and later an iron caliper, for the next eighteen months of his life.

***

Oddly enough, there was no inquest into what had happened. Eck just said he cut his leg on some glass and that was it. There was however, one terrible, bitter irony. I was hailed as a hero for carrying him home.

"How on earth David carried him all that way I don't know," said my Ma, patting my head proudly.

I felt very, very low and vowed never, ever again, to be a vandal.

THE RECORD PLAYER

One hot summer evening, Eck and I were out playing in front of our house. He was watching me skimming Tar over O'Brien's sheds, when I turned and saw our Dad was walking up the hill towards us.

"There's Dad!"

I ran off to greet him, while Eck limped along behind me on his caliper.

Dad was carrying something. It looked like a small green suitcase.

"What's that you've got Dad?"

He grinned. "Wait and see."

This was exciting.

We followed him home. At the door Ma was waiting. He kissed her and went into the house without explaining what the case was.

Inside the dining room he lifted the case onto the table.

"What is it?"

"Go on Dad. What is it?"

"Come on Harry, tell us!"

Ma was as excited as we were. She stood there expectantly, wiping her hands on a tea towel.

"What's that you've been wasting your money on?"

Dad unhitched two metal clips and lifted the top off. There were two parts to the machine, a lid section and a mechanical part.

There was a neat, round metal disc and a long, curved arm.

"Dad. What is it?"

"It's a record player."

The disc was a turntable. There was an arm with a needle at the end, which Dad unclipped from its secure base. He plugged the machine into the socket. An electric record player. It was new and clean and up-to-date.

PHILLIPS ELECTRONICS

It was the first piece of modern electrical equipment any of us had ever seen.

Dad opened his briefcase and took out a small square thin package. This was a record, we recognised.

For years we had had an old mechanical record machine that you had to wind up with a lever. It had great big thick black records of ancient Swing Bands like Harry Roy. But this machine was something completely new - small, neat and modern. None of us had seen one of these 45rpm records before.

Dad had bought the record player from a soldier who had been out in Hong Kong.

The record was *Two Hearts Two Kisses (Make One Love)* by someone called Doris Day.

Dad switched it on. The record began to spin. Dad lifted the arm onto the record and MAGIC! We had music!

Oopy ooo ooo, Oopy ooo ooo!
One heart is not enough baby,
Two hearts make you feel crazy!
One kiss makes you feel so nice,
Two kisses put you in Paradise!
Two Hearts, Two Kisses,
Make One Love!
Oopy ooo ooo, Oopy ooo ooo!

Even I, aged eight, realised it was nonsense, but it was such fun! And compared to the awful rubbish on the radio - I particularly detested the Billy Cotton Band Show, with its lame jokes and Alan Breese - compared to that, Doris Day was a glimpse of a whole new world.

***

Eventually we had two more records. *The Harry Lime Theme*, by Anton Karas on his zither (an unlikely hit record at the time) – which I was given for my birthday.

And one our Ma bought in the market called *Claudette*, by the Everly Brothers. It was the beginning of the pop revolution for us!

To be more accurate, we didn't have three records, we only had two we could actually play, *The Harry Lime Theme* and *Two Hearts Two Kisses (Make One Love)*.

Claudette would slip all over the turntable. Ma had bought it cheap on the market as an ex-jukebox record, and for this reason *Claudette* didn't have a middle to it, so when we placed it on the turntable to play and put the arm and needle onto the record, it would spin off asymmetrically.

Claudette sounded really weird, the music fluctuating wildly. As I had never heard what it sounded like when played properly, I thought it was a terrible song and the Everly Brothers were terrible singers. I couldn't understand why anyone would want to listen to them. Only years later did I discover that they were excellent close harmony singers.

The Harry Lime Theme I liked. We often played it and sang along to it, though it had no words.

"*Da da ta da,*

Da da ta da," it went.

We often joined arms, Ma, our Eck and me, and danced around the room singing along.

"*Da da ta da,*

Da da ta da!"

Times were changing.

SANDRA MARCHAM

O ur Eck had to make two visits a week to the hospital in distant Darlington. These were long and expensive journeys on a winding bus route and it meant he missed a lot of school. He had pot legs or a caliper on for over a year, so he missed months of school which he was never allowed to make up.

Eck had to suffer stiffness and pain for years after and he wasn't able to play sport until his final year as a Junior. And he had a permanent lump on the back of his ankle to remind him of the time I encouraged him to be a vandal.

There were other effects of this terrible event. I didn't forgive myself for my part in it. I knew it was my fault and I was determined to look after our Eck with special care from then on. He would never get hurt if I could help it.

Nor did I forgive Alex Marcham for his part in it. If Alex Marcham hadn't made me lose my temper in the first place, none of it would have happened. And of course, and most unforgiveable of all, he had run away and left us when we needed him most.

Marcham kept well away from our house for weeks afterwards, no doubt scared that I might have told adults about his part in the affair. I hadn't done so, because I wasn't like him. I felt he would no doubt have blamed it all on me and come out of it lily white himself.

Then one day, looking out of my bedroom window, I saw him mooching about in our back lane.

The next day he was there again. I could tell he wanted to be friends again.

The third time I went out and said hello.

"Do you want to come round to our house?" he asked. He knew I liked to play on the steep grassy bank at the back of their house.

I had an exaggerated sense of devotion to our Eck, due in no small part to my guilt over my previous neglect of duty.

"Bring him along too," said Alex Marcham generously. "I'll wait."

This was more like it. I hadn't liked being out of friends with Alex Marcham. I ran back to our house to fetch Eck, who was already fretting at being housebound so much.

"We're going round to Marchams," I said to our Ma. She made a face but said nothing. I understood, it meant Take Good Care Of Him.

Marchams lived in a big house on the far side of Hubberholme Road. They were an odd family. I don't think I ever saw the father and the mother was never at home. She had a car of her own, which was very rare at that time.

Marchams went to a different school from us, being something called Methodists. They wore green uniforms and went to school in a church hall, so we didn't see much of them except at weekends and holidays.

Alex was the same age as me, but he wasn't as strong as me – as both of us knew. He was a strange boy and was often left on his own. To tell the truth, he didn't have any friends apart from me and our Eck, and at the moment we didn't like him all that much either.

His big sister Sandra was very different. She was a year or possibly two years older than me, a tall, blonde, very pretty girl. Unfortunately we didn't see her very often. She had to do lessons – what they were I had no idea, but she told me once she hated them. As a result Sandra couldn't come out with us as much as I would have liked.

This was one of my big regrets. I always had the feeling with Sandra that although she didn't say much, there was inside her a kind of bottled-up rebelliousness. She had spirit. She would suddenly do something unexpected – she could fight like a boy for instance – then she would just switch back to being normal, law-abiding, lesson-attending Sandra, always having to do jobs in the house, leaving no trace of that wildness of soul I had detected for a moment.

The grassy bank was a steep slope of lovely soft grass, long and sweet and warm, where we loved to slide, or daydream or tell tales. There was no harm in the grass and we could roly-poly down it without fear of injury. We could shut our eyes and roly-poly blind, a dizzying and exciting experience only rarely attempted.

On this particular day Sandra was free of the numerous tasks and lessons she normally had to do, and she joined us out on the grassy bank. She was wearing a red check tartan shirt and blue jeans. Sandra was the only girl I had ever seen who wore jeans, which were at the time a real rarity, even among the boys.

For a couple of hours we played happily, sliding and roly-polying, then chewing the grass, or having competitions to make the best screeching noise with a blower. I had shown Alex how to do this when I first met him, but he was still useless at it. Patiently I cut a blade of grass, and stretched it taut between my thumbs, holding my fists together. I forced the blade as thin and tight as possible, and blew sharply onto it. A horrible screech resulted.

"Giz a go!" Alex pleaded.

I passed him the blade. He held it too softly and no noise resulted. We all laughed good-naturedly at him.

This was a good game because our Eck could join in too. At the other games he had been left out, because of his pot leg. Now he picked some grass himself and soon Sandra, Eck and I were vying with each other for the loudest screech.

Alex, just to be awkward, picked a thick and soft piece of grass, held it limply between his thumbs, and made a nasty farting noise.

"Stop it Alex," said Sandra.

Alex ignored her and made a louder fart, then another and another until Sandra moved to hit him. Then he jumped up out of range and started farting again.

"He's an idiot," Sandra said to me. She made as if to chase him, gave up, and came back to sit beside me.

I felt a sudden thrill of excitement. She was very attractive was Sandra Marcham. She had blonde hair cut short and boyish. In fact she was very tomboyish, I had heard my Ma say. She had blue eyes and a small dark spot on her cheek.

I sat and looked at this spot for a long time, until she said, "What are you staring at?"

"Nothing," I lied, not wanting her to think I'd been staring at something she might feel self-conscious about. All of a sudden I was aware that she was a girl.

Now so far Alex had been quite well-behaved, mainly because he was wary of me. He knew he had done wrong and he knew I hadn't completely forgiven him for it – so he had gone out of his way to be civilised to Eck and myself. But Alex couldn't be like that for long. His natural self soon started to re-assert itself. That was the main trouble with Alex, he never knew when to stop.

We were all blissfully happy just lying there watching the clouds change shape, but not Alex. Alex had to sneak up on Sandra and pull her hair.

"Go away Alex," she said, mildly irritated. "You are a pest."

He didn't go away of course, Alex would never do anything so sensible. He pulled her hair again, causing her to sit up angrily.

"Stop it. That hurt!"

"Oooo!" he mocked.

"If you do that again Alex I'll hit you."

And suddenly, there it was, that glimpse of another Sandra. She really meant that she would give the annoying Alex a good belting without care of the consequences, not just a mild sisterly admonition.

Alex knew it and I knew it. Alex backed off hastily, without looking where he was going. And in doing so, he trod on our Eck's pot leg.

"Watch it!" Eck howled.

"Watch it yourself Cripple!" Alex retorted.

Our Eck, pot leg or no pot leg, wasn't going to take this from anyone, certainly not Alex Marcham. He stood up, pivoted on his bad leg and squared up for a fight.

"Come on then you Spaz!" taunted Alex, beckoning to our Eck.

I jumped up and moved quickly between them, determined that I wasn't going to let our Eck get hurt, not after recent events.

"Mind your own business," said Alex to me.

This was just being silly and I said so.

He sniggered.

"Alex, you're only brave cos he's four years younger than you and he's got a pot leg."

This hit home. He bent down as if to sit, and I assumed he'd given up all thoughts of fighting, but he was sly was Alex. He brought his fist up into my guts when I wasn't expecting it. My muscles were slack and his fist sank right in. I sat down, winded.

Taking advantage of my temporary defeat, Alex took a swipe at our Eck. At this cowardice I really lost my temper, jumping at him, determined to smash my fist into that infuriating face as hard as I could.

He fell back with me on top of him, while Eck sat down to cheer me on. We rolled over and over, wrestling with each other, not able to get in a punch. I was really mad now and I wanted to beat him to a pulp. But at that moment Sandra intervened.

As I said before, Sandra was a tomboy. She was athletic and taller than me, and probably heavier. I didn't want to fight her, but I did want to fight her brother, boy did I want to fight him. If she was going to stop me doing that, then I would fight her too.

I think latent guilt about our Eck's pot leg played a big part in it. I wanted to show him and everyone else how much I thought of him and how much I was going to do to stick up for him.

Sandra Marcham started pulling me off her brother.

Unlike most TV fights, few words are exchanged in real fights, and this was quite the most real fight I had ever been in. I shrugged her off. I had got Alex Marcham down now and was going to smash my fist right into his face.

Sandra had an arm round my neck, and was trying to pull me away to stop me hitting him. Alex seized his chance and kicked at me, catching me just below the knee and sending shooting pains up my leg.

I fell over backwards, on top of Sandra, who fell heavily on her back. Locked together, Sandra and I rolled over and over down that grassy bank, rolling and wrestling, fighting each other and fighting to be free. Alex was forgotten now as we fought and twisted, not knowing or caring why we were fighting.

At the bottom of the grassy bank we came to a stop, side by side, face to face. I got a hand free and put it over her mouth, giving her Rubberlips, rubbing my hand up and down over her mouth, nose and eyes.

I climbed on top of her and pinned her down, with my knees on her shoulders. One of her hands was pinioned underneath her body and I held the other one tight in mine. I had her trapped! I could do what I wanted to her with my free hand!

Then, in the thumping, heart-pounding madness and anger of the fight, I caught sight of her eyes. She was looking at me most oddly. It was as if we froze – as if a photo had been taken of us – she was looking into my eyes and suddenly I no longer wanted to gouge her eyes out.

I wanted to kiss her.

We both sensed it at the same time, and all the struggle went out of us.

Something had happened during our fight, something neither of us had ever felt before. All I knew what that it was strangely exciting to be kneeling over Sandra Marcham with my knees on her shoulders and her face gazing up at me. I felt twinges run through my body. There was an electricity about me that I had never experienced before.

Without speaking, I let her free. We both stood up and dusted ourselves down. We went and sat separately from each other on the grassy bank.

"What happened?" asked our Eck. "What's wrong with you?"

"Nothing," I said.

I couldn't tell him, as I didn't understand it myself. I kept glancing at Sandra, and from time to time she would glance at me. Neither of us spoke again that day.

MRS SNAITH

To the boys of our kid's school, Mrs Snaith was a nasty, sneering, sarcastic hulk of a woman who would give them a hard slap without needing a reason. However, to the girls she was kind and motherly, the woman they liked to chat to when she was on playground duty.

She would stand, cup of tea in hand, watching the girls skipping, with an indulgent smile on her face. Should the boys venture near with their tennis ball she would snarl, "Go away! Get away from here! Shoo!"

Turning to her female disciples she would say, "Horrible boys!" And the girls would laugh with her. The boys would flee to the far side of the playground, safe from her vicious tongue. The girls would once again gather round her, and the kind smile would return.

Mrs Snaith was the class teacher of the six year olds. She had never taught me but I knew of her reputation and her vicious and vindictive nature. She was quick -tempered and handy with her fists. All the boys kept well away from her.

Mrs Snaith always addressed the girls by their first names, so she would call them Jane and Catherine, Susan and Mary. Boys were snapped at by their surname. "You!"

she would call, pointing at a boy. "You! Longster! Get in line boy!"

My little brother Eck, who was three years younger than me, was in the five year old's class when he had injured his leg very badly. He had severed his Achilles tendon, the big tendon at the back of the heel. He had been rushed to hospital and the doctors had attempted to save his leg, for without a functioning Achilles tendon he would be unable to walk.

They had been able to catch the two halves of the tendon, which had retreated inside their sheath, and had pulled them together. Then the severed tendon had been sewn together. It was, they had warned my parents, a particularly nasty injury, and one which would need careful nursing if he was ever to walk again.

To this end he was put in a metal caliper. This was a huge and heavy structure which ran from his hips to his ankle. It completely immobilised his leg, not allowing any movement which might otherwise disturb the slowly-healing tendon. Once he was encased in the caliper there was no flexibility. He was told he would have to cart his leg round in the stiff and awkward caliper for a year.

He was still in the caliper when September came. I had dreaded this date ever since the injury, because when September began he would move into Mrs Snaith's class.

***

Our Eck was a very tough little boy. He hadn't cried at any time during the injury itself, nor during and after the operation. When he returned to school after being fitted with the caliper he had been mocked and laughed at, as was usual at the school. Boys had called him names and mimicked his limping walk. However, my brother just laughed off their abuse. He joined in all their games, lurching round the playground dragging his stiff leg in its iron frame. For this he earned the grudging respect of even the toughest of playground gangs.

I worried what Mrs Snaith would say to him. Knowing her hostile attitude to boys I felt sure there would be trouble. Our Eck was not one to take her sarcastic comments lightly, but there was little I could do to protect him. As a boy three years his senior I was now in a different school. However, I warned him about Mrs Snaith, and her vicious and uncompromising attitude to boys. I told him to do nothing to provoke her. He promised to be careful. I consoled myself with the thought that even Mrs Snaith, bully and boy hater as she was, would do nothing to hurt a five year old boy cripple.

How wrong I was.

∗∗∗

After a week of term, our Eck had said nothing about what was going on. It was some of the boys in his class who came to me and told me the story. Mrs Snaith was making him do Games!

Games in Mrs Snaith's class was Boys versus Girls. There would be teams of six, competing in races against each other. Each contestant would have to run carrying a bean bag, place it on the ground and run back to the next person in line as fast as he or she could go. Or there would be races where they had to run balancing the bean bag on their heads.

Unbelievably, Mrs Snaith was making my brother take part in these activities.

"Go on! Run!" she would shout. "Faster! Go go go!"

Of course the shouting was always at the boys. The girls would be encouraged with a smile and, "Well done girls! Well done."

What could I do? Ma had already written a letter to the school asking for Richard to be excused Games. Mrs Snaith had simply chosen to ignore it. Characteristically, my brother was trying his hardest. He competed as well as he could, running on his good leg and dragging the stiff one behind him. Even bending to pick up the bean bag was difficult for him, but he persevered. However the rest of the boys in his class were uneasy about what was being done to him, and had come to tell me.

It went without saying that his leg injury was an extremely serious one. If he was to tear the tendon and re-open the wound, that would be the end of any chance of recovery. He would be a cripple for life. Everyone it seemed, could understand this. But not Mrs Snaith.

At home, out of the hearing of our parents, I asked him, "How's it going with Mrs Snaith?"

"OK," he said noncommittally. He wasn't going to say anything, I could tell.

"What about Games?"

"It's OK."

"Can you do it?"

"Yeah, fine."

There was no further pressing to be done. He was resentful at his unfair treatment, but he wasn't going to let her have any satisfaction. I let it drop.

***

It was no more than a week later when matters came to a head. Mrs Snaith's class were doing Billy Goat Gruff. This is the story of a troll who lives under a bridge. There are three Billy Goats Gruff, a mother, a father and a baby. They all want to cross the bridge, but have to avoid the troll's attentions. I never understood the attraction of the story myself, but it was a favourite of Mrs Snaith's.

Mrs Snaith read them the story, and then instructed the class that they were to act it out.

"Jane, you can be Mummy Billy Goat Gruff."

Jane smiled coyly at the honour.

"Mary you can be Baby Billy Goat Gruff."

Mary blushed and smiled.

Mrs Snaith's whole manner changed, as she came to the next role.

"Now we need a Daddy Billy Goat Gruff." She scanned the boys with relish.

Big Bob Longster was slow in getting his head down, and caught her eye. Who better to be her figure of fun than big and lumbering Longster?

"Longster!" She pointed delightedly at him. "You can be Daddy Billy Goat Gruff."

Poor dull-witted Bob was big and clumsy and would look foolish, so all the girls laughed.

Seeing Longster wasn't smiling, Mrs Snaith snarled and snapped, "For goodness sake smile boy!"

She next selected the boys to lie on the floor, manhandling them into position.

"You boys are the bridge. KNEEL!"

The boys knelt.

Now she needed someone to play the part of the troll. The boys lowered their heads, dreading what might come next. She took her time, then inspiration came to her nasty warped mind.

"Clough!" she exclaimed with a smile.

Hearing his name called, my brother raised his head.

Mrs Snaith waggled a finger at him.

"You! Yes you boy!" She beckoned to my brother. "You can be the horrible troll!"

The boys couldn't believe it. Even the girls looked at each other. Mrs Snaith took hold of Eck, and indicated he was to get down on all fours and hide beneath the bridge. This was clearly impossible for him, given his heavy caliper. Then she busied herself with getting the girls ready, rehearsing their lines with them.

When she turned back, my brother was still standing there. He hadn't moved.

Her face turned red.

"Go on boy!" she shouted. "Do as you're told."

My brother didn't say a word. Nor did he move.

Mrs Snaith's face started to go vivid red.

"Go on! Get on with it!"

She advanced towards him, hands on hips, adding menacingly, "I'm waiting."

Our Eck stood still. The class fell silent. Even the girls excited at being Mummy and Baby Billy Goat Gruff stopped chattering. The boys watched in fear as to what was going to happen next.

Mrs Snaith shouted, "Do what you're told, you wretched boy!"

Still our Eck did not move.

Mrs Snaith launched herself at him, grabbing him by the front of his shirt. It tore and all the buttons popped off.

Eck just stood there, saying nothing, not moving. This seemed to incense her further as she drew back her meaty arm and fetched him a mighty slap right across the face.

The class was shocked. He staggered backwards. Mrs Snaith had by now lost her temper completely and seized him, shaking him violently.

Every child in the class was horror struck.

Suddenly she seemed to exhaust her tantrum, and with a sigh, released him. My brother just turned his back on her and limped out of the room without saying a word.

***

At the end of school our Ma came to collect him. She took one look at my brother's swollen and bruised face, and exclaimed in horror, "Who did it?"

"Mrs Snaith," he said.

Then she noticed his torn shirt. Grim-faced, she took my brother by the hand, and marched him into school.

***

Next morning at registration there was no sign of Mrs Snaith. The class sat silent, fearful, waiting.

Then Mr Davidson, the Headmaster, came in with a young lady.

"This is Miss Taylor," he said. "She'll be teaching you from now on."

The young lady smiled. The class relaxed.

That morning she read them stories, and in the afternoon they did numbers. Miss Taylor smelled nice and smiled a lot. The girls liked her. The boys liked her. The class began to forget Mrs Snaith.

***

It became a legend in our family, the way our Ma had stormed into school to do battle with Mrs Snaith; our Ma, our gentle, loving, Ma had stood up to the bully, had stood up for justice, terrified as she probably was by that evil old dragon Snaith.

From that day on, if ever Ma showed signs of losing her temper with Dad, he would say, "Oh oh boys, take cover! Here she goes again! Just like she did with Mrs Snaith!" – and we would pretend to run and hide.

This was usually enough to bring a smile back to her face and make her forget all about being angry with him.

Our Eck's iron caliper came off after a year, but it was years before my brother could walk or run properly.

Eck never spoke of Mrs Snaith. I think she had hurt his spirit. He was never quite the same boy again.

TICKLING A TROUT

Masham Abbey was where I tickled the trout that made my reputation. It all happened so unexpectedly, on a day when I had other things on my mind - like being down at our secret Mill Race in the dark wood with Sandra Marcham.

Trout are, as everyone knows, the best fish in the river. Clever, crafty and hard to catch, they also cost a lot of money. People have to buy expensive fly fishing tackle to catch them, as well as having to join expensive fly-fishing clubs in order to fish for them. All that was way beyond our means, or the means of any of the kids at our school. We were lucky to have wellies, never mind posh waders – which are an essential part of fly-fishing.

As we lacked the tackle to catch trout, the only way we could trap them was by hand – by 'tickling the trout' as it was known. This was a legendary skill, possessed only by a few ancient adepts, and mentioned in hushed tones by the boys of Ravenscroft school. The method supposedly included being able to sneak up undetected on the wary trout, then, by gently stroking the stomach of trout, so lull him into a state of reverie that it was possible to get both hands round him and flip him out onto the riverbank.

Everyone in my class, Johnny Hopper, Teddy Sherman and the rest of the boys, even Clive Lawson the Pater's son, talked constantly about performing this wondrous act. Everyone in the school knew about tickling trout, but no-one, it seemed, actually knew how to do it. We dreamed nightly of yerking out fat-bellied monsters. We told each other tales of how we had actually done it – though witnesses were somehow never present – we boasted of our skill. But no-one had actually, in front of others, caught a trout by tickling him into submission.

Then came the day I did it.

***

Kenneth, Clive Lawson the Pater's son, Alex Marcham and his delectable sister Sandra and me, were all down at Masham Abbey. We were splashing through the shallows in our wellies, making our way to the weir and the millstream, to watch the trout shooting up and down the Mill Race.

So far we had kept the existence of the Mill Race a secret, but as Sandra was with us today, we thought it was only fair we should show her it. In truth, I just wanted to be near her in the dark secret place that was the Mill Race. We kept bumping into each other, accidentally on purpose, and smiling at each other. Who knew what might happen if we were to be alone together?

It was a warm, sunny day and the water where we were paddling was only a couple of inches deep. It had been a very hot summer and there had been no rain for weeks.

There I was, happily walking in the river, looking down to see what I might find, when suddenly I was distracted. There was a loud yell. Kenneth had slipped and fallen in. It was funny, seeing him sitting there on his backside, soaking wet and wailing away, so we all stopped paddling to enjoy the spectacle.

He stood up, his clothes dark-stained by the water. We all laughed. The entertainment was over. I stepped forward to resume our walk.

Suddenly, I felt something soft underneath my foot. I felt it twist in a muscular way. I reached down to see what it was, and there it was in my hand, a fat, silver, madly-wriggling trout!

"I've got one!" I yelled.

The others, who were only yards away, saw instantly that I wasn't joking and came running.

Grasping it as tightly as I could, I splashed my way to the bank, the silvery bar of muscle jumping and juddering in my fingers. By some miracle I managed to stumble ashore before it succeeded in escaping from my grip. Even then it fell out, only to land on the grass, where I was able to fall on top of it and make sure my miraculous catch didn't get back into the water.

"There!" I said, proudly revealing my trout to their admiring gaze. "Look at that!"

"Woh!"

"Fantastic!"

"It's a monster!"

They crowded round, in awe at such a fish.

For a second I hesitated. Then I boasted. "Yes, I tickled it!" I added dishonestly.

The others bent down close to examine the fish. There could be no doubt about it – they were in awe of such skill. I had tickled it! I was at last a tickler of trout!

All the rest of the day I basked in the glory of being a successful tickler of trout. All the way home I listened as the others marvelled at my skill.

And all the following week at school. Kids would come up to me and say, "Hey Cluffie! I hear you can tickle trout," as if they had met some hero or sporting legend. Kids begged me to recount how I had done it. Kids pleaded with me to reveal the secret of my success. I was at last a tickler of trout.

There was only one dissenter, Clive Lawson the Pater's son. Wickedly, he went round telling everyone that I hadn't tickled the trout at all. I had walked on it, he alleged. I had trodden on it. I had no magical trout tickling skill at all. I was a fraud.

Few people believed him, as I had too many witnesses of my marvellous achievement and anyway his eyes were too close together and he had a Brillo pad on his head, and he spoke with such a posh accent no-one liked him.

Even so, there were one or two doubters of my trout-tickling ability when he said pointedly, "Oh yes. If you tickled it, how come there was a welly-print on its back?"

I don't think I ever truly forgave him.

THE TANK

O 'Brien's Sheds were an old abandoned farm used by O'Briens the builders to store their materials. Even after our Eck's injury this made for one fantastic playground for us kids.

Best of all for playing in, without a doubt, was the tank. This was a tall cylindrical structure, made of metal, rusting and abandoned and turning brown in the sun and rain. It was probably twelve or fifteen feet tall. Once it had no doubt contained some liquids used by the farm, now however, it was empty. We liked to bang the tank with sticks, or best of all with bits of metal, because it made a tremendous clanging noise which somehow pleased us. We were easily amused.

It was next to the old farm building, so it was possible to clamber up onto the roof of the building, edge along the low guttering, and drop down onto the flat top of the tank, which was about eight feet wide. There we would dance around, shouting and yelling and stamping on the metal.

The tank had an opening in the top, about a foot wide, just wide enough for someone to get through had they been mad enough to try. There was no ladder on the tank, either inside or outside. Often we sat on top of the tank, looking into the hole, dropping stones inside, enjoying the sounds we made.

One summer day we were all up there: me, Kenneth Greensit and his bony sister Norma, Clive Lawson the Pater's son and Alex Marcham. Sandra wasn't with us because she had one of her lessons. Our Eck wasn't there because it was one of his days for going to the Hospital in Darlington to get his leg seen to, so he and Ma had left on the bus hours before. Dad was out at work. We were free to do whatever we wanted.

Now what do kids do when they are free of adult supervision? They get up to mischief. Of course they do, that's the fun of it. And that is exactly what we did.

It started by someone saying, "Bet you daren't go inside the tank."

I don't know who it was, it might have been Norma, it might have been Alex, it might have been Clive Lawson the Pater's son. It probably wasn't Kenneth, who was scared of everything. It might have been me. Whoever it was, invited trouble.

We pushed each other out of the way and fought to look down the hole. Inside the tank it was dark. There was a pile of stones at the bottom. No-one in their right mind would want to drop down fifteen feet inside the tank. There was no way out.

Once the conversation had started, it rapidly escalated.

Norma started it, by elbowing me aggressively. "You daren't go in!"

"Who says so?"

"Me. Bet you daredn't!"

"Course I dare!"

"Oh yeah!" she sneered. When she sneered her lips pulled back revealing a lot of teeth. It was not attractive.

Anyway, she had succeeded in annoying me, so I wasn't going to back down, not to her.

"Course I dare!"

"Prove it," said Norma, emphatically.

I elbowed Alex out of the way and stuck my head inside the hole. It was a long, long way down.

"Cowardy custard!" Norma said viciously.

"Shaddap!"

I was too late to stop her. She was off on a rant.

She started capering around, jabbing a finger in my face.

"Cowardy cowardy custard!" she taunted. "Ya feet are made of mustard!"

It didn't matter that the rhyme was ridiculous. It still hurt. Nor did it matter that it was utterly pointless going down inside the tank.

"Shut your face Greensit!" I snapped.

Too late. The others had taken up the chant.

"David Clough, Powder Puff!" they crowed, pointing at me.

"David Clough, Powder Puff!" they chanted, their faces contorted in derision.

I pushed Norma out of the way and sat on the edge of the hole, looking down inside. I knew it was stupid to be forced into doing something which was obviously dangerous. I knew it would end badly, but I wasn't going to be beaten by sheepface Norma.

"Cowardy cowardy custard! Ya feet are made of mustard!" they chanted.

I eased myself through the hole, lowering myself down inside. My arms were hurting. It was such a long way down.

I could hear Norma crowing above me. "Told you he wouldn't do it!"

There was absolutely no chance of me lowering myself gently to the floor of the tank, so I let go and dropped.

***

It was a very, very long way down. I landed on hard stones, stumbled a bit and fell on one side. Miraculously I hadn't broken a leg or arm, so I was relatively unhurt and quickly stood to my feet.

"Yah!" I cried triumphantly. "Told you!"

"He did it!" the boys cried, turning on Norma.

"He did it! I knew he would! Yeah, he did it! Good ole Cluffie!"

She shouted back, "Bastard twatface!" But she was defeated and knew it.

I could hear the others shouting and cheering at my success. I did a war dance to celebrate my achievement. I found a bit of metal and started banging on the metal walls. It made a great clanging noise. Up on top, the boys too found implements and banged on the tank. What a victory! What a great thing to do. See Norma's face! Was she sick!

Suddenly the noise stopped. I stood there panting. I could see millions of specks of dust in the dim light of the tank's interior. Up above, the others had gone quiet too.

"Hey David?"

It was Kenneth. In total contrast to his sister Norma, he was a soft soul, who cared about others. "Can you hear me David? Are you alright down there?"

"Yes, I'm fine."

"How are you going to get out?"

I looked around. I was fifteen feet down trapped inside a metal tank. There was no ladder, no doorway or entrance. No means of escape.

"I dunno," I said quietly.

There was a brief silence, then I could hear snuffling sounds. Kenneth was starting to cry.

Norma slapped him and said, "Shut it you!"

There was a further period of quiet.

"I can't get out by myself," I said.

Kenneth started to cry more insistently. "We're gonna get into SO much trouble!"

"Shut up!" snapped his sister.

I called up, "Is there any rope anywhere?"

"Don't be so bloody stupid," said Norma.

"Well what about at home? Go home and see if you can find something."

"Ooooh!" cried Kenneth. "Our dad's gonna kill us!" And he started to howl in fear.

"You're such a cry baby!" snarled Norma.

Kenneth snuffled. "I don't like this. I'm going!" he cried. "I'm going home!"

"You keep your big gob shut tight, gettit?" Norma snarled.

I could hear him clambering off the top of the tank and hurrying away from the scene of the crime.

Alex too was losing his nerve.

"You're gonna be stuck there for ever," he said. "You're gonna die down there."

"Oh great," I called up. "Thanks Alex."

It was too late. He had already set Clive Lawson off. He would be the next to leave.

"I'm off," Clive Lawson the Pater's son said urgently. "This is NOTHING to do with me."

"Yes it is," said Norma.

"No it isn't. It was your fault. You egged him on to jump inside!"

Alex joined in, "It wasn't me!"

"It WAS you Norma! You started calling him Cowardy Custard. He wouldn't have done it if you hadn't called him that."

I could imagine how fierce Norma looked when she turned on him.

"Shaddap you or I'll give you some fist!"

Clive Lawson started, "Gettoff me! Gettoff I say!"

They must have scuffled because next he said, "That's it! I'm having nothing to do with this. In fact, I'm going home!"

"Ah, go on then! Go on! Go, you quitter!"

"I AM doing!"

Norma was not that easily defeated. "If you go, I'm going too," she said slyly.

That put pressure on Clive and Alex. I wondered if they would be strong enough to resist her.

This was just what I needed. I could hear them arguing away up there, but could do nothing about it.

"I'm going!" said Clive Lawson the Pater's son. "You can't stop me."

"Well go then twatface! I'm not getting blamed. If you go, I'm going too, I'm warning you!"

And with that they were gone.

All of them.

I sat down on my pile of stones.

***

Hours passed. I tried banging on the walls of the tank with a bit of metal, but that just gave me a headache. I sat down on my pile of stones again. I tried to think what would happen next. They would go home and tell their parents and they would come and rescue me. Then I remembered that Mr Greensit worked away a lot and their mum wasn't in either. I didn't know about Alex Marcham's parents, but presumed the father worked somewhere. Surely his mum was at home. She would come to my rescue. No she wouldn't. I remembered then that Alex had said she was going shopping in the afternoon with Sandra, his sister. We never saw the Pater of Clive Lawson. There were no adults to rescue me.

So I sat there and waited.

***

I didn't have a watch, so I had no idea of what time it was. When we had set out in the morning it was quite early, not long after breakfast. I started to get hungry. I thought this was probably because I was thinking about meal times too much, so I thought about other subjects.

Surely one of them would have the sense to tell someone about me? Surely Ma or our kid would miss me when they came back from the hospital?

I must have sat there a long time because I could see through the hole in the roof that it was getting dark outside.

I was becoming tired. Suddenly I could hear something. I strained to listen. It was someone calling out. Then I smiled, recognising the voice. It was my Dad in the distance, calling my name.

"Dad!" I called out hoarsely. "Dad!" There was no reply.

I scrabbled for the bit of metal I'd been using earlier. Grabbing it, I started banging furiously on the walls of the tank.

I could hear footsteps getting louder.

"Dad! Dad! I'm here!"

He was much closer. "Son, is that you?"

"Yes Dad."

"Where are you?"

"Inside the tank."

I waited for him to get mad. He didn't. He was a very calm man my Dad. No matter what his idiot son had done, he didn't lose his temper.

He tapped on the wall of the tank. "Are you in there David?"

"Yes."

There was a pause. Now at this point most dads would have been very angry.... 'How could you be so stupid?'... 'Your mother and I have been worried sick about you'... 'Don't you know you could have died in there...' and so on. But not my Dad.

I could hear a scraping noise and guessed he was sitting down. He was panting. I think he had been searching for a long time and was out of breath.

"Are you alright son?"

"Yeah, fine. Bit hungry. Have you got any grub?"

He laughed. "We'll feed you when we get you home."

"Dad. Why didn't you come sooner?"

"We thought you were out playing with the others. When you didn't come back at bedtime I started looking for you. The other kids said they hadn't seen you."

Hmm. So much for friendship, I thought.

"I've been looking all over. No-one knew where you were."

"They did. They were just too scared to say where."

"Well never mind that. We've got you now."

"Good."

"Stay there," he said.

I started laughing, so loudly he could hear.

"What's so funny?"

"You said, stay there!"

He laughed too. "I'll go get a ladder."

***

And so my dad rescued me. I must have been inside that tank for most of a day.

There were no recriminations. No-one said anything to the other parents. A day later and we were all playing together again as if nothing had happened.

Why didn't the other kids say anything? Because they were scared they'd get into trouble. I thought that they'd have got into a hell of a lot more trouble if I'd died in there, but there was no telling them that.

I didn't do it again though. From now on the tank was strictly for banging on.

Good ole Dad.

ROCK N ROLL

In 1959, Rock n' Roll was going on somewhere. But sadly not in Ravenscroft. No-one seemed to bother with pop music. The only person I knew who paid any attention to it was Daisy Barker, who was bottom of the class. She said she loved someone called Ricky Nelson.

"Ricky who?" was the commonest response.

Or, from the girls, "It was Johnny Hopper last week."

The only boy who was interested in pop music was in fact Handsome Johnny Hopper. Some girl had told him that he looked like an Everly Brother, so we temporarily lost him to the world of pinups and comb-carriers. He grew his hair long on top and raised it into something he called a Quiff. He used hair cream to keep this creation in place, and wouldn't play football for fear of ruining his 'style'.

It didn't last long. Either the bottle of hair cream ran out, or he became bored of being an Everly Brother, because within a month he was back playing football better than ever.

Rock n' roll music wasn't there to be heard. There were no pop music shows on TV (not that many people had TVs.) There was just something awful called Light

Entertainment, set on a boat on a river. It featured a singer called Michael Halliday, who had a funny bent face like a banana. He had a pleasant voice, but the programme was diabolical.

***

There was Perry Como, an American, but somehow he had nothing to do with rock n'roll music or young people's tastes. Perry Como was born old and smiling and cuddly, so he was ideal for mums and grannies. He wore cardigans with letters on. Though he had a reasonable voice, he sang the stupidest songs I had ever heard.

> *"Catch a falling star and put it in your pocket*
> *Save it for a rainy day"*

This was one I particularly detested.
Then there was:

> *"Oh what did Delaware boy, what did Delaware?*
> *She wore a brand New Jersey, she wore a brand New Jersey,*
> *That's what she did wear.*
> *Well what did Missisip boy, what did Missisip?*
> *She sipped a Minnesota, she sipped a Minnesota,*
> *That's what she did sip."*

I used to ponder over these inane lyrics and worry deeply about them. They were quite clever, I supposed, in a silly sort of way. Someone must have spent a lot of time working out which of the American states would fit into the song, and it was a big hit record. Everyone sang it. But the whole thing was just so RIDICULOUS, did no-one see that?

I felt very lonely in my detestation of:

"Oh what did Massachew boy, what did Massachew?"

I couldn't believe that adults would listen to such drivel, and when the Perry Como show came on our TV, I would leave the room.

＊＊＊

Nor was there any rock n'roll music on the radio, amazing though that may sound nowadays. No, in 1959, the only music played for young people was Uncle Mac on Saturday morning radio. Uncle Mac played *Children's Favourites*. That was the official title, I should stress. They certainly weren't my favourites.

Uncle Mac played really whacky tunes like *The Laughing Policeman*, in which some mentally-defective guardian of the law laughed at every crime he was sent to solve. I couldn't wait for him to finish his irritating laughter.

The Laughing Policeman song made me very worried about society. The Laughing Policeman would go BANG BIFF TAKE THAT as he smacked a villain over the head with his truncheon, then he would burst into hysterical laughter HA HA HA HAAAA!

Now that was disturbing.

∗∗∗

Or there was Sparky. Sparky, pronounced 'SPAR – KEEEE', was some American kid who got lost in a cave or something. I was never clear what exactly had happened to him.

There was a mystery piano that played itself - it was a very confusing story. But there were lots of echoing voices and the singer wailed 'Spar – keeee!' for the lost kid. It became a catchphrase for Daisy Barker, along with Perry Como's American states.

That was all the rock n' roll music there was on the radio. Radio One didn't exist. We hadn't heard of Radio Luxembourg. All we had was the Light Programme – why Light – was it the opposite of Heavy?

Somewhere out there, according to the Sunday Express which we had started to read, somewhere out there wild things were happening. Teddy Boys. Rock n' Roll. Elvis Presley.

And what were we getting? Workers' Playtime.

Who dreamed up these titles? Workers' Playtime. For God's sake! What did all the workers do, get in a playpen and skip with ropes? I had a wonderful image of a factory full of workers in blue overalls all downing tools to play with plasticine.

∗∗∗

As well as the Light Programme there was also the Home Service, which no kids in my estimation EVER listened to unless they were in hospital, where you couldn't listen to anything else. And that was it.

The only way you could hear rock n'roll music was by lurking round the listening booths at Woolworth's record department, pretending you were intending to buy a record and were just taking a long time to make up your mind. You might be able to hear parts of three or four records before the manager wised up to what you were doing and booted you out.

I only did this once, as it struck me as a very boring way of spending Saturday afternoons, though Daisy Barker was a fixture in Woolworth's.

***

Then along came *Charlie Brown*. This was a fantastic song by The Coasters, an American group, which somehow swept through Ravenscroft, sweeping up all the kids in its infectious, wonderfully funny lyrics. It was new, it was crazy and it was for kids - a song about the school Naughty Boy, and another sign that times were changing:

All the singers of The Coasters sang:

"*Fee Fee Fi Fi Foh Foh Fum*
I smell smoke in the auditorium
Charlie Brown, he's a clown, that Charlie Brown,
He's gonna get caught, just you wait and see."

Then poor old Charlie Brown (who had obviously been smoking in school) piped up without a trace of guilt,

"Why's everybody always pickin' on me?"

This was something new. It was hilarious and we absolutely loved it. All the kids in Ravenscroft knew the lyrics and whole gangs would march round singing along with:

"Why's everybody always picking on me?"

It was funny, lively and so obviously from a new world, a world away from the awfulness of The Laughing Policeman, The Billy Cotton Band Show and even Perry Como.

Long live the Coasters. They brought joy to a generation of kids.

THOMAS

Thomas Evans used to play with us sometimes, though he was never really a friend. He was one of those poor souls who are the only child of elderly parents. His father worked with my father. I don't know what was said between them, but something was arranged, and this strange quiet boy started arriving at our house, with strict instructions from his mother that he was to 'play sensibly.'

Poor Thomas, I thought.

His mother was his problem. Much younger than his grey-haired and incredibly old father, she was a tough, pushy little Scotswoman. She always seemed dissatisfied with what life had given her, forever determined that it should be better for her cherished son.

Thomas had no idea how to play. He couldn't do anything – being unable to run, fight, play football or cricket, climb trees, throw stones, paddle about in the river, ride a bike or wander out of sight of adult supervision.

He was a pale, dark-haired lad with specs, lacking co-ordination between his limbs and his brain. Mind you, he probably could have done some of the things we did, had he not suffered this blanket injunction from his mother, that he was NOT to ride, run, get wet, go out in the rain, climb trees and definitely NOT do anything more strenuous than breathing.

As a result, anything we did he would just stand there blinking apologetically, repeating, "I'm not allowed to do that. You go on. I'll just watch."

This only made us feel guilty, especially when he added, "I don't mind. Honestly."

Poor Thomas.

***

I went to his house once, with my Dad and Ma and our Eck for tea. It was awful beyond belief, both the house and the tea. Thomas lived in one of those big detached villas on the other side of town, which people apparently aspired to own.

It was big and impressive in size, but it was dead. It even smelled dead. There was no excitement or fun to be had there. Thomas's bedroom was as dull as the dreadful dining room where we sat in awkward silence, nibbling dessicated old buns and meatless sandwiches.

Thomas wasn't allowed to do any of the things we did, as he had asthma. I didn't know what asthma was, but it must have been a pretty comprehensive ailment, as it precluded Thomas's participation in anything more strenuous than chess. Still, Thomas's mother knew what she was doing, I supposed.

Poor Thomas.

***

Then came the day of the joint family picnic, when, for reasons best known to themselves, my parents decided we should take the Evanses with us to the river at Masham Abbey.

"All of them?" Eck and I groaned in unison. It was bad enough having to drag Thomas around with us, without having the deathly father and the restrictive mother along as well.

"Yes," decreed our Dad. "It'll do them good."

I doubted it, as Daddy Evans's idea of a good time was apparently to visit a graveyard. I don't know whether it was to pick his plot or to study architecture, but that was his hobby – graveyards. Bundle of fun, wasn't he? You could see why Thomas was such a handful.

It was a great place, Masham Abbey, and on a boiling hot summer's day, not even Mrs Don't Do That Thomas could spoil it.

We camped out in a field by the river, at a spot where it was wide and shallow and therefore safe. I was sure Dad had picked it for that reason – we could paddle about in six inches of water lifting rocks to find Bullheads - and not even Thomas could drown himself in six inches of water, could he? We shall see.

Of course, the mother started as soon as we got there.

"You're not to go anywhere near that water Thomas!"

Thomas, who had been about to join us in the water, blinked apologetically, backed away from the river and instead sat down next to his mother.

Our Dad intervened. "Oh let the boy play, he'll be alright," he said. I knew he felt sorry for Thomas as we all did.

Anxious looks were exchanged between Mummy and Daddy Evans, before the gravedigger nodded. Mother grudgingly agreed. Thomas could play at the water's edge, but he wasn't to get wet, or go out of sight. He was to stay where she could keep an eye on him.

Poor Thomas.

Well, as I said, the river at Masham was a wonderful place, especially in summer, even when you've got Thomas Evans with you, and his mother has got her gimlet eyes on his back all the time in case he hurls himself headfirst into the water and drowns himself.

Our Eck and I soon had our shoes and socks off and were standing in the warm clear water.

"Come on Thomas," I whispered encouragingly. "We'll show you how to catch bullheads and stone loach. You might even tickle a trout."

Thomas had as much chance of tickling a trout as he had of being an Olympic athlete, but I didn't want to spoil his fun. The poor lad looked quite excited at the prospect of such dizzying amounts of freedom – or as near to excitement as he could get. His pale face went all euphoric and behind his thick glasses his eyes looked brighter than usual.

Eck and I were lifting up flat rocks, trying to catch the little fish which hid underneath. Thomas perched at the water's edge, with one eye on us and the other on his beady-eyed shrew of a mother. It was obvious that he desperately wanted to join in such good fun, as he kept edging that bit nearer the water, hoping she wouldn't notice.

She did of course.

"THOMAS!" she shouted, and poor Thomas sighed and retreated to dry land.

***

Eck and I spent hours in this harmless fun, filling a stock pool with our captured loach and bullheads. Then we had a measuring contest to see which was the biggest we'd caught, before returning the lot of them unharmed to the main river. Poor Thomas hadn't even been allowed to get his hands wet – he'd probably have got typhoid if he had – though he would dearly have liked to have joined in with us.

***

Lunchtime. We had lovely thick meaty sandwiches made by our Ma, and some untouched dry blotting paper sandwiches made by Mrs Dead Body. After that, we returned to the water.

It was now baking hot and the parents lay back and relaxed. Even Thomas's mother, it seemed, slackened her eternal vigilance. Perhaps it was the unaccustomed food she had eaten, for I noticed she tucked into our Ma's sandwiches healthily enough, the miserable old shrew.

Thomas edged towards us. She hadn't noticed. Thomas smiled guiltily and slid down the bank to join us in the water.

At this point I have to confess to possessing a grave character defect. I love wetting people. There is something about water and people standing by it that just screams out to me, "Throw a rock in and splash them!" I had always had this problem, and it hadn't gone away. I just loved water fights.

So, when I saw our Eck bending over intently, searching a pool for crayfish, I couldn't resist picking up a round fist-sized stone and thunking it into the water in front of him.

"Aaaah!" he laughed, reeling back wet-faced. "I'll get you for that our kid!"

And of course, he did. That was part of the fun. We both got soaked, but it was a hot day and we would soon dry off.

Now poor old Thomas was watching all this, and as I have said, he was a lad who didn't know how to play. He didn't know the unspoken rules, which were that you didn't use too big a stone, you didn't throw it too close to your victim and above all, you were careful not to hurt anyone.

For all I knew, he thought we were serious in our fighting. (The art was to get the stone to drop in the water as close as possible to the victim.) I couldn't tell you what his brain was thinking.

I know what he did. He bent down and picked up a large rock, a veritable boulder, the biggest he could carry. He lifted it above his head, and staggered towards me.

I didn't see him coming. All I knew of this was a glimpse of Thomas's insanely-grinning face, his arms held aloft, before he lost control and balance and dropped the rock on my head.

Luckily, some sixth sense had alerted my Dad, and he had seen the whole incident. Though powerless to prevent Thomas's unfortunate assault on me, he was already running towards me as the rock descended. Though I fell unconscious into the water, Dad quickly scooped me up and carried me to the bank, thus saving me from drowning.

I was out for some minutes, but in time, I recovered. I had a huge lump on the back of my head where he'd dropped the boulder on me, but luckily, no permanent damage.

Poor Thomas. Though he was apparently the uninjured party, he suffered far more.

He was never allowed out again.

DAISY BARKER

Though I spent much of my time avoiding the unwanted attentions of Norma Greensit, I was very keen on girls in general, and quite a few in particular. I had already had some stormy affairs with several other nine year olds at my school.

Georgina Palmer was one. She had lovely soft brown hair cut long around her shoulders, big brown eyes to match and a lot of brown freckles. Usually she was only interested in skipping, but I was eventually able to talk to her and declare my passion for her. She rewarded me by letting me hold one end of her skipping rope. I was in heaven.

Then there was the unfulfilled passion for Nicolette Goulding, who was simply too beautiful to exist in our world. She didn't belong among people who went to the toilet. Whenever I saw Robert Chapman with his nose dribbling twin tubes of snot, I used to wince for Nicolette Goulding, knowing how upset she would be at this display of the horrors of humanity.

Nicolette Goulding was so heavenly she never took any interest in any of the boys, not even Handsome Johnny Hopper, so it was no surprise that I never got further with her than distant worship.

***

It was very different with Daisy Barker. Daisy was a plump vivacious little thing, black-eyed and black-haired, a bouncy, cuddly sort of girl. You could imagine her curled up on a sheepskin rug in front of a roaring fire. Daisy Barker fancied me.

It had all started quite innocently. I was having a fight with Clive Lawson the Pater's son, behind the prefab hut, well out of the way of prying teachers. It was unimportant, just one of our constant and usually bloodless skirmishes, caused by the fact that he was such a know it all.

A girl came up to us with a message in her hand, and waited politely for us to finish.

"What is it?" I asked, when I'd got him down.

"Letter for you Cluffie," she said, handing me a folded piece of paper, obviously torn from a school Rough Book. I took it from her and stood up, allowing Clive Lawson to escape.

'Dear David,' it read. 'I really fancy you. Signed, Daisy Barker.'

My heart missed several beats. I looked around in case anyone else might have seen it being delivered. I sneaked another look at this passionate letter.

Daisy Barker. And there were lots of XXXXXs in abundance after her name. Daisy Barker! Woo hoo!

I grinned at my own cleverness (and obvious attractiveness!) and hid the letter inside my pocket. Then I looked around for the escaped Clive Lawson so I could continue where I had left off.

"Any message?" said the delivery girl.

I had forgotten her. I hadn't thought that Daisy Barker might want a reply. What was I to say? I was pretty inexperienced in this sort of thing.

"Tell her 'Thanks'," I said. The girl scampered off back to Daisy Barker.

***

Daisy was my first real date, in the sense that I arranged to meet her. It was very different from going out with any of the other girls I had known. Daisy knew, and I knew, that we were meeting for purposes sexual. Well, as near sexual as you can get when you're nine years old.

I just wish I'd done the choosing of the site for our first date myself. We met outside the chip shop on the new estate. It wasn't my idea of a romantic tryst, but then, Daisy was near the bottom of the class. Anyway, she lived above the shop next door to the chip shop, so I suppose it was handy for her.

It certainly wasn't for me. It was on the Green Howards estate.

The new estate was being built on the hill behind the Green Howards barracks, row upon row of pebble-dashed boxes without a tree or hedge in sight. I was risking life and limb by even going there. If the Green Howards kids discovered me, or worse still, discovered that I was taking one of their prize assets, Daisy Barker, I would be dead meat.

The Green Howards estate and its new chip shop were cut off from our territory by the Ghyll, the steep dry valley full of bramble bushes and frequented only by marauding gangs of Green Howards kids. I was in foreign territory and if caught there I would have to jump over the wall into the Ghyll and just hope I could outrun them before they caught me.

Daisy and I met outside the chip shop and hung about the parade of shops for several nights, for no useful purpose. I don't know to this day what she wanted from me. She did write DAISY = DAVID on the door of the outhouse at the back of the off-licence, but this did little to excite me.

I had hoped we would be kissing. I wanted to feel again the excitement I had felt that day when I held Sandra Marcham so close as we rolled about on the grassy bank at the back of their house. I didn't want to write things on doors and stand about all evening waiting for something to happen.

Then one night I saw a gang of big kids leaning on bikes and talking in close huddle. Among them was Kevin Batty and it was obvious they were talking about me. Kevin Batty kept looking up from the nest of heads and smirking in my direction. I began to prise my hand free of the hot little grasp of Daisy Barker, anxious to leave.

"Where you off?" she asked. This was in itself an improvement, as normally she didn't say anything at all.

"Off home," I replied. We were economical with words.

The gang of big kids broke up and began circling menacingly, swinging their bikes up and onto the pavement. I was surrounded and in trouble.

Luckily, (and I think I'm always lucky) – one of the cyclists tried to show off and do a wheelie at speed. He failed. The bike twisted, then went over on top of him. With a loud crack, his head hit the stone flags. His mates roared with laughter and cursed most foully. Then they realised that he was unconscious and crowded round to look at him.

Taking advantage of their inattention, I sneaked past their outriders and sprinted to the wall which led onto the Ghyll. With one jump, I was over it and tearing down the hill to my home territory.

By the time they'd noticed I was gone, it was too late for them. They chased after me, but had to take time to lift their bikes over the wall and by that time I was running up the hill on the far side of the Ghyll and nearly safe.

I decided there and then that Daisy Barker just wasn't worth the trouble.

***

I gave up girls for a day or two, ignoring plaintive messages delivered by a variety of Daisy Barker's friends. Then I noticed that Colleen Riordan, who had been recently promoted to sit ahead of me in the class, had the most amazing red hair I had ever seen. It must have been nearly a yard long. It spilled all over my desk when she sat down for registration.

To do any school work at all, I had to part hanks of the stuff and of course every time she moved it would all fan out again. I picked some up without alerting her and examined it. This girl was Rapunzel! You could have twisted rope out of it. It was so long she didn't even notice that I was holding it and dreaming. I fell in love with Colleen Riordan's hair.

However, it was another relationship doomed from the start. This time not because the girl was stupid. (Even when I was going out with Daisy Barker I had to admit to myself that she wasn't exactly the most intellectually gifted of girlfriends.) No, Colleen Riordan was clever. She had just joined the school and already she had been promoted to the front desks, because the teacher was interested in her results. No, I failed with Colleen Riordan because she was weird. She didn't like boys.

If any boy, attracted by her pretty face and stunning hair, said to her any of the usual opening lines in use at our school, like, "Will you come tut pictures?" she would snarl and thump her fist into the boy's face.

She was hard was Colleen. She had come to us from Germany. Her dad was in the Duke's (The Duke of Wellington's Regiment) who had been fighting EOKA in Cyprus. She was no softie.

At rounders she was always picked first, because she could belt that rounders ball out of the playground either left side or right side, and no-one else could do that, not even the boys.

Having seen her thump three or four suitors I decided that I would content myself with adoring her beautiful red hair and leave her well alone. No doubt she would make someone a sweet and loving wife one day, but at nine years old she was too fierce and temperamental for me to tackle.

Then Diana Nelson arrived.

DIANA NELSON

Diana Nelson was new to the school and new to the town. Her parents had moved to Ravenscroft and bought a house on Hubberholme Road, near where we lived. As a result she had to walk to school along the same route as I did, down Hubberholme Road, along The Land of Green Ginger, down Kirkgate and turning into Widdybank Wynd. This of course would have to be repeated after school. I therefore had the perfect opportunity to meet the delicious Diana.

I lost no time in volunteering to accompany her, because Diana Nelson was truly lovely.

She was willowy. She a beautiful doll's face, with big round blue eyes and her hair cut short. Her skin was pale like that posh china our Ma always wanted and could never afford.

Because Diana was new, she had no friends. Because she was so pretty the other girls were instantly jealous. Because she was so pretty all the boys were in love with her.

By a miracle, and thanks to our paths to school coinciding, I was in first. Instead of going to school with

Clive Lawson the Pater's son as I usually did, I made some excuse and hung back on Chestnut Grove, walking so slowly that concerned pedestrians stopped me to ask if I was alright. I was alright, I was just trying to time my arrival outside Diana's house with the emergence of Diana.

The door opened and out she came. She was wearing a pale blue dress of light flouncy material. There was something fairylike about Diana, something of Tinkerbelle.

I waved. She stopped talking to her mum, looked for a worrying second as if she didn't recognise me, then she smiled and waved back. I staggered to her side, hampered by quivering legs and a rattling heartbeat.

Diana looked nice and smelled even nicer.

Her mother looked at me. "Who's this, Diana?"

Diana smiled at me and said, "This is David. He's in my class at school."

She knew my name! I stood there shaking, grinning and blushing. A sneaky little fart may have escaped my bottom.

Mummy Nelson held out her hand. I stared at it. Then I realised that she was expecting me to shake hands. This I did, as Diana watched. I felt I was almost married into the family already!

"Bye!" her mum called, as Diana and I set off to walk down Hubberholme Road together.

The news was round school by break time. Clive Lawson the Pater's son was no doubt responsible. He had been suspicious when I made the excuse not to accompany him. He was jealous. His eyes were too close together. He had a Brillo pad stuck on his head. It was no wonder he was a total failure with girls.

The whispering started straight after break.

"How's Diana then?" came a voice from behind me. There were lots of giggles.

"Quiet!" yelled the teacher.

The whispering was stilled for a few minutes. Then it started again.

"Ooo hoo! Who's in love with Diana Nelson then?"

I blushed and prayed Diana couldn't hear the taunts.

"Quiet!" yelled the teacher, scanning the classroom for the perpetrators.

Silence returned, but not for long. Everyone was too excited to restrain themselves.

"Hey lover boy!"

"How's Diana then?"

"Have you kissed her yet?"

"WILL YOU BE QUIET!" the teacher shouted. "Really, I don't know what's got into you this morning."

I was prodded from behind. I could see that Daisy Barker was glaring viciously at me from the back of the class. She was urging her gang of Barkerites to prod me.

***

At lunchtime I tried to play football with the boys as usual, but I couldn't help noticing there was a huddle of girls talking animatedly in their corner. Obviously it was to do with Diana and me. Daisy Barker was there, talking loudly.

She glanced in my direction, saw me and looked as if she wanted to kill me.

I didn't know what to do for the best. I wondered whether I should go to Diana and confess my past affair with Daisy Barker. It might explain to her why they were all being so nasty.

"Hey lover boy!" one of Daisy's gang called to me. "Holding hands yet?"

I turned away and went to look for Diana, but the Daisy Barker gang pursued me, forming a circle of taunting snarling girls whichever way I looked.

"Two timer!" one called.

I could see that I was going to have to suffer for Diana. One glance at the tight little mouth of Daisy Barker told me that.

∗∗∗

It was the same at afternoon break and again at home-time. Angry knots of Daisy Barker supporters gathered at corners of the buildings to report my whereabouts to their leader. I couldn't go to the toilet without Daisy Barker knowing about it.

"Two timer!" they called.

The only moments I was safe from gangs of shrill hate-filled harpies was when I played with the boys. But I didn't want to play with the boys. Marbles and football and fighting no longer held any attraction for me, not when I knew that Diana Nelson was out there somewhere, no doubt being tormented by gangs of Daisy Barkerites.

***

At home-time I waited for her at the school gate, trying not to lose my temper with girls who kept calling me a Two Timing Twat.

Diana came out and joined me without a word. Her lovely face looked set. Together we set off up Widdybank Wynd, side by side up the steep hill, not speaking a word. I thought she must be angry with me.

Girls followed us, skipping about and calling out rude words.

This torture lasted all the way up to the top of Kirkgate, where Daisy Barker and her gang turned off in the other direction, to go up to the Green Howards estate, while Diana and I continued together up Hubberholme Hill.

"Sorry," I said.

She smiled and took my hand. My heart exploded! It was the first time I had ever walked hand in hand with a girl, and it was very exciting indeed.

***

The following morning there was a repeat performance, Daisy Barker's jealous hatred showing no signs of abating. In fact it got worse. In class, messages were being passed around. Vicious messages concerning Diana and me. The girls were giggling and sniggering and trying to upset her. Whispers went round the class. Diana remained calm and unmoved.

That evening we again walked home hand in hand.

At her house we stopped at the door. I noticed that Diana had lovely lips, little pink cupid lips they were. I studied them closely as we stood there hand in hand, looking at each other. She smiled slightly and I could see her teeth were very even and very white. Inside her mouth there was a little pink tongue.

I stared, fascinated, quite out of this world. I had never felt like this about a mouth before.

Diana moved closer to me so that we stood chest to chest. I could feel warmth from her body and my head began to spin dizzily. I wondered what was happening to me and feared for a moment that I might be sickening for something. Growing Pains perhaps? The only time I had felt this light-headed was when I had had influenza, or when Thomas Evans dropped the boulder on my head.

Diana reached forward, opening her lips and bringing me closer to her. We were going to kiss, I could tell!

We kissed.

Kissing Diana Nelson was very exciting indeed! I did it again. I wondered if I should stop, then decided that no, I wouldn't stop. It was too exciting.

It was, in fact, almost too exciting. I felt lights flashing inside my head and a heavy juddering shook my whole body. She was pushing her lithe body against mine and making me quiver. I wanted to go somewhere private with her, feeling that we shouldn't be showing this much emotion in public, that it was too personal for others to see. I was shaking uncontrollably and I knew that I had found that feeling I had sensed that day with Sandra Marcham when we wrestled together on the grassy bank.

I don't know how I managed to walk the rest of the way home that night. I wasn't conscious of my whereabouts. I felt different.

Ma noticed immediately that something had happened. She peered closely into my face.

"You look as though you've been overdoing it my lad. Early to bed for you!"

For once I didn't raise any objections about an early bedtime, so she knew for certain that I wasn't my normal self. Something was wrong with me, but I didn't know what. I felt queasy after tea and went to bed at six o clock, even though it was still light and sunny outside.

I slept for fourteen hours of unbroken sleep and woke next morning with a thick and aching head.

***

The following day, the first signs of Diana's acceptance appeared. At break I noticed that one of Daisy Barker's key hangers-on was talking to Diana and smiling. I guessed instantly that she was changing sides and was trying to be friends with Diana. The girls were like that, very short-lived in their allegiances.

In the lesson after break there were further indications that the tide had turned. No messages were passed around the class. No-one hissed when Diana spoke. I caught her eye and smiled. She smiled back. My God, could I cope with this much excitement?

At home time she waited for me at the school gate, unmolested by anyone. Daisy Barker lurked there, looking wicked, but she was now alone and deserted by her followers. As I approached, she hissed at me. "I hope you die, rat face!"

It was a weak gesture. I didn't look in the least like a rat, and she knew it. I took hold of Diana's hand and off we went, hand in hand, popular at last and unescorted.

Outside her house we kissed once more and I found the experience had lost none of its appeal.

This time however, we were interrupted by Diana's mother.

"Oooh!" she said with a big friendly smile, stepping out of the back door and bumping straight into us, locked together in a passionate embrace.

I blushed so red I nearly burst and in my panic let loose an accidental fart of fear, which I prayed they didn't hear.

"You'd better come inside David," she said. "I've been hearing a lot about you."

I was taken in and seated on the settee. Her mother gave me orange juice and a piece of fruitcake. I decided that this was quite the most delicious food I had ever tasted.

Meanwhile Diana continued to hold my hand. I was astounded at her bravery. I would never have dared to hold hands with her in front of my Ma or Dad.

The only incident to spoil what had been a perfect day was when her dad came in and her mother said, "Diana's brought her little friend home with her."

LITTLE FRIEND!!! I didn't like 'little friend' at all. Had she no sense of what was happening? This was momentous. This was true love!!!

∗∗∗

On my solitary way home I wondered if I should tell my Ma and Dad. Diana had been sitting there in her own house, holding hands with me, so confidently, so utterly without embarrassment. Could I do the same?

I doubted it.

∗∗∗

The following day there was no trouble from any of Daisy Barker's supporters. Most of them had abandoned Daisy Barker and were now keen to be friends with Diana. I wasn't surprised, because quite apart from her stunning looks, Diana was so gentle, kind and friendly that people just liked her. Daisy was left to glower alone.

That evening, I was again invited into the Nelson's front room and stayed there holding hands until her mother said pleasantly, "David, you'd better be getting home. Your mum will be wondering where you've got to." I hadn't realised that I had been there for over two hours.

On my own, I walked up the remainder of Hubberholme Road and into Chestnut Grove, in my usual cloud of love. Only to be confronted by the ultimate horror. There, in huge white letters, chalked on the road outside my house was the message

DC LOVES DN

TRUE

No-one could miss it, certainly not my dad, who was due to walk that way in less than half an hour. I burned crimson with embarrassment. Who could have done it?

Daisy Barker was sitting on Greensit's wall.

She smirked at me. "Serves you right!"

"Get it off!"

"Get it off yourself. Or better still, why don't you get Diana to get it off for you?"

I wanted to strangle her. This would be the end of the world for me. My parents would find out! I would be humiliated!

I rushed to our front door and, avoiding Ma, ran in the kitchen and got a bucket of water and a brush.

I scrubbed and scrubbed desperately at the chalk letters and managed to shift most of it. The rest of it was left unreadable.

By the time that my Dad came up the road all that remained was a large wet patch. Daisy, having succeeded in hurting and embarrassing me, had vanished.

Just in case she should reappear, when Dad came long, I ran up to him, grabbing his arm and hurrying him up to the house.

"Hello Dad! How'd it go today?"

He looked strangely at me.

"Are you in trouble son?"

I shook my head and put on the falsest of smiles.

Dad turned to go into the house, and then I saw it.

DAVID CLOUGH LOVES DIANA NELSON

All written in great big Daisy Barker writing, right across our garage doors.

***

After that, it was never the same with Diana. I didn't know why. I couldn't explain it. Just that I was humiliated at home and as a result I just didn't feel the same way about her, though it was hardly her fault.

We continued to meet, to walk to and from school together and to kiss, but without that thudding sickening passion. We had been strong enough to defeat Daisy Barker and her friends, but I wasn't strong enough to survive the exposure of our love to my family.

I realised then that she was much more mature than I was, because she had been able to tell her mother about me, when I would rather have died than tell my mother about her. I was only nine.

Diana Nelson though, she was some girl.

OUR TELLY

E ven when we got a telly ourselves, we all knew it wasn't a proper one. It was one my Dad had made.

Dad was some kind of electronics expert and he had got the bits from the Army, in much the same way he was later to acquire the tank radio – a massive piece of machinery which could pick up broadcasts from all over the world. It even picked up Radio Moscow, which was a bit odd I thought. Why would a British tank want to listen to Radio Moscow, even if it did broadcast in English?

Back to the TV. Our telly was very different from the Greensit's TV. It wasn't square for a start, nor was it in a wooden box. Our telly was long and thin, about two feet deep by two feet high, but only nine inches wide. It was all built inside an aluminium chassis. You could see all its innards.

The screen was round and about the size of a small plate. It was green. My dad called it a cathode ray tube, though I told him that people who had real televisions, like the Greensits, used the term 'screen'. He did not seem impressed.

Exciting bits had gone into our telly, like a heavy transformer (which got very hot when turned on) and odd-shaped valves which had to fit into special sockets. And best of all, the resisters.

I loved resisters. They were little things shaped like tiny sausages, stuck on bits of wire. They looked like sweets. Their bodies had coloured stripes painted all round them, which, Dad told me, indicated their resistance value. I liked the brown ones with red and yellow stripes best, and my least favourite was one with waxy paper which felt sticky to the touch.

Dad had built our telly and it had worked for months without any problems. It looked a bit odd I supposed, sitting in the corner of our living room. It wasn't square like Greensit's telly, nor was it in a wooden box. But you could see all the bits that were inside it, and little lights came on when it warmed up. It hummed a bit and it gave off a lot of heat. All its working parts were visible and it was probably a lethal risk to health, but we loved it.

You couldn't put a jug of flowers or an ashtray on it like Mrs Greensit put on hers, but at least you could see a picture on it (unlike hers which had a Horizontal Hold which didn't hold.) Greensits spent half their time watching Mr Greensit with one hand inside the back of their TV and his head round the front, watching the picture spin and spin into ziggy black lines as he tried to stabilise it.

We knew that our telly had its limitations. It had only one channel for a start – BBC. But we didn't mind. Our Dad had made it and it worked. We took a perverse pleasure in its odd appearance.

***

Then came the day when Ma dropped something inside it. As there was no wooden case to it, the innards were exposed to the elements and Ma, ever one to be tidying up the house, let something fall inside it. There was a mighty flash and a big bang.

Ma screamed. "Oh my God!" and leaped backwards.

Our Eck looked up from the comic he was reading and said, "What was that?" – so it must have been some bang to get him away from *The Tough of the Track*.

Even then the TV might have survived had Ma not panicked. The sight of the flames flickering out of the TV made her lose all control.

She rushed round and round the room shouting, "Fire! Fire! Oh God help us, the thing's on fire!"

Then she ran into the kitchen, still shouting for the Fire Brigade. Eck and I watched in horror as she returned with a basin full of water.

"No Ma!"

"Don't do it!"

But it was too late. Ignoring our pleas, she swung back and threw the basin of water at the smoking telly. A bright blue flame shot up to the ceiling. Something flashed. There was a loud bang. The cathode ray tube shattered. The telly sighed as if expiring. Eck fell off the settee and I took cover behind an armchair.

I was very sad. All those lovely little resisters were burned black and ruined. The transformer had melted. Nothing could be retrieved.

I think it was a jar of sewing machine oil she dropped inside it. It disappeared at about the same time, and we could never find it after that.

Poor Ma. Her telly had gone forever.

When Dad came home and saw the damage he said, "Ah well. I never liked telly anyway."

THE CANOE

Our Dad was admittedly rather eccentric, which is a polite way of saying that we all thought him slightly unpredictable, or as Ma would say at times of stress, "The biggest eejit that ever walked the planet!"

As proof this there was the sudden advent of Frisky the cat, the Hong Kong record player, the fishing trips where we never caught fish … but best of all his exploits was his canoe.

One evening he arrived home from work at Catterick Army camp in a state of great excitement.

"What's the matter with you?" Ma wanted to know.

He wouldn't tell her. Instead he raced upstairs to our bedroom where we were busy having a pillow fight.

"Hey boys, you won't believe it!"

"What Dad?"

"I've got you a canoe."

"A what?"

"Yes boys, a real live genuine canoe that you can sail up and down the river!"

Eck and I jumped up and down on our beds in excitement. Ma came upstairs to see what was going on and said, "The ceiling's coming down! Whatever's the matter?"

Dad told her about the canoe.

"You haven't got the brains you were born with!" was her retort, and she stormed off downstairs.

Now both Eck and I thought the canoe was great news, apart from the fact that none of us had ever expressed an interest in having a canoe, or even wanted a canoe, or could even use a canoe. And we lived seventy miles from the sea and miles from the nearest lake or anywhere we might be able to use it. The river was out of the question – it was the fastest flowing river in England.

"And neither of us can swim!" we both shouted together.

"Never mind," said Dad cheerfully. "You can soon learn."

∗∗∗

Later that evening a large Army lorry appeared in Chestnut Grove. We were out playing on the road at the time and when we saw it was an Army lorry we guessed it might be something to do with us.

Norma Greensit said, "What are you stupid lot up to now?"

We ignored her. Kenneth Greensit tagged along with us as we approached the lorry.

"Are you looking for us mister?" I asked the driver. It was not brilliant guesswork on my part. About ten foot of the pointy end of a canoe was sticking out of the back of the lorry.

We called our Dad and he came out to supervise the unloading. Ma came out too. Her face had that sort of sour twist to it round her mouth, which meant that she was really really angry about something. We hadn't seen her as mad as this since Dad bought her the slippers for Christmas.

We didn't care. It was all a big adventure to us.

I hadn't seen many canoes before that day, but I did know one thing. That canoe was the biggest, heaviest canoe I had ever seen. Other canoes I'd seen had been lightweight boats, made out of fibreglass. This one wasn't. It was made of wood, and four big brawny soldiers struggled to lift it out of the back of that lorry and to carry it down our drive.

Our Dad led the way with his magnificent new toy following behind.

"Got it off a pal," he said to my mother with a great big grin on his face.

Ma did not respond. She just folded her arms with solemn emphasis.

The four soldiers managed to carry it down our drive, manoeuvred it past the garage with difficulty, and deposited it in our back garden.

"Well," Ma said heavily when they had gone. "Whatever do you think you're going to do with a canoe?"

"Sail it," beamed Dad, patting the very solid-sounding side of the canoe.

"You great daft article. Where do you think you're going to sail it?"

"Oh, on the river," Dad said airily. "Or we might take it to the Lake District. It's a great canoe, isn't it a great canoe boys?"

"Yes Dad!"

Dad took us on an inspection of his canoe. It was about fifteen feet long, had room for three grown men inside, and was too heavy to be moved.

"Sit inside it boys."

We climbed inside, me in front, our Eck behind me and Dad bringing up the rear.

"There," Dad said proudly, beaming up at Ma. "See that! We can go on expeditions in this canoe!"

"You could," said Ma. "If you had any paddles."

Ma was right. We had no paddles.

That didn't stop my Dad for long.

"Use your imagination boys." He paused, while we used our imaginations. "There - isn't that great now!"

It was indeed. We loved his canoe immediately. No-one else had a canoe. The kids at school would all want to come round to our house to have a go. Dad was delighted with his purchase.

Ma, however, wouldn't let it rest. All evening she was on at him. "But whatever made you get it?" she asked.

"Have you no imagination woman?"

"Oh yes," she said between tight lips. "I've got imagination alright. I imagined I was married to someone normal."

"Hah! How wrong you were!"

Ma went wild. "Well, ye great eejit! Have you ever thought how you're going to get it anywhere you could sail it?"

A cloud of unhappiness came over the face of Happy Harry.

"I thought not," Ma said triumphantly. "You need a car and a trailer to tow it! What do you think you're going to do – sail it to the Lake District?"

"Well," he admitted. "Now that you mention it……"

The canoe stayed there in the back garden. It never went to the river, nor to the Lake District. In fact it never got near any water at all. Only once was it moved.

When we had some spare green paint left over from painting the garage roof, our Dad thought it would be a good idea to paint his canoe with it. We turned the canoe over and painted both top and bottom. It looked great in its bright new green coat.

Dad was really pleased. He sat and admired it for ages.

"There," he said proudly. "You'll never see a smarter canoe than that!"

***

The canoe lasted remarkably well, all things considered. Dad was very pleased with it. He never thought he'd made a mistake, because it never rotted, or leaked, or sank, so as canoes went, it was a pretty good canoe.

He used to say to Ma, "You know love, I'm glad we got that canoe."

And she would smile at him and nod.

"You're a complete eejit, d'you know that Harry?"

So he was happy and she was happy too, all because of the canoe.

FRISKY

Frisky the cat spent the daylight hours with us, playing contentedly and doing whatever we wanted him to do – he was a very good-natured cat – but when our bedtime came and the sun went down, he began to get restless. He would start washing his face, stretching his claws and testing them out on the settee and you knew his thoughts were turning to the fields and woods, to smells of vole and trails of mouse, to a fearsome battle with a cornered rat. For Frisky the cat was on the prowl!

I have always admired cats for their strong personality and single-mindedness. Not dogs. Dogs are dependent. Dogs crave affection. Dogs lack that self-confidence that cats have instinctively. Cats take what they want from humans, then they say, 'Right, that's it. I'm bored with being stroked and your pet names, I'm off to be a cat again.' A dog daredn't do that.

And of all the cats I've ever known or kept, Frisky was the best. Bigger, stronger, cleverer and cleaner than any other. More self-possessed yet more willing to give of himself, that is, when he felt like it. There was no beast that frightened Frisky. Frisky was all cat.

***

Mrs Burton was the lady who lived at the back of our house, on Hubberholme Road. She was a district nurse and had a car. It was Mrs Burton who had driven our Eck to Darlington when he severed his Achilles tendon. We were friendly with her but she had never been to our house.

One Saturday morning, Mrs Burton called. This was unusual. My Dad answered the front door and stood there talking to her. I saw them and I knew, I knew straight away, that something was wrong.

She and Dad talked in the doorway in low voices. I was hiding in the kitchen. Dad looked round several times to see if anyone was listening. I was.

I heard her say, "On the road. I think it's yours."

I felt a knife through my heart then. Frisky wasn't yet back for his breakfast. I knew straight away what she was saying.

Dad said, "Thanks for letting us know. I'll deal with it."

Then he shut the door and turned back to face us two, by now sitting at the bottom of the stairs. He wasn't his normal smiling self. He looked serious.

"You stay at home," he said to our Eck. "David, you can come with me."

We went out to the garage and Dad picked up his spade and an empty cardboard box. He didn't say anything. He looked grim-faced. He gave me the cardboard box to carry. Together we walked down Chestnut Grove to the main road.

On Hubberholme Road was an object. I didn't want to think of it as our Frisky, our lovely Frisky who we had cuddled as a kitten, who stroked his whiskers so delicately, who curled up in the folds of our bodies when we went to bed.

It had a little trickle of blood by its nose, but otherwise appeared uninjured. It was dead of course. Already stiff and cold. I had realised that as soon as I had heard Mrs Burton's low voice say, "On the road. I think it's yours."

My Dad scooped it up gently on the spade and I held open the cardboard box. The body slid in with a heavy thunk.

Silently, Dad took Frisky's collar and name tag off and put them in his pocket. Then he closed the box lid and lifted it. He carried him home without saying a word.

When we got home Ma and Eck were waiting. Ma didn't say anything. Dad just nodded. Eck started crying.

Frisky was buried at the bottom of our garden, where once he had lain among the spinach rows, looking with such disdain at the sparrows. There were no public tears. But the house was very quiet for many days afterwards.

I said prayers at night for Frisky.

"No more cats," said Ma. "Definitely no more cats."

STRANGE MEN

M y parents often warned me about 'strange men' who 'liked to talk to little boys' – but somehow I never made the link in my mind between these 'strange men' and sex. I knew what sex was of course – I spent most of my time avoiding Norma Greensit. But I had never heard of perverts or child molesters, or of paedophiles. I don't think the word existed then. Instead, when Ma or Dad warned me about 'strange men' who liked to talk to little boys I always wondered what they might want to talk about. It never occurred to me that they might want something more than a friendly chat.

So, I was never quite sure what 'strange men' looked like or did, but I had a feeling it was something unpleasant, and it was something to do with public toilets. I had no reason to fear these men, as I never went near public toilets. I hated the smell of them, so I would never go. I wouldn't dream of going into one of the cubicles, for a Number Two, as Kenneth Greensit called it. I either went at home, or not at all. Perhaps I was very innocent, or perhaps they were just very innocent days. I don't know. Even when the toilet incident happened, I didn't realise its significance.

At this point I should have mentioned that my Dad was an expert on public toilets. He collected them in the same way that other people collected ancient monuments. If you mentioned the city of York to my Dad he wouldn't think, 'Oh yes, York. Roman name Eboracum. Viking name Jorvik. Capital of the North for two thousand years, has wonderful city walls, the Castle Museum, the Shambles, Clifford's Tower and a huge railway station.'

No. My Dad would say, "Got some great toilets York. Especially the ones in the Railway Hotel." And off he would drift into hazy memories of the last time he had a pee in York.

You might say that was very weird, our Ma certainly did. She covered her face in shame and refused to walk with him when he started on about public toilets, but as my Dad said, "Why be embarrassed about it? We all have to go – even the Queen."

It all came from the days when as a young man he used to tear about the countryside on a variety of high-powered motorbikes: Broughs and Nortons, and his favourite, his beloved AJS. In those far-off days he used to drink a lot of beer with his pals, and of course, they would have to get rid of it. That was how he became so acquainted with the public toilets of Great Britain. If ever there was an Egon Ronay *Guide to Britain's Toilets*, my dad would have written it, you could bet on that.

***

One day we went on a trip out on the train to Knaresborough. This was a rare treat for us all and one my Ma had looked forward to for months. We hadn't – we were perfectly happy where we were, never being bored with our adventures. It was different for Ma though. She had no-one to play with and she had no friends in Ravenscroft. We didn't have a telephone, so she often felt lonely. She had lived happily in Knaresborough after her marriage to our Dad, before our Dad had got posted. She had friends there. This was the result. A day trip on the train to Knaresborough.

Ma wanted to go to the market and do some shopping. Then she wanted to meet her friends and maybe go to the Castle Yard and the Gardens and then go for a walk along Riverside and maybe if we were lucky we would all go for a trip on the river in a punt.

Dad wanted a pee.

Ma went crazy. "It's always the same, wherever we go!" she shouted furiously. "I don't know what's wrong with you!"

Dad grinned.

Ma was not amused. "Go on then, go if you must! But don't expect me to hang around waiting for you. I'm off to the Market." So off she went on her own.

Dad laughed ruefully and set off up the High Street, to the public toilets near the Bus Station.

Eck and I stood undecided as to which one to follow. Ma had the money so we were most likely to do well out of her, but she was in a bad mood now and hell-bent on shopping, so we picked Dad. He might only be heading to a smelly old toilet, but that wouldn't take him long and after than he would be good fun. He always was. So we raced each other to catch him up.

Dad was in such a good mood because Knaresborough was his home town and he liked being back there. He was also in a good mood because one of his all-time favourite public toilets was in Knaresborough. It was stone-built, marble-tiled, had its own diligent attendant, and was very well equipped with modern machinery like weighing machines and a hand towel dispenser. We all marched in together, us boys swinging from his arms like pendulums.

Dad went off to stand in the line with the other men, while Eck and I played on the weighing machine.

I noticed a man was watching us. He hadn't seen that we had our Dad with us and must have thought we were on our own. I guessed that the man had been irritated by our noisy laughter and that was why he was staring at us. I tried to play more quietly.

As it was summer Eck and I were both in short trousers, our legs burned brown by being out in the fresh air all day long. We were trying to weigh the two of us by using only one coin.

Suddenly I felt cold and goosepimply and stopped playing. I turned and the man was standing right behind me. His face had an odd expression, but even then I only thought that he was angry because we'd annoyed him.

I felt uncomfortable in his presence, and grabbed Eck's arm and tried to pull him away from the man and outside into the sunlight. The man stepped in front of me and put his hand on my neck. I was too frightened to speak. Eck didn't understand that anything was wrong and he was laughing.

Suddenly, my Dad was there. I'd never seen my Dad angry before, but he was mad now.

He pulled the man off me. "What do you think you're doing?"

The man let go of me and tried to smile and laugh it off.

My Dad pushed him in the chest. "Don't you touch my kids!"

"I didn't know they were your bloody kids, did I?"

Dad pushed Eck and then me out into the sun, said, "Stay outside!" then turned back to face the man, who was swearing horribly.

I'd never seen my Dad fight and he didn't look the fighting type as he wore spectacles. But he was so angry he forgot all about his spectacles, or maybe he remembered his own Dad, who was an army boxing champion and was a legendary fighter and terror of the town in his youth.

I do know what he did next, because I disobeyed his orders and put my head round the toilet door to see what was happening. And what he did next made me shout with happiness (because secretly I had sometimes regretted that my Dad was not a big tough soldier. I had sometimes been ashamed that my Dad was not bigger and without specs.)

Not now! Not any more!

He whacked the horrible man right on the chin - wham wham, both hands!

And the man spat blood and tried to speak. "I never meant anything! I'll get the cops on you!"

"Bollocks!" said my dad.

The man turned and ran off.

We all three went off down the High Street to meet Ma in high spirits, though we never told her why.

THE MILL RACE TROUT

G ulliver Tower, our very own private castle, was probably our favourite place of all, but as a secret haunt it lacked one vital ingredient – water. All the best secret haunts had a hidden well to shout echoes down, or a murky bottomless pond with untold victims sunk in its depths, or a scummy sluice full of scurrying rats to terrify even the biggest kids. Gulliver Tower had none of these.

The Mill Race had however. It was dangerous – not as dangerous as the Goathland estate where we'd gone to try and find a swan's nest and where we'd been chased by a keeper and had to hide holding our breath in laurel bushes as he beat about angrily shouting for us just yards away from discovering us and where we found the swan's nest only to be attacked and pecked at by a furious adult swan which nearly broke my arm because I was trying to save Kenneth Greensit who had fallen in the lake and got himself covered in stinking slime and his father had beaten him later and had come and complained to our Dad about his wild kids and suggested that he beat us as well. Not as dangerous as that, but dangerous.

The Mill Race was down at Masham Abbey. It was a cut-off from the main river, running under low overhanging trees to the old mill itself. A wooden lock gate held back the water, which nevertheless seeped through the bulwarks, sprouting through in white fountains in the dim light of the under-forest.

The Mill Race was very quiet. It was a six foot wide stonewalled channel, eight foot down and twenty yards long, containing a foot or so of clear water. The water moved swiftly over a flat stone bottom. The air was cold and chill. In the distance could be heard the voices of workmen. Occasionally a figure could be seen moving about, carrying something indistinct. The Mill Race had mystery and it had danger, and it had monstrous trout.

At first we'd sworn to leave them alone, but the merest thought of them haunted my dreams so much that I succumbed to the lure, and decided I would try to catch one. The others were only too keen to join in the attempt.

To reach the Mill Race we had to enter surreptitiously from the river, scrambling over slippery river stones until we were level with the lock gates. Then it was a steep climb up and over, pulling ourselves up on the great black iron levers that had once been used to wind the lock paddles. Everything had to be done silently and slowly or the trout would see us and would vanish under the walls, where they lived in impregnable holes.

Once up and over the high lock, we were inside the wood. The ground was green with a carpet of moss. On hands and knees we edged forward, peeking over the rim of the stone wall until we could see down into the water. With a bit of luck, if Kenneth Greensit hadn't shouted, screamed, nettled himself or waved his arms about, and if the weather conditions were right, the Mill Race would be full of immense brown trout, slumbering peacefully.

It was best on hot, bright days, when the sunlight would slant through a hole in the tree cover, and there, in a patch of golden dust amidst the dark gloom, river flies would hop and jig their silent dance of death. And the fish would wait for them, open-mouthed.

It was little wonder they were so fat. No-one fished for them, few people even knew they were there. At the slightest movement on the bank, they would shoot under their walls and vanish. They wouldn't reappear all that day.

Of course, we all dreamed of catching them, of staggering home with our arms full of record-breaking trout, trout so long they would hang over the plate when they were cooked and their heads and tails would flop over onto the tablecloth.

We tried everything. Firstly, conventional float and worm tackle – which the trout laughed at for its crudity. Next we took off our noisy floats and used worms with just a single hook. The trout disdained even to look at these. Cunning strategy was called for – that difference in brain power which divides us from the lower forms of animal life.

We threw in handfuls of worms, carefully culled from Greensit's cowshitty manure heap – worms so tiger-striped and appetising no self-respecting trout could fail to be attracted by their alluring wriggles. The worms hit the water. The water boiled with feeding fish!

We hugged each other with excitement and prepared to throw in another handful of the marvellous worms – only this time among them would be that single worm with a hook in it, attached to my line and rod.

Wham! In went the worms.

Once again the water boiled with frenetic activity as the greedy trout gorged themselves on our free food. We hugged each other in excitement. This was too easy, too good to be true! I almost felt sorry for them. The trout were clearing up every worm as if they were vacuum cleaners. Every single worm.

Except one. The one worm with a hook in it, the one miserable useless worm which had failed to get itself eaten. To our disgust it was left forlornly wriggling alone at the bottom of the Mill Race, while the trout lay gorged and belching, waiting to see what we were going to give them for dessert.

Eck wanted to net them.

Kenneth Greensit wanted to get an atom bomb and drop that on them.

It was just so incredibly frustrating, seeing those great fat trout lying there, untouchable as ever, just laughing at our pathetic attempts to trap them.

But no, I decided, if we couldn't catch them by legitimate means, we couldn't catch them at all. I explained my reasoning to the others and, reluctantly, they agreed. Anyway, we didn't have a net, and we certainly didn't have an atom bomb.

We left them alone, immense, slumbering, undefeated, kings of the Mill Race for ever more.

BUNK BEDS

The summer of 1959 was the hottest any of us had ever known. It began in April, not long after the snow had melted, and it lasted until October and the conker season. As kids we ran around for months in short trousers and T shirts and were burnt brown. It was the longest summer there ever was and I was nine years old.

The year had begun with the snow and sledging and our Eck limping around on his caliper, but when the sun came it was day after day at Masham Abbey for us, splashing about in the river catching bullheads or trying to tickle trout or creeping on our knees through the dark undergrowth surrounding our secret Mill Race, where huge trout slumbered tantalisingly out of reach. We had no need for holidays or for going away, every day was a holiday we never wanted to end.

In the evenings Ma used to have to threaten us to get us up to bed for the night. We were so lively and so hot the windows were flung open and the beds had only a thin sheet as cover. We couldn't sleep, so we fought pillow fights until Dad would be sent up by Ma to sort us out, then we'd attack him and forget our own fights and all three of us would wrestle and whack each other until Ma lost her temper and would come up to see what all the row was about.

"Harry! You're worse than the kids!" she'd rage, while Dad stood looking guilty, a pillow in his hand.

Then Ma would go off in a huff and we'd resume where we left off, me holding Dad around the knees so he couldn't run and Eck trying to clout him with a pillow.

***

Those were the days I remember – when we had never heard of rape or mugging or drugs (I didn't know what rape was until I was sixteen) - Eck and I standing on our twin beds with the matching quilts Ma had made, matching to stop arguments between the two of us. There we'd fight night after hot night in the front bedroom where I'd tried to fly and had cut my tongue in two.

For a change we were moved into the little bedroom at the back of the house. This had twin bunk beds, bought for some mysterious reason without any explanation being given. I think our parents were hoping for an addition to the family, though this was never mentioned. These twin bunks always provided promising sites for our adventures – as they could easily resemble the cockpit of a fighter plane, the rear turret of a Lancaster bomber, a wrestling ring, or a trampoline.

There wasn't much room in the little bedroom, in fact anyone coming through the door had to open it very carefully, edge his way past, and then close the door again before he could sit down.

This lack of space prevented us having the massive pillow fights with Dad that we'd had in the other bedroom, but, as if in compensation, it meant that Dad would sit down with us and tell us stories. If we couldn't tire ourselves out by fighting, Dad would have to talk us to sleep, not that he ever minded doing that.

I remember many nights when he'd talked to us until we felt sleepy, and we'd still beg him, "Just one more story Dad, just one more!"

His stories were wonderful, and we never tired of them. I think mainly they were so good because he was so natural. As a kid he'd been just like us – he'd done the same things as we did; he thought the same way as we did. He didn't try to moralise or make us better people; he didn't patronise us, nor did he give us any of that fantasy rubbish which I so detest. Dad was just like we were. Only older. And that was his secret.

As a lad he'd had three great pals, Jackie Lee, Ginger Brown and Patchy Bowes. These lads had got into scrapes just as bad as our own – even the one I haven't mentioned when I was four, in a field of long dry grass at the back of our house with Moira McKenzie and we'd been playing with matches and had accidentally set fire to the field and the fire brigade were called out.

Dad and his pals had gone swimming naked in the river - why not, it was a hot day and they didn't have any swimming trunks and there was no-one about, and the river looked so cool and inviting.

A girl had been with them, the daughter of the local vicar. We understood. She had tagged along just like Norma Greensit did with us. They had had a fantastic time, diving into the water off a cliff and swimming all the way up to the weir.

Then some nasty nosy individual had come along and had seen them. The vicar had been informed, there was a great scandal, and for weeks afterwards parents pointed the four of them out as children to be avoided.

Dad didn't say "it was very wrong of us" or "we learned our lesson" as so many adults would have done. We understood well enough who was right and who was wrong.

One night in the back bedroom he'd been telling us stories about Jackie Lee and Ginger Brown and Patchy Bowes until very late. It must have been eleven o' clock, an unimaginably late hour for us. Ma had eventually to come up and drag him away, otherwise we would never have gone to sleep.

"Night Eck," I said sleepily, when the lights were out. He was on the top bunk. It was his turn.

"Night Kid," he said.

We fell asleep.

Some time later I heard him stirring restlessly.

I called up, "Are you alright Eck?"

He was groaning.

I sat up, concerned at the odd noise he was making.

"Hey kid," I called in alarm. "Are you alright?"

He made no reply, only groaning even more loudly.

By now I was thoroughly frightened, as he sounded really ill.

"Eck," I hissed, putting my head out from underneath his bunk. "What's wrong with you?"

He leaned out and threw up all over me.

***

Ma blamed our Dad for keeping us up so late. "It's all your fault, ye great eejit. Telling them silly stories."

I didn't mind nearly as much as Ma did. Once I had been cleaned up I forgot all about it. I didn't blame Dad at all. It was our Eck's fault for eating oranges in bed.

How did I know?

The evidence was all around me!

And a couple of days later Dad was back telling us stories.

WOZBEE

I had been overhearing an unfamiliar word from Ma and Dad for some days. And once or twice when I had entered a room where Ma and Dad were talking they stopped discussing whatever they had been talking about, and changed the subject.

"Something's going on," I said to our Eck.

He didn't reply, being stuck in a comic as usual.

"Put down that comic for a minute and listen."

"What? It's Matt Braddock. He's fighting the Germans. Everything depends on him."

"Eck. They are only stories."

"No they're not!" He held the comic close to my face.

TRUE WAR STORIES.

"Shutup and listen. Ma and Dad. They're up to something. They've been acting funny all week. I heard them talking about a Wozbee."

"A what?"

"A Wozbee."

"What's a Wozbee?"

"No idea."

He hadn't any more idea about what was going on than I did. He was only six. But I was sure I was right. It was all very suspicious. What was a Wozbee?

And I'd heard the word Selection. Selection was a word I associated with those lovely packets of sweets Father Christmas brought us, the ones they sold in Woolworths. I was sure they were talking about a different type of Selection.

In 1959 parents were parents and children were children. They inhabited two different worlds. Parents never discussed anything with their children, and children were by and large content with that arrangement. They did as they were told. Well, most of the time they did.

I wondered what our parents were up to.

***

Matters became even more mysterious the following week when Dad announced he was going away for a few days. Going away? Dad had never gone away. We had never been apart. Now he was going away. We were upset.

"Where are you going Dad?"

"London."

"Why?"

He glanced at Ma. "On Army business."

Hmm. I suspected it was something to do with this Wozbee. No further information was forthcoming from either of them.

***

A couple of weeks passed. Then one night when Dad came home from work, he told us to put down the books we were reading. Ma stood beside him. This looked serious.

"I've been posted," said Dad. He glanced at Ma, who looked oddly nervous.

Eck and I waited for more details.

"Posted away," he repeated.

Judging by the expression on Ma's face this did not look like good news.

"Where to?" I asked.

He paused. "Germany."

My heart missed a beat.

Eck, used to flying with Matt Braddock and shooting down Messerschmitt 109s and Focke Wulfs, which were of course German, looked confused.

I struggled to understand the implications of what Dad was saying. Did he mean he was going to Germany by himself – which would be terrible for all of us. Or did he mean we were all going – which would be even worse.

"It's a big promotion," he added.

So that was what a Wozbee was. It was about Selection, to see if he should be promoted.

A Wozbee was a War Office Selection Board.

"What do you boys think?"

I couldn't say anything. I looked at Ma for guidance. For once she seemed lost for words.

"It'll mean more money."

That would be good, I supposed, but I still couldn't think of anything. It was all so confusing.

Then Dad said, "You'll soon settle in there."

That was it then. We were to leave our beloved Ravenscroft and to go to live in Germany.

***

Later, in bed, I tried to think of it from their point of view. Ma had hated Ravenscroft from the very start. She knew no-one here. Her friends were in Knaresborough and London. Her family was in Ireland. She wanted to live in civilisation, and Ravenscroft, in her estimation, was emphatically not civilisation. She wanted to leave.

Dad was clever, I knew that. He should have done much better for himself than just instructing soldiers in the Royal Signals. It was just his bad luck to be 18 in 1939. If war hadn't broken out, he would have gone to Cambridge and become a top electronic engineer. Instead he'd spent six years of war working in communications for the Post Office on RAF Bomber stations all over Yorkshire. And after that he'd been an instructor for the Army. Now he was being offered the chance to really fulfil his potential.

He wanted to go. He deserved to go.

The next day he explained that he had a few days in which to make up his mind. If he turned down this promotion, he would not get the opportunity again. That was the way the Army worked, he explained. You didn't get a second chance.

Things were very tense.

***

Two days later a letter arrived unexpectedly. It was blue and had red and blue stripes round the edges.

AIR MAIL it said.

We had never had an Air Mail before. It was from Canada.

At first I felt a rush of panic as I thought it might be something to do with Ma's Canadian. It wasn't.

It was from someone Dad had taught years before. After leaving the Army he had gone to Canada and set up an electronics business in Vancouver. It had been a great success. Now the man, remembering how clever Dad was at electronics, wanted Dad to come and join him in the company. He would pay him a lot of money and Dad would be a partner. He would pay for our flights to Canada and would find us a house. We would, he assured us, live like kings in Vancouver.

"Vancouver," said Dad, totally stunned at this news.

We awaited Ma's reaction.

"Vancouver," she said, equally shocked at this extraordinary news.

"What's going on?" asked Eck, emerging from his latest comic.

My mind was racing. Dad would have the opportunity that the war had denied him.

We all drifted off to separate rooms. I sat alone in the sacred front room.

***

"Telecoms are just beginning," he said to me later, clearly excited. "One day soon we'll have microwaves and home computers and colour televisions. We'll all have phones and you'll be able to talk to people anywhere in the world. In ten years' time the world will be unrecognisable from what it is now."

(Telstar and the satellite revolution were in fact only three years away.)

Dad was excited. He was animated. This was what he had dreamed of doing all his life, ever since he had made his first crystal set. And now, by a miracle, he was being offered that chance.

He wanted to go.

Then there was the Army promotion to Germany. What would he do about that? He wanted it, I knew he did.

Ma? Ma just wanted to leave Ravenscroft.

So would it be a move to Germany or to Canada?

And what about our beloved Ravenscroft?

Eck and I didn't want to go.

What was going to happen to us all?

———

ABOUT THE AUTHOR

David Clough is a born and bred Yorkshireman, proud of his county, its history and its people. His interests are writing, cricket, fishing and football.

He is the author of award-winning short stories, most recently as a finalist in the Colm Tóibín International Short Story Award.

David currently has three novels in preparation for publication.

He has written many plays and musicals and was for a time Associate Writer at the Royal Court Theatre in London. His plays have always been well-received and popular with audiences.

Now that David has retired he is, at last, getting round to publishing some of his works. Hopefully, this is the first of many.

Available worldwide from Amazon
and all good bookstores

---

http://mtp.agency

http://facebook.com/mtp.agency

@mtp_agency